HOW TO PACK FOR THE END OF THE WORLD

Also by Michelle Falkoff

Playlist for the Dead

Pushing Perfect

Questions I Want to Ask You

HarperTeen is an imprint of HarperCollins Publishers.

How to Pack for the End of the World
 For information address HarperCollins Children's Books, a division of HarperCollins Publishers, 195 Broadway, New York, NY 10007.
www.epicreads.com

ISBN 978-0-06-268026-6

Typography by Ellice M. Lee
20 21 22 23 24 CPIG 10 9 8 7 6 5 4 3 2 1
❖
First Edition

HOW TO PACK FOR THE END OF THE WORLD

MICHELLE FALKOFF

FOR EVERYONE WHO IS AFRAID,
AND FOR EVERYONE WHO IS TRYING TO MAKE
THE WORLD BETTER ANYWAY

1.

Gardner Academy used to be one of the most prestigious private schools in New England, if not the whole of the United States. Its list of esteemed alumni included presidents, senators, judges, and winners of prizes and fellowships from MacArthur to Nobel. For years, acceptance to Gardner meant near-guaranteed admission to the Ivy League school of your choice, as long as your parents could pay the massive tuition checks.

But place a bunch of kids under the not-particularly-watchful eyes of badly vetted, overpaid teachers and coaches, and before you can say "Penn State," you'll have exactly the scandal you'd expect. *The Boston Globe* broke the story of how Gardner's administrators covered up rampant sexual abuse in both its academic and athletic programs, and the school seemed doomed to go under.

Thanks to its enormous endowment, though, Gardner

had time to weather the crisis and strategize. How could it regain the people's trust while remaining solvent, let alone profitable? One option was to focus on the money, accepting any students who could pay, no matter the history of inappropriate behavior or limited evidence of literacy. This would keep the doors open, but the school would hardly be minting an impressive alumni class.

Another option was to emphasize academics, seeking out the best and brightest students who would never otherwise consider private school and offering them full scholarships, burnishing Gardner's reputation as a feeder school for the finest universities. It could create a rigorous, goal-oriented curriculum for future leaders of America, whether in politics or business, making classes available that were rarely offered even at the best of its competitors. Not only would it salvage its mission to educate the most promising young minds, it would be serving a public-interest function, satisfying the clamoring voices of alums who wanted to be proud of their school again.

Gardner, in its infinite wisdom, chose to do both.

Enter yours truly, Amina Hareli, scholarship student. I did not want to be here, and yet here I was, sitting on a mattress so thin I could feel the springs under my butt, watching my mom unpacking my clothes as she valiantly tried to shake out the inevitable wrinkles that had formed when I stuffed everything I owned into garbage bags. I wasn't about to do a whole bunch of fancy folding to go someplace against my will.

"I know you're not going to just sit there and watch your mother do all the work," Dad said, giving me a dark-eyed glare that I gave right back. He was better at stare-downs than I was, so I got off the crappy bed and began throwing clothes into random drawers. My little sister, Shana, took my place on the bed, only instead of sitting she jumped up and down like she was on a trampoline. The springs squeaked. I would never be able to sleep here. I was having enough trouble sleeping at home.

"Minnie, honey, you could fold the clothes one time," Mom said.

"Don't call me that," I said, as if by reflex. She'd named me after her grandmother Minnie, but while she'd been kind enough to recognize that Minnie was a terrible name, she couldn't seem to stop herself from using it as a nickname. "Amina" wasn't awful; it made me the only kid in Hebrew school with the same name in both Hebrew and English, so that was a plus.

"I'm just saying that if you set up the room nicely at the beginning, it will be easier for you to keep it clean." Mom was a neat freak. Everything in our house had a place, and she'd tried desperately to make me into someone who lived that kind of orderly life. She even looked the part, with her tailored clothes and smooth mask of makeup and sleek dark cap of hair. I was more like my dad, all dark messy frizzed-out curls and shirts left untucked and mismatched socks. His study and my bedroom even looked alike, piles of papers and books everywhere, tucked away behind closed doors so Mom didn't have to see how she'd failed in molding us to her will. I wouldn't have to worry about that now, I supposed, though that might depend on my roommate.

"Shana, stop jumping so I can make the bed," Mom said. "Min, give me a hand."

I'd trained myself to live with "Min," if only to keep the peace. I grabbed two corners of the extra-long-twin white jersey sheets we'd bought on sale at Target and acted like I cared about the difference between the fitted and cover sheets, as if this bed would ever get made again once my family left. Once we'd tucked the sheets in so tightly I wasn't sure I'd be able to undo them, Mom draped a brightly colored patchwork comforter on top. She'd bought it for me as a present, which is to say it was the complete opposite of what I would have picked for myself. At least it was reversible, so I could flip it over as soon as she was gone and just deal with the bland pink underside. It would still be awful, though, as would all the matching stuff she'd bought to go with it: throw pillows, a desk lamp, a new journal.

"I trust you're going to adjust your attitude when you're

on your own." Dad sat at the bare wooden desk, setting up the laptop the school had provided. I'd never had my own computer before. "I understand you want us to see you sulk to punish us, but you should at least pretend to be open-minded when it's just you. You'll have a much easier go of it."

What if I didn't want to have an easy go of it? I was tempted to ask, but I figured they knew that already. Last year had been a nightmare, and yet I'd made it very clear that I wanted to deal with my issues at home, not at some random school I'd never even seen before. We'd been over this a million times, and yet somehow I'd still landed here. I was fine with keeping the almost-silent sulking going for a while.

"Don't ignore your father," Mom said. Ugh, they were such a unit. Intellectually I knew it was better to have parents who were still together and who still got along, even loved each other, but seriously, did they have to agree about everything? Couldn't they have debated this decision, for example, and left open the possibility that one of them might listen to my arguments for why I should have been allowed to stay home? Wouldn't they want the family to be together if the world as we knew it was about to end?

"I will improve my attitude," I said, fighting the urge to use a robot voice. "In fact, I'm going to go to a pre-orientation thing. Some sort of game night. It starts in about an hour and I should probably get ready, so maybe it's time for you to go."

Mom and Dad gave each other one of those looks that

I knew meant they were trying to decide whether to yell at me for trying to kick them out, or to act like they believed I was going to give Gardner a shot. "We do have three or four hours' drive ahead of us," Mom said. My hometown, Brooksby, was in the northern suburbs of Boston, a couple of hundred miles away from Gardner, which was located in nowheresville, Vermont.

"Can we stop for ice cream?" Shana asked. "Please please please?"

Oh, to be ten again, to have your biggest worry be access to sugar and not the impending collapse of civilized society. I was still mad enough at my parents to think I wouldn't miss them, but I really would miss Shana. They'd better get her ice cream.

In the hour before Game Night began, I loosened the sheets, flipped the comforter, organized my clothes (without folding them—I wasn't ready to go that far), and briefly met my roommate, Brianna, who looked me up and down, checked out my Target sheets, sniffed, and asked if she could use the extra closet space. I nodded, and she ignored me until it was time for me to leave. I hadn't even been sure I'd meant it when I told my parents I would go, but the thought of spending the night in a room with Brianna proved worse than the thought of meeting some new people, which honestly didn't sound all that bad. And I liked games.

"Do you want to come to Game Night?" I asked Brianna. She scrunched her nose without even looking at me and continued hanging up clothes that seemed way too fancy for school. I got the feeling she was not a scholarship student.

According to the flyer I'd seen in the dorm, Game Night would take place at the Rathskeller. I'd looked up the word online and immediately gotten confused—the word was German and referred to basement bars located in government buildings. Gardner wasn't German, I was pretty sure there wasn't going to be a bar at a high school, and the town center was miles away.

As it turned out, the only connection Gardner's Rathskeller had to any real Rathskeller was its location in a basement. After Brianna turned me down I wandered over on my own to what turned out to be the rec center, heading downstairs with a crowd of other students. Gardner was a three-year institution—we'd all had our chance to either excel at or screw up our first year of high school—so I had to get used to the idea of first-, second-, and third-year students, rather than sophomores, juniors, and seniors. A group of second years had organized the event, but I figured the rest of the students filing into the basement were first years like me.

The room was filled with couches and chairs from eras long past, and ranging in fabric from tattered basket-weave tweed to pleather. It definitely felt like a hangout for scholarship kids. I chose a faded floral-print armchair and sunk in, craning my neck to face a raised platform in the middle of the room. On it stood a pair of second years, one male and one female, both knobby-kneed, the girl nearly a foot taller than the boy, both looking far younger than I'd have expected sixteen-year-olds to look, both staring out at us with bug-eyed intensity.

"Welcome to Gardner!" Both boy and girl clapped their hands together as they shouted their greeting in unison. They'd clearly practiced. The fact they'd needed to practice something so basic made me wonder how smart they could possibly be.

"We know orientation doesn't officially start until tomorrow, but we thought it would be fun to do some get-to-know-you stuff first and get the party started down here at the Rat!" The girl talked through a toothy smile. "We're going to split the room in half, and each of us will lead the first game."

I looked around, trying to figure out if there was a side I wanted to be on, but how could I tell in a basement full of strangers? Any one of them could be my future best friend or someone I would completely despise. Back home I knew who my friends were, or had been; I'd been hanging out with the same group of girls since kindergarten, expanding the group only slightly once middle school started and we met kids from the other public schools. Here I had no one, so I just stayed where I was. Worst-case scenario I could always take a nap.

Maybe forty kids had shown up of the hundred or so in the first-year class, so we ended up in groups of twenty. The first game wasn't much of a game at all; it was more of an ice-breaker. We had to introduce ourselves, say where we were from, and then say something unusual about ourselves. After the first few people spoke I could tell we were all trying to figure out who the scholarship kids were, but it wasn't as easy to tell as you'd think. The intros went by so fast I couldn't keep track of anyone's names, so I was grateful for anything memorable. My group included an extremely good-looking Asian boy wearing glasses and an argyle sweater who claimed the TV show *Breaking Bad* had inspired a love of chemistry; a girl with upsettingly perfect hair who was some sort of internet fashion influencer; and a too-pale boy who appeared to be twelve years old who was, in fact, twelve years old.

The introductions got everyone talking, so they served their purpose, even if their more lingering lesson was to teach us to be skeptical of one another. (I, for one, had convinced myself the chemist was here for cooking meth.) Our next game was a round of Assassin, in which one person is designated the killer and has to murder the other players by winking at them without getting caught in the act. From this I learned quickly that (a) Gardner students were as aggressivley competitive as one might expect, and (b) a very cute red-haired freckled boy's gentle smile belied his ability to decimate the population. I took him down, but it was less about my ability to solve mysteries and more about the fact that I was staring at him the whole time. Still, I liked the fact that I'd been the first person to win something here. I could tell people were impressed.

After a few more rounds of Assassin people got bored, and several first years wandered off, presumably to find more interesting things to do. People tossed around ideas for more games, and eventually we settled on a round of Would You Rather. I stuck around, even though I'd always hated that game.

The game started as it usually did, with gross questions ("Would you rather eat worms or maggots?") quickly devolving into sexual questions ("Would you rather sleep with your best friend's significant other or your middle school principal?") I held back and watched as my fellow classmates revealed their preferences for worms and friendship betrayal. This game was the worst.

Once people ran out of questions that were both gross and sexual, the room fell quiet for a moment. "Can I ask one?" a boy asked. His skin, eyes, and hair were all nearly the same shade of light brown, and he had an intense look on his face. I had a feeling his question would be neither gross nor sexual. "If you knew the world was going to end tomorrow, would you rather die along with your friends and family and everyone you've ever known, or live among strangers to rebuild civilization?" The boy's eyes widened as he spoke, flirting with the line between curious and creepy, inching a toe past and then pulling back. He must have been stewing over his phrasing the whole time we'd been playing.

Finally, a question I was interested in hearing the answer to. Given how I was feeling about my parents these days I was pretty sure I knew where I was at, but more information couldn't hurt. "How's the world going to end?" I asked.

"She speaks!" the red-haired assassin said, and I hated myself for blushing.

"Will there still be technology?" asked a wiry girl with short, bleached-out hair.

"How can you be sure we wouldn't know anyone?" asked the terrified twelve-year-old.

"Is it, like, the Rapture or something? Where everything would be exactly the same but the people would be gone?" This from the meth chemist.

"I'm not sure it matters how things end," the shaggy-haired boy said, "but I can make it interesting, I guess. Let's say plague. The survivors are immune but there are few enough that the power grid goes down. No power, no internet. Not enough people to keep the world moving as it has been, though we would work together to bring it back." He flushed red. "Guess I've told you where I'm at."

The twelve-year-old immediately said, "I'd want to die." He looked like he wanted to die right now.

"I'd live for sure!" shouted the meth chemist. "I'd go steal an Escalade and then raid the grocery store for all the food and water. Then I'd charge people so much money I'd be the richest person alive."

"Because Walter White over here would definitely be the only one to think of that," said the wiry girl. "Yeah, you're a real genius."

It wasn't hard to hear the sarcasm, and yet the meth chemist beamed. "Exactly."

"We'd need some way to protect people from guys like him," the redhead said. "I'm going to be a lawyer someday. I'm all about making rules and making sure they're fair. Put me on Team Survival." He'd somehow gotten even cuter while he was talking.

"What about your family, your friends?" I asked. "Wouldn't you be lonely?"

He shrugged. "Making friends is easy. And my family sucks. I'd miss my brother, but not enough to want to die. I'd be fine."

"You and me both," I said, though I was only referring to the family part. I'd miss Shana, but I wasn't about to give up trying to save the world for her.

The redhead gave me a high five. "Team Survival!"

From there the remaining kids weighed in. Only a few were on Team Death, nearly all girls. This was more likely a matter of honesty than true gender difference; the scared twelve-year-old was probably the bravest person in the room, given his willingness to say what I was sure many others were thinking.

Everyone else felt they had value when it came to rebuilding society, but their reasons varied so radically we might as well have been having different conversations. The meth chemist wasn't alone in wanting to run a black market food-hoarding enterprise, which helped identify some of the kids who'd gotten kicked out of other schools, but the obvious scholarship students weren't much better. Their reasons to survive were equally gratuitous, even if they knew how to make them sound virtuous. "The world is going to need great art," said a boy wearing conspicuously paint-spattered clothes. "Wasn't it Churchill who refused to cut funding for the arts during wartime because he said that's what they were fighting for?"

The wiry girl snorted. "Snopes debunked that one like ten years ago, Picasso." She already intimidated me, but in a way that also kind of made me want to hang out with her.

"Someone will have to rebuild the tech," said a girl so pale and stooped it wasn't hard to picture her hunched over the glowing screen of her laptop, forever.

"Not necessarily," said the fashion influencer.

I wasn't expecting that. Not from her, anyway.

"Tech as we understand it now isn't something we need," she said. "It's just something nice to have. We'll need to go back to first principles when it's gone, to think about skills. Hunting, gathering, gardening."

"Sewing," said the redhead.

Crap. He'd probably noticed the influencer was gorgeous, with her hair like a box of Honey-Nut Cheerios come to life, and clothes that fit her body perfectly. I was going to hate her, I was sure of it.

"Sewing, sure," she agreed. "But leadership too. From really smart people." I thought she'd be looking at the redhead, but instead she was looking at me.

"Nerds, you mean," said the meth chemist.

The influencer rolled her eyes, and I laughed despite myself.

"Nerds will save the world," said the wiry girl. "I bet some lawyer nerd your dad paid off got you out of whatever trouble landed you here."

The meth chemist stood up. He wasn't all that tall, but he was broad, and since the wiry girl was sitting down, he towered over her. "What makes you think I didn't get in because I'm smart?"

The wiry girl jumped up so fast I barely saw it happen, and she got right in his face. They were about the same height now that she was standing, so she could look him directly in the eye. And she spoke so quietly he practically had to lean in to hear her. We all leaned in too, because she was definitely about to say something good.

"First of all, you opened your mouth," she said. "Second, you're wearing fake glasses and that ridiculous sweater but you're jacked underneath, and while it's not impossible for a scholarship student to have that kind of time to spend at the gym, it's not common. It's like you're trying to play a smart person rather than actually being one."

The meth chemist's mouth had fallen open. He couldn't even bring himself to interrupt.

"Third, and I'm sure our resident fashionista can back my play here"—she nodded at the influencer—"your watch alone could cover tuition for at least a semester." She paused, as if giving him time to answer, but he seemed as mesmerized as we all were.

"Not to mention the shoes," said the fashion maven. "Prada penny loafers. Every new scholarship student's go-to footwear."

The wiry girl nodded. "You could have found the other losers to go drink or get high or whatever you think is more worth doing than hanging out with nerds like us, and yet here you are. Because you know"—and here her voice got even lower, even quieter—"that if you go out with those people, or back to your room alone, the drugs are going to call to you.

You're a rich kid, so what was it? Coke? Fentanyl? Mama's Percocet? You haven't been off long, but you promised you'd stay clean, didn't you?"

The meth chemist was no longer making eye contact. The wiry girl reached out one finger and placed it under his chin, lifting his head back up to be level with hers. He still didn't speak, but now it was more like he couldn't. Instead he tried, and failed, to keep his nose from twitching.

"Cocaine, then," the wiry girl said. "That's a tough one to kick. You did good." She sounded like she meant it, too; her finger moved away from his chin to gently stroke his cheek.

But the spell broke. The meth chemist shrugged her hand away. "Screw you. All of you." He turned around and walked off.

"Guess making friends won't be as easy for me as it will be for you, Prince Harry," the wiry girl said to the redhead. "Maybe you can give me some tips."

"I'll do whatever you want," he said, and he might as well have been speaking for all of us.

I had to get to know her. She might be the only thing that could make Gardner interesting.

2.

The nightmare wasn't the same every time. Sometimes it started with me and my family sitting at Friday-night services at our synagogue, Temple Emanuel. I'd be listening to the cantor sing, staring at the Hebrew words above the ark that translated to "Know Before Whom You Stand." The bronze fixture that held the ner tamid, the eternal light, hung right above the ark, and I could see the tiny fire blazing in it. And then the fire blazed more brightly, and then it wasn't contained by the fixture, and before I had time to realize what was happening, the walls had caught fire and the screaming began.

That wasn't real, though.

In another dream my family wasn't there; it was me and my friends, in one of the classrooms across the hall from the sanctuary, waiting for the rabbi's wife to come and begin our Hebrew school class. Until high school started I'd gone three times a week, despite my protests. The rebbetzen was never late, so even in the dream I knew something was wrong. In this version I smelled the smoke before I ever saw the flames, and I ran to the door only to find it locked from the outside, the handle so hot it singed my fingers. It was only when one of the boys kicked it down that we saw fire everywhere, with no path for us to escape.

That wasn't real either. None of the versions I dreamed were real, because I hadn't been anywhere near the temple when it burned. No one had been except the rabbi and a man he'd been counseling after the death of the man's wife. They'd met in the rabbi's office after the daily minyan ended, despite the fact that there had been arson attempts at several local synagogues in recent weeks. My mom had been at the minyan, as she had been every night since my grandfather died six months before the fire, nearly two years ago now. She'd left the temple less than half an hour before the fire started.

The rabbi and the man he was counseling would ultimately be fine; they'd suffered mostly from smoke inhalation. But the temple itself needed a tremendous amount of repair. I'd seen pictures of the scorched sanctuary and the sooty classrooms in the newspaper. I knew it could have been worse, but all I could think about was how my mother had been there only moments before some awful man, someone they'd never caught, had thrown a Molotov cocktail through the stained-glass window that spanned the back wall of the sanctuary. She could have died. The thought of it left me breathless and sent my brain into nightmare-creation overdrive. My therapist said my subconscious had taken the images I saw and combined them with everything I was afraid of to make dreams that were worse than reality, and I was sure she was right, but that knowledge was insufficient to make the dreams stop.

The funny thing—to the extent you could call anything surrounding these events funny—was that until the fire I'd had what I would call a complicated relationship with Judaism. Sure, I'd gone to Hebrew school for years, had a bat mitzvah and all that. But I'd never believed in the idea of God, and it struck me that lots of the world's problems were grounded in religion. I respected that my ethnicity was Jewish, that my culture was Jewish, but religion? I wanted no part of it. I'd started complaining about going to services, even though my parents felt strongly that Shabbat was family time and insisted we all sit down for dinner on Friday nights and then go to shul together. "It's not up for debate," my mother would say, and though I'd look to my father for backup—many Israeli Jews, like my father, are more secular than people realize—he'd always get behind her.

But now, in a world where synagogues were the sites of mass shootings and arson, where torch-wielding men shouted "Jews will not replace us!" and the government did nothing, I felt more Jewish than I ever had, in good ways and bad. I didn't complain about going to services anymore, in part because we now had to go to a different temple, one that had reinforced its windows with bulletproof glass and hired full-time security guards, and there was something intensely comforting about hearing the familiar prayers every week after our usual family dinner. I realized it didn't matter whether I believed in a higher power but not for the reasons I'd thought; the people who wanted me dead didn't care about the complexity of my belief system. They wouldn't be checking to see whether I'd really prayed during the silent Amidah or whether I'd let my mind wander. Judaism was my birthright, and that didn't mean a free trip to Israel; it meant there were people who hated me just for my existence, and there was nothing I could do about it.

That's when my obsession started. I'd always believed knowledge was power, so I set about empowering myself, thinking knowing more would comfort me. At first I was just reading about anti-Semitism in the world, about the Holocaust, the rise of the Third Reich, and I tried to move forward and study how Germany had come back from its dark past and reinvented itself as a more humane country. But I couldn't help but look even further back as well, at empires and what had caused them to collapse. There was so much going on in the world, and in the United States in particular, that resembled events that had happened before, and those civilizations hadn't always survived. I thought about how often I'd been taught that those who forget history are condemned to repeat it, and I wondered whether we were in danger of becoming yet another failed democratic experiment. It was all I could think about, all I could talk about, all I could write about. I scribbled so hard in my journal my pen often ripped through the pages.

My obsession was frustrating for everyone around me. One by one my friends backed away, some so subtly I barely noticed, others with a little more fanfare, reminding me I wasn't the only person the temple fire had affected, but you didn't see anyone else becoming a full-blown conspiracy theorist, did you? I didn't think that's where I was headed, but it didn't matter. Friends were a distraction. There was so much I needed to know, and without them I had more time for my reading, more time to write in my journal.

"Amina, honey, this isn't healthy," my mother would say, after I'd yet again woken her with my nighttime screaming.

"You're frightening your sister," my father would say, when it was his turn, hoping the thought of my impact on Shana would make a difference.

Nothing helped with the nightmares—not therapy, not drugs—but what my parents and friends and therapist and psychiatrist didn't seem to understand was that I was okay. Maybe I wasn't happy, but who could be happy with everything going on in the world? I was home and I was as safe as I was going to be and I had my research to do and that was really all I wanted right now. I wasn't the one who needed to change; the country needed to change. I just needed to try to figure out how.

My family didn't agree. The fire had taken place while I was in eighth grade, and my parents had hoped that my obsession with history would burn out over the summer and I'd be distracted by starting high school. No such luck. My English class was reading Elie Wiesel's *Night*, I'd signed up for World History so I could study World War II, and I'd expanded my daily reading to include so many political websites I got headaches and eventually had to start wearing glasses.

"She can't go on like this," I heard the rebbetzen tell my parents at services one night. The new temple we'd joined had welcomed our whole congregation, even allowing our rabbi and cantor to participate in services so we felt like we were a part of things while the renovations continued. "You need to get her out of there. There's a Jewish high school in Brookline—I can help you get her admitted."

I didn't hear what my parents said in response, but they'd apparently decided the rebbetzen was right about getting me out of Brooksby but wrong about sending me to an all-Jewish school, where there was a good chance my obsessions would be shared by much of the student body. Before I knew it they'd filled out all the paperwork to get me into Gardner, a school there was no way they could have afforded without the scholarship I ultimately received.

"You can't do this," I told them. "I don't want to leave."

"You can't live like this," Mom said. "The nightmares alone . . ."

"We can't live like this," Dad said. "And Shana can't either."

Even my sister was against me? It was too much. "I'll miss you," she had said. "But I don't want you to be so sad."

"I'm not sad!" I wasn't sad; I was furious. All the time. It felt kind of nice to have something tangible to be angry at, and so I spent the rest of my time in Brooksby raging at my parents for sending me away, even as I tried to rein in my obsessiveness, just to show them I could. I'd resolved to hate this place, to try to get home as quickly as possible, but even my few hours at Game Night had made me wonder whether maybe I should give Gardner a shot. Maybe there was more for me to learn here than there was at home.

One thing was for sure, though; being at Gardner was not going to automatically stop my nightmares. I woke up on the first day of classes to Brianna shaking my shoulder so hard my teeth rattled. "What is wrong with you?" she asked. "Is this going to be a thing every night? Because this is totally not okay."

I felt tears drying on my cheeks. It had been a variation of the classroom dream this time, which made sense given that classes started today. "I'm sorry," I said. "I can fix this." That was only sort of true, but I'd brought all my prescriptions with me, and I'd try them all again if there was any chance they'd help.

"You better," Brianna said.

I hadn't exactly won the roommate lottery.

But to my surprise, I soon discovered I had won the class schedule lottery. It hadn't occurred to me that someone who wanted to be a lawyer would probably take the same kinds of classes I did, but the first person I saw in my first class the day after orientation (Intro to Political Science) was the red-haired guy. To my even greater surprise, he recognized me immediately. "You busted me at Assassin!" he said, and took the seat right in back of me, which guaranteed I'd spend the whole year self-conscious. I learned his name was Hunter Fredericks from roll call; when he turned up in my class on the American Revolution and sat in front of me I learned the freckles that dotted his face also covered the back of his neck. And when we got assigned to be partners for our European History class and had to move our desks together I learned he smelled green—some combination of mint and grass, maybe—and I knew I was doomed.

We didn't have all our classes together—he was taking Spanish, while I was taking Chinese, and I was in a higher-level math class than he was—but we did have the same lunch period. "Save me a seat!" he said, and I watched him head straight for the sandwich station. It took me less time to make my peanut-butter-and-jelly-on-whole-wheat-toast than it did for him to put together a massive and truly disgusting-looking roast beef sub, complete with four different kinds of cheese and every condiment in the world. "What?" he asked, when he saw me eyeballing the mess on his tray. "I haven't even put the potato chips in it yet."

"I don't even know where to start," I said, but he wasn't looking at me anymore; his eyes had wandered to some vantage point behind my head, and his mouth had gone slack. I turned around, and in less than a second I knew exactly how things were going to go.

"Well, well, well, if it isn't the Game Night crew!" It was the fashion influencer, because of course it was. She was wearing a flowered sundress as if she were headed to a garden party, her Honey-Nut-Cheerios hair bundled under a floppy sun hat. I, in contrast, was wearing my usual uniform of black leggings, plaid shirt, and red Converse, and I wondered whether the fact that I'd noticed her outfit meant I was starting to care more about my appearance, like my mother always told me I should. Somehow I doubted it.

Hunter couldn't stop staring, and his obvious admiration was a huge downer. Since he didn't seem capable of speech, I'd have to take over. "Come sit," I said. "I'll scooch."

The girl didn't hesitate for a minute, plunking her Instagram-ready salad down on the table in front of her. "It's so great I ran into you guys! I was afraid I'd have to sit with my roommate. She kept me up all night talking about how much we were going to love it here—her brother graduated already—and honestly I'm exhausted."

"You don't look exhausted," Hunter said, which was true, and also enraging. "But we'll do our best to keep you awake. I'm Hunter."

"I'm Chloe," she said, and smiled so we could see her mouthful of almost-perfect white teeth. Her bottom two teeth had a teeny overlap that even I had to admit was adorable. This lunch was turning out to be a disaster. The two of them were just going to stare at each other until little cartoon hearts started dancing around their heads.

But then Chloe turned to me. "And you are?"

"Amina," I said. "Nice to meet you." I waited for her to give me the up-and-down look I'd expect from someone who clearly cared about fashion as much as she did, but to her credit, her eyes stayed on my face.

"Nice to meet you too," she said. "How are your classes so far?"

From there things got easier. Hunter and I took turns telling her what we were discovering about our shared schedule; we agreed that our poli sci class was sure to be the favorite, given that our teacher was a former State Department official who'd quit after the latest election. I admitted how nervous I was about taking a Chinese class and showed them the vocabulary flash cards I expected to be carrying around with me until graduation. "What about you?" I asked. "Do we have any classes together in the afternoon, maybe?"

"I'm going to guess no," Chloe said. "My schedule is super

specialized—I'm taking an intro course in 3-D design, and it's got a geometry add-on, plus anatomy, economics, journalism, Italian, and French."

One of the things I had to admit (grudgingly) was exciting about Gardner was how many classes were available. The school was committed to preparing us for whatever our future career plans might include, though I had no idea what that meant for the non-scholarship kids. Chloe's schedule sounded kind of all over the place, but she seemed to have a plan. "When you say specialized . . ."

She laughed, and I noticed her lipstick hadn't so much as smudged, even though she'd made it most of the way through her salad while Hunter and I geeked out over our classes. "I want to start my own clothing line. I've already got a pretty good internet presence, so now I need to go next-level and learn more about the business. The major players are all still in Europe."

I was starting to see how the pieces fit together. "So the design classes and anatomy are about the clothes themselves, economics is about the business, and the language classes are so you can talk to the big guns. What about journalism?"

"Everything's happening online now," Chloe said, "and the fact that I'm good at taking Instagram pics isn't enough. I need to learn how to talk to people through my writing."

Hunter was practically drooling. "You've given this a lot of thought."

Chloe laughed. "You have no idea. But I have to say, it's really nice to be around people who get it. My family totally doesn't."

"Mine either," I said, though we were talking about completely different things. "They made me come here." The words slipped out before I even had a chance to think—I hadn't meant to share that with anyone, let alone people I'd just met.

"Really?" Chloe's eyebrows shot up. "I had to fight my way here, all claws out."

"Me too," Hunter said. "My family was super not into it. They wanted me to stay closer to home."

"Where's home?" Chloe asked.

I hadn't asked him this yet, I realized, and I had no idea what the answer would be. I definitely wasn't expecting what he said. "Texas. Houston, specifically."

"Where's your accent?" I sounded more skeptical than I intended.

"Not everyone in Texas has one," he said, with an exaggerated drawl. "But if that's what you ladies are looking for . . ."

"Does the sexism come with the accent?" Again with the sharpness. I had to get it together. I added a little drawl of my own. "Or is that just a cowboy thing?"

Thankfully Hunter seemed to get that I was joking, or trying, anyway. "That's where 'y'all' comes in really handy," he said, accent now eliminated. "Gender neutral, all-encompassing. The language of the people."

"Oh, I don't know," Chloe said, taking off her hat and shaking her hair out. "I kind of like being called a lady. No one back home has that much class."

I found that hard to believe, given Chloe was probably the classiest person I'd ever met, at least appearance-wise. I wasn't convinced people who dabbled in casual misogyny were the classiest people, though. But I didn't feel like getting into it with people I hardly knew. My friends back home had ditched me for being too intense, having too many opinions about things they didn't care that much about, and there was no need for me to wreck my potential friendships here before they'd even gotten off the ground. I wondered whether I should change the subject, but before I could think of a topic, Hunter had already jumped in.

"Have either of you met that girl from Game Night, the one who got all up in that guy's face? She seemed cool."

"She's in my econ class," Chloe said. "Her name's Jo. Short for Josephine, but best to never call her that. She gave our teacher an earful."

I was glad Hunter had asked about her; I wanted to meet her too. "We should all hang out," I said. "But maybe not in the Rathskeller. That place was shady."

"Wouldn't make a bad place to hide if something terrible

happened," Hunter said. "I'd rather hang out there and hide behind a sofa than barricade a classroom door with desks."

I'd done the same active shooter drill back in Brooksby. The Gardner student handbook had a whole section on school shootings, instructing us to memorize exit routes and find closets to hide in where the walls around them were reinforced. "Sofas can't stop bullets all that well," I said.

Hunter shrugged. "Bullets aren't what's going to get us, anyway. Do you know we've got less than twenty years to fix what we've done to the environment before we're completely and totally screwed?"

Interesting. I, like most kids I knew, was way more worried about school shootings than the environment. And that wasn't even taking into account my more pressing fears of anti-Semitism and complete governmental collapse. I had a vague recollection of reading something online about what Hunter was saying, and I knew that some newspapers and climate scientists were pushing for changes to terminology that would help people understand just how disastrous a time we were living in—climate crisis versus climate change, for example. But all I'd done to help so far was to quit using plastic straws. Hunter was obviously more committed.

Chloe, in contrast, was not. "That stuff is so overblown," she said, with a wave of her hand. "We're way more likely to get blown to bits by a nuclear bomb well before the environment does us in. Or we'll build too many nuclear power plants because we're so anti-coal, and the meltdowns alone will turn us into cancer-riddled walking death. Do you even know what happened in Chernobyl?"

"Are you serious right now?" Hunter asked. He seemed genuinely shocked by what she was saying. Maybe they wouldn't be a perfect couple after all. "No one in their right mind is arguing for more nuclear power. It's all about wind and solar energy. It's the only way we'll survive, and we have to change now."

Before I could jump in, the two of them had launched into a full-on argument about whether coal really was bad for the environment. It turned out Chloe was from western Pennsylvania, and though her family had been more affected by the steel mills closing, she had a lot of sympathy for coal miners who'd lost their jobs. Maybe they weren't really arguing—they didn't seem angry with one another. In fact, it soon became clear they were having a good time. "Never would have pegged you for a hippie," Chloe was saying. "And aren't you pretty much destroying the planet with that hot mess of a sub? Aren't cow farts, like, the greatest threat to mankind's survival?"

"And those shoes aren't made of leather?" Hunter shot back. "Along with however many other pairs of shoes you own?"

"You can't even count that high," Chloe said, but she was laughing. "Don't forget all my handbags. Besides, I'm not the one who's trying to reverse centuries of planetary destruction in, like, two weeks."

I sat and watched them debate, trying to keep my mouth from hanging open. Here I was, all worried about whether I'd be too intense for them, and the two of them were battling out energy policy like it was no big deal. Their obsessions might not be entirely the same as mine, but they had obsessions, and it was so exciting to watch. For all my dread about coming here, it had never occurred to me that I might meet people who I'd want to talk to, who might share some of my concerns, or at least understand them. Could I actually be a part of this?

"Our government is going to go down in flames well before North Korea bombs us into oblivion or global warming fries us to a crisp," I said.

Hunter and Chloe both stared at me for a minute. "It's global heating now," Hunter said, finally, and then the yelling began again. Only this time, I was yelling too, and I loved it.

3.

The first thing I did after classes got out that day was to go back to my dorm and look up my new friends online. I couldn't find much on Hunter; his social media was limited and locked down, and all I could access was the occasional tagged photo of him playing soccer on someone else's feed. He did look super cute in soccer shorts, though. No shock there.

Chloe was a whole other story. I thought about what she'd said about having a good online presence, but that turned out to be the understatement of the century. Her blog was called *Chloe's Closet*, a name that struck me as childish until I clicked on her bio and saw that she had literally started it when she was a child—she'd been interested in fashion since she was ten years old. The site was basic but professional, not cutesy like the title might have indicated, and it mostly existed to direct people to her Instagram.

That's where it became clear how massive her online

following really was. Like, over a million people massive. Seriously? That many people cared what a teenage girl thought about fashion? I scrolled through the photos, and while I could see she was really talented, it was weird to think she'd amassed that kind of following even before turning eighteen. I clicked on a post of Chloe wearing the sunhat-and-flowered-dress ensemble from earlier today, assuming she'd put it up in the morning, but she'd gotten her outfit together last night and described each component of it, complete with a ton of hashtags. Thousands of people had already commented on how cute she looked and how they were going to buy every last item. I saw that it was marked as a sponsored post, and I wondered what that meant. Were the clothes free? Did she get a cut if people bought them?

Apparently I could ask her if I ever got up the nerve to be that nosy, because somehow Chloe and I were becoming friends. The three of us had exchanged cell phone numbers at lunch and had agreed to meet the next day as well. Dinner was more complicated; Hunter was obliged to sit at a table with the soccer team as a kind of bonding activity, and Chloe had promised to hang out with her roommate, in whom I had less than no interest. That was fine, though; I needed alone time, and besides, at least once a week I wouldn't be eating in the dining hall anyway. Friday nights were reserved for Shabbat dinners with Gardner's Hillel group.

I'd had high hopes for making friends with some of the other Jewish kids at school, who I assumed would share some of my fears about the rise of anti-Semitism. But from the very first Friday night I spent at Hillel, it was clear to me the kids at Gardner were nothing like my former friends back home. They were mostly from New York and Los Angeles, and I could tell few of them were scholarship kids, though my guess was that the misbehavior that got them sent here might have been as simple as not making the kinds of grades their parents expected. They were sophisticated in ways I was not, telling stories of bar and bat mitzvahs that sounded more like that MTV show about wealthy sixteen-year-olds. Their parents had hired aging rock stars to perform at their parties; mine had rented out the basement floor of our temple and put my sister in charge of making a playlist on her phone. They were fashionable and beautifully dressed and I was scared to talk to them. In some ways, they reminded me of Chloe. I supposed I should give them a chance; they'd invited me to hang out with them after dinner, but I really just wanted to go to my dorm room and be by myself for a while. Being around them made me miss my family, especially Shana, and I thought maybe I should call home. I could always hang out next week.

When I got back to my room, there was a note taped to my door.

Dear AMINA*,*

Would you rather spend three years at Gardner studying on your own? Or would you rather hang out with some like-minded people, have some fun, and add an extracurricular to your college transcript at the same time? If you're on Team Fun, then find the most secret, safe place on campus and meet there next Saturday at midnight and we can get started.

Hope to see you there!

I had no idea what to make of this. I put all thoughts of a family phone call out of my mind and read the note over and over again, trying to figure out what was going on. Did Gardner have a secret society? If so, why would I be invited? Maybe that wasn't it. Maybe it was just some sad, desperate person who needed friends. But why make it a game, then? And why such a hard game? I had no idea what the most secret safe place on campus was. Although I was reminded of the conversation Hunter, Chloe, and I had had at lunch, about how the Rathskeller would not be the safest place to hide if something bad were to happen. Was this Hunter's way of showing that he'd known that already? Or perhaps Chloe calling his bluff?

I debated whether to check in with them. The note hadn't specified that I had to keep it secret, though it seemed implied. I had some time to think, anyway, and I decided to use it. Maybe one of them would bring it up.

The following week flew by in a whirlwind of classes and homework and lunches with Chloe and Hunter, who'd fallen into a routine of finding topics to fight about ranging from the trivial to the serious and everything in between. It was hilarious to watch them argue about whether rap and country went well together; I didn't really listen to either, but Hunter was obsessed with rap/country collaborations, whereas Chloe thought they should always be kept separate. "There's a reason Taylor Swift didn't start bringing rappers into the mix until she was all pop, all the time," Chloe said, at which point Hunter got out his cell phone and played a clip of her doing a jokey rap with T-Pain from way back that had all of us laughing so hard people started coming up to our table to see what was so funny.

I tended to have opinions about the more serious topics, like when they debated whether you could separate art from the artist. Chloe thought the artist was completely irrelevant, but I didn't. "I had to stop watching one of my favorite TV shows when I found out the star was a rapist," I said. "I couldn't pretend he was someone else anymore. And I tried to watch this comedian I used to love and his act just comes across so different now, like all his pro-woman stuff was just a way to get access."

Hunter's eyes got all sparkly, and even though I'd only known him a short time I already had a sense of what was coming. I was in trouble. "All the examples you just gave are for people who you liked and then found out were awful," he said. "What about people everyone always knew were awful? Do they count?"

"What do you mean?" Chloe asked.

"Well, we know Amina's a big reader," he said. I'd told them about growing up a huge bookworm and how that basically hadn't changed at all, though now I read different stuff. "I bet you liked *Charlie and the Chocolate Factory* when you were little, didn't you? What about *Matilda*? That's, like, bookworm candy."

My real Roald Dahl favorite was "The Wonderful Story of Henry Sugar," but I didn't see the need to argue details. "Sure, I'm a fan."

"You know Roald Dahl was a massive anti-Semite, right?" His eyes were super wide now, reminding me of the boy who'd asked the apocalypse question at Game Night.

"That sounds familiar," I admitted.

"Did you stop reading him?"

"I didn't have to," I said. "I grew up."

"Okay, fine. What if Ms. Cavanaugh assigns us T. S. Eliot or Ezra Pound? You going to just refuse to read? What about other kinds of art? Are you going to stop going to museums?"

Now Chloe looked interested. "No more Picasso?" she asked. "Why stop at art? What about music? And what do we do about Michael Jackson?"

They both watched as I tried to come up with an answer. Hunter was onto something, but it wasn't everything. "Okay, fine, I hadn't really thought about the older stuff. But there's a difference between people who did horrible stuff way before I was even alive, people who are dead now, and people who were doing bad things at the same time as they were making the art I like—books, movies, whatever. It doesn't feel like the same kind of betrayal, you know?"

Chloe nodded, but I hadn't convinced Hunter. "Just because the standards were different back then doesn't mean what they were doing wasn't wrong," he said. "Is it really okay to let them off the hook just because they didn't know better? As if being anti-Semitic or horrible to other people was ever really okay?"

"You have a point," I said. "You're going to be a really good lawyer."

He grinned. "If I even get into college. I'm going to have to find some extracurriculars, and soon."

Funny that he'd bring up extracurriculars. Was that some sort of hint? Had he sent the note? Was he waiting for me to figure it out? I watched his face but it was as open as it always was. Chloe hadn't responded either, except to say that extracurriculars were the least of her worries. "Speaking of which, I have to go," she said. "Did you know there's an amazing greenhouse on campus? It's perfect for photo shoots. I'll join the Garden Club to get access if I have to, but I am fully taking that place over."

I didn't doubt it for a second.

The breakneck pace of those early days of school made me realize succeeding at Gardner would be a lot harder than succeeding at my old high school. I had an astonishing amount of work to do in every single one of my classes, and I was already wondering whether taking Chinese rather than sticking with Spanish was a mistake. I'd been half kidding about walking around with flash cards initially, but now I was deathly serious—I brought them everywhere and reviewed them constantly.

The good news was that my teachers were all pretty great. They might have ended up at Gardner because they'd made mistakes or bad choices or were too stubborn to leave when things got bad, but that meant we had teachers with interesting backgrounds who were committed to making sure the students who cared got the best possible education. Sure, that meant a ton of work, but that had already turned into weekly study dates with Hunter, so I couldn't complain.

The bad news was that I had no idea how I was going to do academically, which meant I was going to have to build up my résumé with more than just classes. Which meant I didn't have the option of ignoring that note. I needed to join a club of some kind, and I didn't care what it was.

Except I'd run out of time to figure out where to go. I'd planned to come straight home from services and dinner Friday night and get to work, but I was exhausted from a week of studying, and I fell asleep before I could even start to plan my research. I'd have to find the place on Saturday.

I hoped there was time.

I started early, bringing my journal and a pen to the dining hall, where I drank cup after cup of sweet, milky tea and worked through the options. The safest place on campus depended on what kind of bad thing might be happening, and given that we were at a school, I immediately went back to thinking about shootings. But the safest place in a school shooting was relative, and there wasn't always time to get picky—the note's phrasing indicated there was a specific place to go, so the event probably was something that came with some notice. Could it be a biohazard, in which case I'd be looking for a nurse's office? That wouldn't necessarily be safe; it would just be obvious, which didn't seem right. We had to be looking for someplace that was completely blocked off from physical harm of any kind.

I tried to imagine the worst possible thing, which made me think bomb. And the safest place to be in the event of a bomb was a bomb shelter. There had to be one on campus, but where? Gardner was big, the size of a small college, between dorms and faculty housing and academic halls and the gym. I wasn't going to be able to guess where a bomb shelter might be.

I decided I'd had more than enough tea and went back to my room to get out my laptop. The new student information packet had nothing about bomb shelters on campus, though it did provide evacuation instructions in the event of fires or other catastrophes. Not super helpful. I'd have to find it myself. If there was a shelter somewhere on campus, it had to be in a basement, right? I hadn't been at Gardner long enough to do much exploring, so first I had to figure out which building was most likely to have a basement. I was up for the challenge.

I made a map of the buildings as best as I could remember them in my notebook and then decided to start in the place I'd identified as the best option: the gym. It was gigantic, with multiple basketball courts and a swimming pool, not to mention the fitness center and the indoor track. With all that space taken up already it seemed like you'd need to go underground for storage, I figured.

The sound of basketballs echoing off lacquered wooden floors assaulted my ears the moment I opened the massive front door of the athletic building. I'd thought maybe it would be relatively quiet because it was the weekend and the weather outside was shockingly warm for mid-September, but the practice courts were filled with students playing weekend pickup games. Maybe I'd just underestimated people's love of basketball.

I walked past the practice courts and turned a corridor

to pass athletic department offices, my flip-flops flipping and flopping on the concrete floor, though there was no one working on a Saturday to hear me. I tested every unmarked door I could find in the hopes there would be some secret basement entrance, but it wasn't until I reached a stairwell that I realized I'd made things harder than necessary. Though ostensibly the stairs only went up, there was a door, painted the same gray as the cement blocks that made up the wall of the stairwell, right where one might expect a set of stairs leading down to be. Even the handle was painted gray; the door almost blended right into the wall, which was clearly the intention of whoever painted it. I was sure it would be locked, but it wasn't.

The stairs did lead down into a basement, as I'd expected, but the basement was really just another set of offices that were no longer in use. Long fluorescent lights flickered over a dropped ceiling, with those white tiles that looked like they had holes punched into them at random. I wandered the halls looking for some sort of room that might function as a shelter, but I saw nothing but offices and bathrooms that hadn't been cleaned in a very long time. There was some evidence other students knew the basement existed; I saw condom wrappers and empty beer cans in one of the bathroom trash bins, and all of a sudden I felt how alone I was, hanging out in this basement by myself.

When I got back to the staircase, though, I noticed another

gray door, again where a down staircase would be. And when that door, too, was unlocked, I had a feeling I might be onto something.

There were more stairs this time, or maybe it just felt as if there were because there wasn't as much light. I stepped into a hallway with the same cement brick walls as the staircase, the same concrete flooring as the main floor, though it was scuffed and dirty with years of use and little cleaning, as far as I could tell. Gone were the ceiling tiles and flickering fluorescent lights, replaced with lightbulbs trapped behind what looked like little steel cages and set at intervals along the narrow walls. I'd found some sort of hallway. No—it wasn't a hallway; it was a tunnel.

This had to be the place. But the lights were dim and the tunnel seemed to head in both directions and I had no idea which way to go. I didn't want to get lost, but I hadn't exactly brought breadcrumbs with me, so I decided to go right and then keep going right any time I had to make a choice.

After about fifteen minutes of taking right turn after right turn and seeing nothing but hallways only occasionally interrupted by a storage closet or yet another door leading to more stairs, I decided it was time to change my strategy. I started going upstairs every so often, popping my head aboveground like some sort of gopher, orienting myself to where I was on campus. It quickly became clear the tunnels tracked the buildings, serving as an underground means of getting around campus. There was no way a school with the foresight to maintain these tunnels didn't have a bomb shelter, or several, but I wasn't going to find it wandering around aimlessly like this.

Instead, I made my way back to the dining hall to get a sandwich, then went to my room to check the campus map. If the tunnels went everywhere on campus, then a shelter would probably be closest to where people lived. And not just any people—important people. Most likely it was under one of the administration buildings, or the Gardner president's house.

I felt so sure I'd solved the problem I was tempted to take my chances and show up right at midnight, but it wasn't in my nature. Instead, I headed back underground. It was almost anticlimactic to find, just under the president's house, the black-and-yellow sign indicating the presence of a fallout shelter. It was the only distinguishing feature drawing my eye to yet another gray door blended into yet another cement-block wall, but it was enough.

I didn't try the door to see whether it was unlocked; it was one thing to show up a few minutes early, and quite another to miss the mark by hours. I went back to my dorm, grabbed some dinner at the dining hall, and spent the rest of the night trying to imagine what this group might be about. I was feeling pretty confident that either Hunter or Chloe had started it, but who else would they have invited? The soccer team? Chloe's roommate? I'd noticed some girls had figured out who Chloe was and were starting to shadow her around campus, wearing outfits similar to hers; would this end up being a club of her followers?

I showed up just before midnight and got part of the answer to my question: both Hunter and Chloe were there, along with the wiry girl from Game Night who I'd so wanted to get to know. Jo, Chloe had said. "Amina!" Hunter yelled, clearly both surprised and happy to see me, and gave me a hug.

I had not expected this—so far we were class-and-lunch friends, not hugging friends—so it took me a minute to hug him back. "Hey, Hunter," I said, bringing my conversational A game, as always. "Hi, Chloe."

"So you're not in charge of this," she said, frowning. "I'd been so sure."

I laughed. "Funny, I thought it was you." I wondered why neither of us had been willing to ask the other, but I supposed we didn't know each other that well yet.

"We've already established that it wasn't Hunter or Jo," she said. "Have you two met yet?"

"I'm Amina," I said. "Did anyone knock?"

Before she could answer, the door swung open. Standing in front of us was the shaggy-haired boy from Game Night, a huge grin on his face. "Come in, come in," he said, practically bouncing up and down. "I wasn't sure how many chairs to set up, but it looks like there'll be plenty. Any trouble finding the place?"

The place in question was indeed a fallout shelter, a square space I estimated to be the size of two dorm rooms, with a little door in the back corner that most likely led to a bathroom. The floor was the same concrete gray as the tunnels, the walls covered in the same cement blocks, but in front of two of them were floor-to-ceiling metal shelves filled with canned goods, bottled water, and first-aid supplies, along with what appeared to be tool kits. The shaggy-haired boy had set up seven or eight spindly folding chairs in a circle in the center of the room, but there were only five of us, including him, which meant he'd sent out more invitations. Had the others gotten lost? Or were they just not into it? It didn't matter to me; I was happy to be among the few and the proud who'd made their way here, and I didn't love big groups anyway. The shaggy-haired boy plunked himself down on one of the chairs, and we all followed suit.

Hunter spoke first. "It wasn't that hard, getting here. I started on Google and tried to figure out what kind of place would be safest, and bomb shelter seemed like the obvious choice. From there it was just a matter of finding it, and here we are." He opened his arms to indicate the room. How had he found it so fast? Had he already been underground?

"I went straight for the blueprints," Chloe said. "The

originals were on the town hall website."

"Such high-tech activity for a low-tech task," Jo said. "The blueprints are in the library, dorks."

"I bet it took Chloe half the time to find it," Hunter said. I was not loving how he jumped to her defense, especially when I was pretty sure she didn't need that kind of help.

Chloe smirked, and I waited for her to lay into Hunter. But her half grin was for Jo. "Your nicknames were much more creative on Game Night."

Jo stared at her for a moment, and I wondered whether the group was doomed before we'd even gotten going. But then she laughed. "You're absolutely right," she said. "I went for the low-hanging fruit. I'll do better next time, I promise."

I was relieved she'd cleared the air, but that meant it was my turn. "I wish I had all your confidence. It took me ages to find this place." I told them about working through all the different theories before spelunking underground. "I started making my own map, but I'm sure the blueprints are better. I'll have to print up a copy myself."

"I can do it!" the shaggy-haired boy said. Such enthusiasm! "I've got copies already, and I made a map of just the tunnels, too. I'm so glad you made it here! This is the only fallout shelter on campus, and it was built back in the eighties, when everyone thought nuclear war was right around the corner. It was designed for just the school's president and his family, which is why it's so small."

Exactly what I thought. "And everyone else could just crawl off and die?" Jo asked. "This school is cold, man."

"And it's not even winter yet!" I said, though I regretted the dumb joke immediately.

Hunter was the only one who seemed amused. "Dad jokes," he said. "My favorite. Maybe because my dad is completely humorless."

I admitted my dad and I had a competition, ourselves. "But we go for groans more than laughs."

"Lucky for you," Chloe said. "Put me on Team Humorless Dad."

"That's my team too," the shaggy-haired boy said.

"Not mine," Jo said. "My dad's dead. Mom, too."

The room got very, very quiet.

Then she laughed. "Oh, come on, it's fine. You'll laugh at dad jokes but dark humor is too much?"

"So your parents aren't dead?" Chloe asked.

"No, they are, but I've had time to get used to it. Don't worry, I'm okay. But if we're already getting into family stories then maybe we need to get better acquainted." She turned to our fearless leader, whose name we still didn't know. "I got everyone's names in the hall except yours, Shaggy."

The boy touched his hair, and I felt bad she'd made him feel self-conscious. "I'm Wyatt," he said. "If you all got to know each other already, then maybe we should just get started."

"Sounds like a plan," I said.

"That's great!" Wyatt nodded enthusiastically. I got the sense he did everything enthusiastically. "So here's the thing: this is the first school I've ever been to. I grew up on a kind of commune, but my parents split up and they told me I could pick whatever school I wanted, as long as I could get a scholarship."

It was refreshing to hear someone talk so openly about being a scholarship kid. I wondered whether I'd have the courage, if it came up. It's not that I minded, or was embarrassed by it, but the culture around here didn't really lend itself to being so up-front.

"Anyway," Wyatt went on, "I've never really had to, like, go out and make friends. But after Game Night I thought maybe I could find the people who seemed to be having fun and we could start a club. We could play some other games, or just talk, or whatever. And I know it's early to be thinking about college, but it can't hurt to get involved in something, right?"

"What would we talk about? Like, what's this club about, exactly?" This came from Jo, who'd stretched out so far in her folding chair she seemed to take up half the room. I'd been trying not to stare at her, convinced she'd be able to see how intrigued I was by her, but it seemed okay to look at her while she was speaking. She'd been so edgy with the meth chemist at Game Night that I'd been sure she'd be all sharp and sarcastic, but she just seemed curious about what Wyatt was saying. Not at all what I'd expected.

"Well, I asked that question during Would You Rather about surviving the end of the world, and that's because given everything that's happening these days I feel like maybe we don't have that much time left. Like, as a species, you know?" He looked nervous, like he was worried we'd think he was a freak. "My family's always been . . . um . . . concerned about end times and that kind of stuff, but it feels more . . . real now." I wondered whether his commune had been more like a cult, but now definitely did not seem like the time to bring that up. "We could always talk about that sort of thing, if you all were interested."

"You're serious," Chloe said. "Are you one of those prepper types?"

Wyatt shrugged. He wasn't saying no, I noticed. I bet I was right about that cult. "I am serious, but that doesn't mean we have to do it. We could just talk about it. As a group. If we wanted."

"Like how?" I was starting to get excited, despite myself. Maybe I really had found my people. My parents had sent me here so I'd stop thinking about the terrible stuff going on in the world, but there was no getting away from it. And I hadn't wanted to get away from it in the first place.

Wyatt jumped out of his chair and started to pace, except

there wasn't really room to pace, so he ended up taking two steps forward, spinning around, and then taking two steps back. I hoped he didn't get dizzy. "There are just so many things! We could think about all the ways things could go wrong, and what we'd have to do to survive, and we could learn what to do to help ourselves."

"This is all sounding really intense," Chloe said. "What happened to the whole we-could-all-just-hang-out-and-play-games part? Maybe we could get to know each other a little before we start officially packing for the end of the world? I don't know about you people, but I haven't spent a ton of time away from home, much as I've wanted to, and I'm a little freaked out. We all have to survive here before we can think about surviving the apocalypse, so maybe we could strategize that?"

I wanted to learn how to survive the apocalypse, but she had a point. "I wouldn't mind a little help surviving here."

"I don't know," Jo said. "I came here to get a diploma, not to make friends."

Chloe giggled. "You literally sound like you're on one of those survivalist reality TV shows."

"They're hardly reality," Jo said, but she was trying not to laugh herself. "You must know the producers of *Survivor* got busted for cheating the very first season. They kicked off the girl who ate bugs because they wanted to keep the senior citizen."

"I remember that!" Wyatt was bouncing up and down again. "The eating bugs part. I didn't know about the cheating. That sucks."

"Aw, he thought it was all real," Jo said. "Poor thing."

Wyatt was sweet, but he did seem a little sheltered. I hoped we'd learn more about what his life had been like before he got here. It wouldn't be boring, that was for sure.

"I'm not that naive," he said. "I just haven't watched all that much TV." He was starting to look a little dejected. Even his curls were drooping. I felt the impulse to cheer him up.

"I think we should make this a survival club," I said. "It can be about surviving school or surviving the apocalypse, I don't care. I just like the idea of having some people to talk to, and the college app thing can't hurt. If you all are up for it, I'm in." I looked around the group to see how everyone was reacting, and I was relieved to see mostly nods.

"Here for the friends, at least," Chloe said.

"Me too," Hunter said.

That left Jo. She was the person I'd most wanted to get to know that first night, and I found myself holding my breath waiting for her to say something. Finally, she sighed. "I guess it can't hurt to try."

Wyatt had gotten so excited he'd started bouncing again, making his way over to the shelf of bottled water and grabbing a handful to pass around. I was relieved to see that they appeared to be newer than some of the other bottles; Wyatt must have brought these himself. "I'm so happy everyone is into this! We're going to have so much fun!"

"Cool it, Twitchy," Jo said. "You sold us, okay? Now chill with the exclamation marks. I can practically see them."

Wyatt calmed himself down and sat in his chair. He uncapped his water bottle and held it in the air. "To survival!" he said.

"Man, you really need to calm down," Jo muttered, but she held out her bottle anyway, as did the rest of us.

"To survival!" we all repeated.

The survival meeting had completely energized me. I couldn't believe I'd actually found a potential group of friends, two of whom already seemed to like me and one who clearly shared my obsession with the imminent demise of society. Not to mention that Jo had joined too—I was getting everything I wanted, all in one place. True, I'd be feeding the fixation that had gotten me sent here, which was definitely not what my parents had in mind, but I didn't care. For the first time in forever I wasn't afraid to go to sleep. I skipped my Ambien and was fine, and I woke up feeling rested and happy.

Chloe and Hunter weren't quite as enthused as I was. "That Wyatt is kind of off the wall," Chloe said. "Maybe it's just that I've never met any homeschooled kids, but he is extra."

"He's just excited," I said. "You're still going to be in the club, right? We'll make it fun, I promise."

"Oh, it's we now, is it?" Chloe smirked. "You and Wyatt start doing some planning without the rest of us?"

My face got hot. I hoped Hunter didn't notice. "Not at all. I just want this to happen. It's not like I've joined any other groups, and Wyatt's right—we'll have to do that eventually, even just to fill up our résumés."

"My résumé's doing just fine," Chloe said.

"We know," Hunter and I both said at the same time. Chloe never let a chance go by to remind us how internet-famous she was.

"What would make it worthwhile for you guys?" I asked. It was so weird how quickly I'd become invested in the success of this group.

"I like you both, and I definitely need to hang out with people who care about more than fashion," Chloe said. "But I don't want to spend all my free time talking about the apocalypse. If you can keep that from happening, I'm good."

Not exactly the answer I wanted to hear, but I understood. I didn't want to lose any more friends to my own single-mindedness, either. Back in Brooksby it had gotten so bad the only person I hung out with regularly was Shana. And she was five years younger than me. I reminded myself to send her an email—she didn't have her own phone yet.

"I wouldn't mind talking about some of the things we're afraid of," Hunter said. "I went to one of the Environmentalist Club meetings and I don't know if I can spend three years hanging out with those people, but I can't just pretend I'm not scared we've all but screwed up the planet."

"We're not the ones who screwed it up," Chloe said. "That's on our parents, and their parents, and everyone before them. They just left a mess for us to clean."

"Sure, but if we don't clean it, we're done," Hunter said. "Just because it isn't fair doesn't mean we can pretend it's not happening."

I sensed they were about to get into yet another one of their lunchtime debates. "See, here's the thing—you both love talking about this stuff. I do too. So does Wyatt. I don't know Jo yet, but if we come up with some way to make thinking about survival fun, then this club can be everything we want. We can get to know each other, have people to hang out with that we like and who aren't annoying like the Environmental Club, and we can learn some things too, about how to survive both here at Gardner and in the world."

"I don't know," Chloe said. "Who's to say we won't be as annoying as the Environmental Club?"

"First of all, we're just not," I said. "You already know that. Second, Wyatt started the whole thing because we met at Game Night. What if we made this into a gaming club? Like it would still be about survival, but we'd turn survival into a game. I've got a little bit of a competitive streak, and I know you both do too."

Hunter started nodding. "We could take turns planning.

The games could teach us about survival strategies for all sorts of situations. I'd do something about the climate crisis, and you can teach us how to win the internet."

Chloe narrowed her eyes. "Underestimate me at your peril. I'll destroy all of you."

"Don't count me out so quick," Hunter said. "I've got years of team sports behind me. I hate losing."

I wanted to chime in with some pithy explanation of my own competitive impulses, but all I could really point to were some vicious family games of Boggle. I invariably beat my father, though he was pretty good given that English wasn't even his first language, and I still could stomp my sister, though she was getting better very quickly. It was Mom and I who really fought it out, most of the time. I loved that it would never occur to anyone in my family to throw a game; we'd been playing since I was a little kid, and while it used to upset me terribly to lose, my parents considered failure an important lesson. "There will always be people better than you, so you're going to have to work your hardest all the time," Mom would say.

I'd been reminded of that Saturday night, when I realized everyone had figured out how to find the bomb shelter a whole lot faster than I had. I may have been a scholarship kid, but that didn't make me smarter than anyone here.

Chloe let out a dramatic sigh. "It is a little bit of a downer, though, isn't it? All this worrying?"

How could she not worry? Did she not see what was happening all around her? Maybe the world was different for beautiful blond people who spent their real-life time being perfect online, but it felt like the rest of us were under siege. How could I make her see that? "I mean the world kind of sucks right now, so isn't that the point?" I asked.

"True, it sucks," she said, somehow cheerfully. "That's why we have to make it better. But I don't intend to spend the whole time here obsessing about the end of the world. We've got to mix it up a little. I'll stay in your club and play your games, but you've got to promise me it won't be all we do."

"I totally agree," Hunter said, before taking a bite of his sandwich. It was becoming a ritual, watching Hunter concoct and ingest his horrific lunch, a rotating mélange of pinkish deli meats, orange and yellow cheeses, colorful condiments, and crushed chips of some kind, all stuffed into a foot-long grinder roll. I no longer tried to guess any of the contents except for the chips; today's appeared to be Cool Ranch Doritos, based on the smell.

"Well, then, let's talk about what else you have planned. Hunter, I know you've got soccer, but is that it? Are you sure about ditching the Environmental Club?" Chloe leaned forward while at the same time tossing her hair back as if she were in a shampoo commercial. I wondered whether she'd practiced that move at home.

Hunter frowned. "They're the worst," he said. "I don't

know, I've got to find something else, at least for college apps."

"I'm good," I said. "Between the club and Hillel I've got enough, I think. And I'll need time to study."

"Hillel?" Hunter asked.

I was so used to spending most of my time with Jewish people that I'd forgotten not everyone would know what Hillel was. "It's a group to organize Jewish kids in schools. Mostly colleges, but they have a branch here. It's where I go for dinner and services on Friday nights."

I waited for one of them to say something about me being super religious and started getting anxious at the thought of trying to explain, but Hunter just nodded. "Cool."

"I don't think it's enough," Chloe said. "Our club has just five people, and how many kids are in Hillel? Like fifty?"

"More like twenty," I admitted, and I wasn't even sure how long they'd all keep coming to Friday-night dinners. "But I don't see why I need to be in big groups. It's not like colleges are going to care."

"I'm not talking about college. I'm talking about influence," Chloe said. "I've decided the two of you should run for student council." She laughed when we both shot her the same glare. "Oh, come on. You both stepped up right away to save the world but you can't imagine saving our class from having loser reps?"

"Who cares if they're losers?" I asked. "What do they even do, anyway?"

"Does it matter? The whole point is that you'd get to see how government works from the inside—isn't that your whole thing, learning about how governments work? And you"—she turned to Hunter now—"you're applying to law school. It's either student council or Debate Club for you, if you want to be smart about it."

Chloe could be very convincing when she wanted to be. "Why wouldn't you run? It seems like you've already got half the school under your thumb as it is." It was true—we hadn't even been at school a month and already girls were imitating Chloe's hairstyles, her makeup choices, her clothes. The Chloe Burns look, they called it. There was that group of girls our year who seemed to float around her like butterflies, leaving her alone only at lunch; she must have directed them to stay away when she was with Hunter and me.

"Exactly," she said. "I've already found ways to exert my influence if I want. Now you both need an outlet." There were so many assumptions built into that statement I didn't know where to start, but Chloe didn't give me a chance to open my mouth. "I'll be the campaign manager for both of you. I need that kind of experience for my own résumé, especially if I want to go to business school someday. We'll make this as painless as possible, I promise. We'll start next week."

A chance to spend even more time with Hunter, even if Chloe would be there too? I wasn't about to pass that up. Chloe wanted to have strategy sessions once a week, so we agreed on Tuesdays. The rest of the weekdays were reserved for studying, Friday night was for Hillel, and Saturdays were for the club, though we'd agreed at our first meeting that we'd vary whether we met during the day or at night. That meant Sunday was the only day I truly had to myself, and I had my weekly call with my parents in the afternoon.

"It sounds like school is going great!" Mom said, during our call the next weekend. "I'm so pleased to hear it!"

I'd managed to avoid talking to them the week before, but this week Mom had adopted the strategy of calling every fifteen minutes until I picked up. She was relentless.

"It's fine," I said. "I'd still rather be home." I told her about classes and joining clubs but not about making friends. I wasn't about to make this easy for them.

"Well, you can come home for the holidays. We'll pay for the bus." Rosh Hashanah was my favorite holiday—we celebrated at my house, where my mom made brisket and kugel and tsimmes and my aunt baked apple cakes with honey to ensure a sweet new year for everyone. We'd go to services in the morning and then my sister and I would help my mother set up the big buffet table so everyone could pile food onto the fancy paper plates my dad insisted on ("Silver and gold is festive!" he'd say, when we complained the plates were tacky). We'd stuff ourselves the first day and do it all again with the leftovers on the second, and my grandmother would always stay until after everyone else left so she and my mom had time to gossip.

But this year wouldn't be the same. The temple renovation wasn't done yet, and the shared temple was too full to let us in for the holiday, so services would be held at a Unitarian church that had volunteered its space, which I found both lovely and depressing. I'd only just started getting the nightmares under control, and as badly as I wanted to go home, I worried that going to a church for the High Holidays would send me into panic mode.

"They're having services here," I said. "A dinner, too. With brisket."

"Not as good as mine," Mom said. "I trust you plan to fast for Yom Kippur as well." She didn't even pretend it was a question. "Is the school closed?"

"It's not closed, but I don't have to go to class. And yes, I'm fasting." I was skipping services, but I had no intention of telling her that.

Skipping meetings with Chloe was not optional, as I soon discovered. We didn't have long to campaign; the election was in mid-October, and it was already three weeks into September. Our first mission, Chloe informed Hunter and me at our initial strategy session, was to get on the ballot. It wouldn't be difficult, given that we only needed twenty-five classmates' signatures, but they were due the following week, so we had to get started. Hunter had it easier than I did; between his popularity in our shared classes and his access to the entire soccer team he'd practically be done.

I, on the other hand, would have to work a little harder. We tag-teamed our classmates, at Chloe's direction—"We want people thinking of you two as a set so you both win," she told us—but we still needed a dozen signatures apiece. "Go hit up your Hillel people," she said. "And do more than just get them to sign—find out what they want. You're looking to represent them, after all."

She had a point, though I wasn't excited at the idea of talking to the whole group. Attendance hadn't dropped off at all in the first few weeks, to my surprise, but I hadn't done any better at getting to know people. Now was my chance.

At that Friday's dinner, I tapped on my water glass to get the group's attention before services started. There were about fifteen of us arranged around a long makeshift dining room table in the back of the chapel; we'd finished our usual dinner of roast chicken, potatoes, and challah. The room went quiet. "Um, hi, everyone, my name's Amina, and I'm running for student council as a first-year rep." There was a little whispering as a couple of girls I knew to be third years resumed their conversation quietly, uninterested in newbie politics. I powered ahead anyway. "I was hoping some of the first years might be willing to sign my petition to get on the ballot. I can come find you later if you don't want to write on

Shabbat." Some giggling now; this wasn't a very observant group. "And also, if there's anything you want me to know, you know, about what you'd want. If I won." It felt presumptuous to even say it.

The silence was palpable now, which was unusual for this crowd, at least so far; I was usually the quietest person here. But then, as if the silence had just been a dam for all the water gathering behind it, there was a flood of everyone talking at once. I couldn't hear anything other than the occasional word breaking through—"church," "kosher," "unfair." This had been a terrible idea.

"QUIET!" A voice broke through the cacophony. I saw a girl stand up at the other end of the table, someone who'd been at the previous two dinners, though I'd never spoken to her. "One at a time, okay? It's obvious you all have a lot to say, so give Amina a chance to hear you."

I gave the girl a grateful smile and listened to the more orderly list of demands that followed. There was little consensus: some of the kids wanted a dedicated synagogue space that wasn't part of the chapel, complete with security, while others didn't care; some wanted kosher meals offered in the dining hall, while others argued there was plenty to eat if you went pescatarian or just ate kosher-style, and there were so few of us it wasn't worth fighting. The only thing everyone seemed to agree on was how unfair it was that we had extended breaks for Christmas and Easter but no days off for the High Holidays and Passover, and it didn't seem to be a good time to point out that we were excused from classes and Christmas was a national holiday anyway.

But everyone seemed thankful to have had a chance to speak, and I was thrilled that I'd made it through the evening without passing out. It felt good to listen, to express genuine concern for what people wanted and to feel like maybe there was something I could do to help, even if in this case I might not accomplish much. I couldn't have done it without the girl who'd stood up and yelled at everyone, so I went over to thank her after dinner was over.

"Oh, it's no big deal." The girl waved her hand, and I saw that her nails were perfectly manicured, painted sky blue with clouds, a sun peeking out on each thumb. She saw my eyes widen. "Not bad, huh? I'd say it's not as hard as it looks, but it's probably even harder."

My own nails were clipped as far down as I could stand it, in part so I didn't get annoyed hearing them click on the keyboard and in part to keep me from biting them. I'd given up the habit years ago but it could come back in a second, I knew. "They're incredible. You must be ambidextrous."

"Nah, I'm Tamara, but it's nice to meet you." She held out her hand to shake mine.

I gawked at her. I had a feeling I'd met another member of Team Dad Jokes. "Anyway, nice to meet you. Thanks again for helping me out."

"No problem," she said. "Glad you decided to speak up at one of these things. It was getting a little boring hearing about what's on sale at Bergdorf's this week, you know?"

It had never occurred to me that anyone would want me to talk. Tamara had struck me as one of the girls who would care about what was on sale at Bergdorf's. Perhaps I'd read her wrong. "Maybe we can sit together at services? Or at dinner next week?"

"Sure thing," she said. "And good luck with the election."

"Thanks." I'd need it, I was sure.

In the meantime, I still had to contend with my list of signatures. After services were over a bunch of kids signed the petition for me, which brought me into the low forties, but I still had a handful left to go. What did people even do around here on Friday nights? For the first two weeks I'd gone straight back to my dorm after services to keep up with my reading projects; I imagined I'd need the time for studying once the quarter heated up. But I was feeling cheerful and not in the mood to read about the fall of the Roman Empire, so I texted Chloe.

Hillel went well, I wrote. Forty-two down, eight to go.

You're so close! she texted back. Get your butt over here and finish the job. She'd attached a picture of a basketball game, which I assumed was taking place right now. As much as I was not excited at the thought of watching sports, I'd definitely be able to finish off my petition. Besides, maybe Hunter would be there. Soccer games didn't happen at the same time as basketball games, did they?

The basketball gym wasn't that large, and even with the other team's fans the stadium wasn't half full, though there were still enough people that I had to scan the crowd to find Chloe. She was sitting high up in the bleachers with a bunch of girls who all looked like slightly faded photocopies of her. They were wearing pale blue jeans, beige suede booties, and light sweaters in shades of pastel, complete with varying shades of pink lip gloss and pale ribbons woven through their uniformly blond hair. Did they all just run back to their rooms and change as soon as Chloe showed up somewhere or posted a picture of herself online? Or were these bigger trends I was completely oblivious to?

Chloe stood up and pointed as soon as she saw me. "Get up here!" she yelled, and I could hear her over the sounds of the game and the buzz of conversations. She was so bossy, I thought, even as I followed her directions and ascended the bleachers.

As soon as I got to the top she gave me a big hug. "I'm so glad you're here!" She turned to her group of follower-friends—I recognized her roommate Lauren among them—and told them to get out their pens. "You did bring the petition, didn't you?"

Of course I had. Why else would I put myself through this? The girls passed it around, and in minutes I had enough signatures to get on the ballot. It had been easy, just as Chloe said.

"You going to just stand there, or are you going to sit down and hang out for a while?" Chloe patted the seat next to her, causing one of the followers to scooch down, though she didn't look too happy about it.

Truthfully, I wanted to go back to my dorm and read, or write in my journal. I couldn't say I didn't like Chloe's friends, since I'd never really spoken to any of them, but there was something about being around such uniform bland blondness that made me feel even more out of place than usual. I'd made peace with my dark, wavy/frizzy hair, my fire-hydrant body that could never pull off the kinds of delicate, willowy outfits Chloe's crew favored, and I had no desire to change anything about myself. But that didn't mean I wanted to stay, a bee among the flowers.

Still, they'd helped me out, and I needed to learn how to be more accepting, especially if I was entering the world of politics. "I can hang out." I sat down next to Chloe, and she gave me a squeeze. I'd never had such affectionate friends before. "Which team is us?" I nodded at the game below.

"We're the ones in white because we're the home team." She was matter-of-fact, as if this were something people just knew, which, I supposed, most people did. I'd never watched any kind of sports before, though; my parents weren't into sports, and as a consequence Shana and I weren't either.

I looked over at the scoreboard, where the *H* number was higher than the *V* number, though not by much. "We're winning?"

"For the moment. We're not very good, but the other team isn't either. But you don't really care about this stuff, do you?"

I was trying, but she was right. "Nope."

"Then let's not pretend we're paying attention. The girls are just here because they're already hot for some of the guys on the team, but that's not us, right?"

For a second I wondered if she knew how I felt about Hunter. I hadn't told her, though it would have been nice to be able to talk to her about it; I was too worried she might be into him as well, and then we'd have to deal with the fact that we both liked the same guy and he most likely was only into her. "Right," I said.

"So let's talk about what's important. How did Hillel go? You've got all your signatures, so I assume it was okay."

"All good." I told her about what everyone wanted, how they didn't all agree but how I'd realized I might actually be able to help with some of their requests. It had been a good feeling. I didn't tell her I might have made a new friend; I wasn't yet ready to share that.

"That's excellent!" Chloe was so great at making me feel like I'd done a good job. I wondered whether she'd literally been a cheerleader before, whether that's how she knew so much about sports, if she even did know a lot—I knew so little it was hard to tell. "Hunter and I have been checking in with our groups—the soccer guys all want late-night access to the dining hall so they can get snacks, and the girls want softer lighting in the bathrooms and a better system for receiving packages, since there's no good shopping around here." She rolled her eyes. "They're all delusional. Your stuff is more fun because we might be able to get it done. Now we just need to wait for the next phase."

"What's that?" I asked.

"That's for me to know and you to find out," she said. "Just check in with me when the list of candidates comes out and we can start to have some fun."

I wondered whether our idea of fun was the same, but I had a feeling I knew the answer.

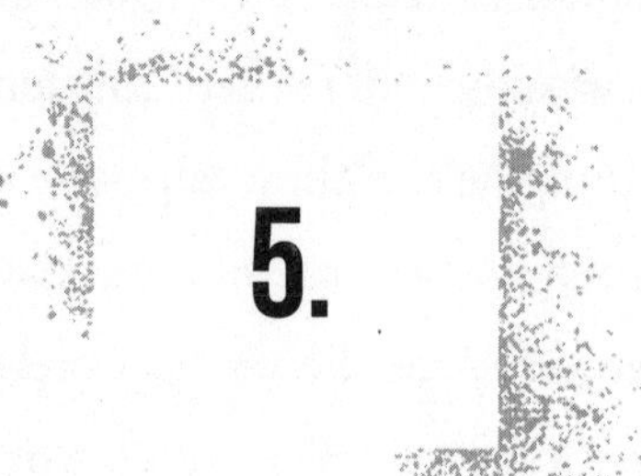

5.

The next day was our first official club meeting, and I had to figure out how to convince Jo and Wyatt to go along with the plan we'd developed. Chloe, Hunter, and I had agreed on it so readily I didn't think we'd have trouble, but it seemed weirdly disrespectful that we'd made a plan without Wyatt, given that the group was his brainchild.

We met in the bunker, though thankfully this time the meeting started a lot earlier so we didn't have to sneak around after curfew. Though we'd had no communication other than to set the time, everyone had taken it upon themselves to bring something with them, and I got a kick out of what each person brought. Wyatt and I had gone with a similar strategy: we'd hoarded snacks from the dining hall. His were mostly salty (chips, nuts, pretzels) while mine were sweet (gummy bears, M&M's, cookies), but we'd made the obvious choice for scholarship kids who didn't have a lot of disposable income. Chloe brought a pile of blankets and throw pillows and within ten minutes had turned the sterile bunker into a makeshift living room, though it was way more stylish than my living room at home. Hunter brought board games—Risk, Settlers of Catan, Scrabble—and I was pretty sure he'd done it to get Jo and Wyatt ready for the idea of turning the club into a gaming group, and it was so cute I wanted to make out with him. Though, to be fair, I pretty much always wanted to make out with him.

I wasn't sure what to think about what Jo brought. At first I wasn't even sure she was going to show up—she came later than everyone else, and she was carrying a black plastic case and a shopping bag. She didn't apologize for being late; she just rolled in and said, "Can you all hang on a few more minutes before we get started so I can take care of this?" Without waiting for us to answer, she went back outside with both bags, and we heard a bunch of banging noises, followed by several metallic clicks.

No one wanted to be the first to even speculate about what Jo was up to, so without discussing it Hunter opened up Settlers of Catan and started explaining the rules to the rest of us, since we didn't know how to play. He'd barely gotten through describing all the game pieces and cards when we heard the sound of a door unlocking and Jo came back in the room.

"All done," she said, and handed each of us a shiny silver key.

"What's this?" Chloe asked.

"I put a hasp closing on the door. Come look." Jo led us back into the hallway and, sure enough, she'd secured what looked like two metal flaps across the door, and then she showed us how they could be held together with a padlock, for which we now each had keys. "I wanted this to be a space we could trust. Now we're the only ones who can use it."

Wyatt looked a little panicked. "What if someone else wanted to come in? It's not really ours."

"You're the one who scoped the place out," Jo said. "Did you run into anyone? Did it seem like anyone had been using it, or cared that you were bringing in chairs, water?"

"No," he admitted. "It was filthy, too. I scrubbed the place down before I even sent out the invites."

"Good job, Mr. Clean. I think we're safe." Jo locked and unlocked the door and we all went back inside and sat down, not even bothering with chairs anymore. Chloe's blankets and pillows were enough to make us feel at home.

I wasn't sure whether I felt more or less secure now that I knew we were the only ones with access to the room, but I supposed I'd figure it out in time. I was intrigued by the fact that Jo had come up with the idea and bought the supplies and brought the tools and made it happen, all of which were way beyond anything I'd ever have come up with. The real question was why. I'd have to add it to the list of things I wanted to learn about Jo.

In the meantime, we let Hunter keep explaining the rules of the game, and we played until we got the hang of it. The three of us weren't the only competitive members of this club; Jo was, unshockingly, fierce, though I was surprised how into the game she was; she got so intense she even dropped the sarcastic nicknames. Even gentle, enthusiastic Wyatt wasn't above shouting "That gives me longest road!" when he'd made a good trade. We played well together, which made it easy to transition into a conversation about where the club was headed. Hunter was some sort of genius.

"So I was thinking, now that we've got this club and all, that maybe we'd want to combine some of the things we're into," I said. "I know some of us were into talking about different kinds of survival strategies, and some people were more about getting to know each other and having fun, but why not do both? We could describe some of the things we're afraid of, and then we could make up games to help us learn how to deal with them."

I could tell I had Wyatt from the minute I said "survival strategies," but Jo was frowning. I'd have to do more to convince her. "We'd make it a real competition," I said. "We'd keep track of who won each game, and maybe there could be a prize at the end or something."

Now I had her attention. "What would the games be like? What would the rules be?"

We hadn't gotten that far in our lunch talks. "I don't know.

Could be anything, I guess. Maybe Wyatt could be in charge of that—this was all his idea. Thank you for that, by the way." I didn't want him to think I was trying to take over.

"No problem," he said. "This is terrific. I already have so many thoughts about what we could do!"

"And the exclamation marks are back," Jo said.

"I don't think there was ever any stopping them," Hunter said, and gave Wyatt a friendly punch on the arm.

"I just get excited," Wyatt said. "But seriously, I'm happy to go first. I could even plan something for next week—I'm going to want to go outside, so we should do it while the weather's still good."

Glad I wasn't the only one worried about the Vermont winter, though intellectually I knew it was unlikely to be all that much worse than winter back home. "I'm in if everyone else is."

"Can I request that we do one thing first?" Chloe asked. "We haven't come up with a name for ourselves yet. We're not really cool enough to just call ourselves The Club."

Wyatt clapped his hands. "I was totally thinking about this! What if we called ourselves the Post-Apocalyptic Survivalist Society?"

"That's quite a mouthful, Shaggy," Jo said.

"The acronym would be PASS, though," Hunter said. "That's not so bad."

"It's not the sexiest thing I've ever heard," Chloe said.

"Let's see if we can do better."

This coming from the person behind *Chloe's Closet*, I thought, but was smart enough not to say. "How about the Hunger Gamers?" I asked.

Jo groaned. "Ugh, terrible jokes again."

"The Gardner Rebuilding Society?" I suggested.

"That doesn't even make sense," Hunter said. "How about Team Survival?"

"Too basic," Jo said.

"How about the Pyrophytic Association?" Wyatt asked, which earned him blank stares from the rest of us. "Pyrophytic plants need fire to survive, whether it's so their seeds can grow, or so they can resprout, or—"

"You realize we'll sound like we want to set fire to stuff, right?" Chloe asked. "Besides, I thought we'd agreed we were going metaphorical when it came to survival."

"What about Phoenix instead of Pyrophytic?" Hunter asked. "That gets at the fire and rebirth stuff."

"It's so overdone, though," I said. I didn't want us to be a cliché. Not before we'd even gotten going.

"I've got it!" Wyatt said. "The Eucalyptus Society. Eucalyptus plants are pyrophytic in lots of different ways, but they've also got a million uses, including as biofuels and bug repellent and food and so much other stuff I can't even remember. They'd be super useful in a real apocalypse. Also they're pretty and they smell good." He tried not to direct this last part at Chloe, but we all knew what he was up to.

"That's not bad, actually," she said. "It's not really easy to shorthand, though."

"You can live without a nickname, Princess," Jo said.

I was surprised to hear her stick up for the name, but if it was good enough for her, I was in. "That sounds great, Wyatt."

"Works for me," Hunter said. "Looks like we are now the founding members of the Eucalyptus Society."

"Eucalyptus it is!" Chloe said. I guess she'd found a way to make it a little shorter.

I was surprised at how much I was looking forward to Wyatt's game. He was so enthusiastic about everything it was hard to imagine it not being fun, even if being outside was not my favorite thing. My parents had had to crowbar me out of the house, bribing me into learning how to ride a bike when I was a little kid and then bribing me into teaching Shana how to ride hers when I was older. In truth, they didn't have to bribe me for long once Shana came along. Lots of people find their younger sisters annoying, but not me—I'd always wanted a sibling, and I knew my parents wanted more kids too. It took me years after Shana was born to figure out that my mom had had two miscarriages before Shana arrived; I just remembered a couple of times when I'd been sent to my grandmother's house because Dad told me Mom was sad.

"You'd like this club," I told Shana, during my weekly

family phone call. "You'd probably win all the games. Especially the outdoor ones."

"Games like kickball?" she asked.

Sometimes I had to remind myself how much younger than me Shana was. "Maybe," I said. "But maybe a little harder."

"Tell me about your new friends!"

I could tell she really wanted to know, but I wasn't sure how to describe any of them. Shana was one of those ten-year-old girls who thought boys were gross, so I wasn't about to tell her I had a crush on Hunter. I'd already sent her to Chloe's Instagram, and she'd informed me that she preferred my red sneakers to Chloe's fancy shoes. And how was I supposed to explain Jo? Jo, who seemed to be cultivating a kind of scary look on purpose, with her cropped, bleached hair that emphasized her cheekbones but clashed with her skin tone. Every time I saw her she was wearing the same thing: black jeans and a white T-shirt and a black leather jacket and black Docs with rainbow laces on one side and purple laces on the other. I was pretty sure the laces meant she wasn't straight but I didn't know much else; Brooksby was a pretty retrograde town when it came to gay rights, though we did have a Gay-Straight Alliance that had the best bake sales. But none of that would be relevant to Shana.

I decided to keep it basic. "They're really nice. Maybe someday you'll come visit and you can meet them all."

I could practically hear her jumping up and down over the phone. "That would be so great!" She reminded me of Wyatt.

I told Shana she could tell Mom and Dad everything I told her and got off the phone, hoping it would be an effective strategy to help me avoid talking to them myself. I wasn't angry anymore; I'd only been here a few weeks but it was already clear they'd been right to send me. I just didn't want them to know that yet. Stubbornness is a Hareli hallmark.

It was nice to have the game to look forward to, given that the week itself was a nightmare. I had a quiz in Algebra II on Monday, a paper due for my English class on Wednesday, endless Chinese phrases to learn, and a European History project to finalize with Hunter by Friday. At least I got to work with him, though I was having trouble convincing him that we should choose fascism as our topic.

"It's so broad," he said. "Can't we narrow it even a little?"

"Of course we can narrow it," I said, "but we have to start somewhere, don't we?"

"If we're starting broad, why not socialism? It's totally relevant now, especially with everything going on in politics. Aren't you, like, obsessed with that?"

Seriously, he was cute but he could also be kind of dense. Yes, I was obsessed with politics, which was why I was also obsessed with fascism. Socialism was a misunderstood word that had been bad and was now neutral for a lot of people;

fascism was still awful, and yet we seemed to be creeping closer and closer to it every day. How did he not see that?

I took a deep breath and thought about how to answer. I didn't want to antagonize him, and not just because of my crush; he was becoming my friend, and I wasn't about to lose a friend over a school project. I had to make this about something other than my own feelings. "I think fascism generally will be easier to research because it's less complicated," I said. "Socialism has all this negative stuff attached to it, and if we're going to compare European socialism to what's happening in America right now, we're going to have to do a lot of explaining. If we look at Italian fascism around World War One and what's happening in America, we'll have an easier time making the comparison."

He was already nodding before I said the word "easier." I'd figured out what made Hunter tick: he wanted to take on hard topics but find ways to make them simple. A useful skill for lawyers, based on what I'd seen on television—juries didn't exactly know much about law, and yet somehow they were in charge of deciding whether people were guilty.

Convincing Hunter to pick the topic I wanted felt like such a huge victory it completely made up for the rest of the week. I ended up telling Tamara about it at services Friday night, which she immediately and correctly translated into me having a crush on Hunter. In a way, it was a relief that someone finally knew. Not talking about him was just about impossible, but I couldn't tell anyone in the group. "Now we're in this club together, so I'll get to see him even more," I told Tamara, realizing only after I said it that we'd never talked about whether the club was a secret. It probably wasn't, though I didn't know what I'd do if she said she wanted to join, or if she told other people. I liked having a friend who wasn't connected to the group, someone who was just for me. I'd never had that before.

"Does he know you're into him?" Tamara asked.

I shook my head.

"Are you going to tell him?"

I stared at her. "Why would I ever do that? It could ruin everything."

"How will you find out if he likes you?"

She made it sound so straightforward. Maybe it was. Maybe I just had no idea how to be a person. "I have no idea," I said.

"Well, you might want to think about it."

She had a point, but it wasn't going to happen anytime soon.

Saturday morning finally arrived, and we all met in front of the statue of Gardner Academy's founder, Jacob Hawthorne Gardner. He was an imposing man on a bucking horse who looked like a Revolutionary War hero but who was really just a wealthy dilettante whose parents had bought him a school. Fitting, given what kind of institution Gardner had turned out to be. The woods stretched out behind us, the ground covered with red and orange leaves, making it appear to be on fire, which paired well with the smoky smell that filled the air.

Wyatt stood before the statue, bouncing with joy and anticipation, as it seemed he always did, his hair flying everywhere in the wind, his backpack in place. He could use a haircut, really, but we didn't yet have the kind of relationship where I could tell him that. I was surprised Jo or Chloe hadn't; they both seemed far less inclined to hold back their criticism. "I'm so excited we're finally starting!" he shouted, as if the wind were loud enough to require shouting, which it wasn't. "I'm going to teach you some things about the woods here and then we'll start?" He had this habit of turning statements into questions that I knew came from insecurity about speaking, not from the contents of what he was saying. But I saw some of the others frowning, and I knew they weren't all convinced Wyatt knew what he was talking about. I was tempted to remind them that he'd literally grown up in the woods, but whatever—perhaps I could use my faith in him to win the game.

We followed Wyatt as he moved away from the statue and onto a path leading into the woods. "As you all know from orientation, Gardner's been around for over two hundred years, and the surrounding land has belonged to the school the whole time, so there are lots of paths in and out of the woods. I'm going to teach you some techniques for finding your way out if you get lost, but as long as you haven't taken too many turns, most of the time all you need to do is turn around and go back the way you came and you'll end up at school."

This was only somewhat comforting given how directionally challenged I knew myself to be. The others looked equally skeptical, except for Jo. It was hard to imagine her seeming not confident. I wondered what, if anything, she was afraid of. I wondered whether the lock on the bunker door was a clue.

The path started out wide, so at first we could all walk next to each other, with Wyatt just ahead. Jo walked on one end next to Chloe, with Hunter on Chloe's other side and me next to him. That meant that, on the one hand, I got to be near Hunter, so close I could smell his grassy green scent, but on the other hand, I couldn't see him and Chloe with us in a horizontal line like that. I tried to just enjoy the feel of him walking next to me, the occasional brush of his jeans against my leggings, sending the hairs on my arms into military formation.

Wyatt walked backward so everyone could see him, impressing me with his apparent ability to see what was behind him and to avoid treacherous situations, like fallen tree branches or roots growing in the path with leaves covering them up. He was in his element. "Today we're going to talk about the basics: how to tell where north is when you don't have a compass, how to find good places to camp out, how to find things to eat."

"How do you know so much about the woods in Vermont?" Hunter asked. "Aren't you from California? I may be just a lowly Texan, but the trees are different here, right?" He'd let a little drawl slip into his voice, like he had back when I'd learned where he was from.

Wyatt's ears and cheeks turned pink. "I've been doing a lot of hiking since I got here," he said. "And yeah, some of the trees and stuff are different, but north is still north."

"Good point," Chloe said. "Hunter, don't be a jerk."

"Wasn't doubting your skills, bro," Hunter said.

"It's fine," Wyatt said, and I wanted to give him a high five. "Follow me and I'll show you how to find north." As we continued traipsing through the woods, he showed us how to read the position of the sun, how to look at trees and gauge north by the dense patches of moss and south by looking at where the flowers grew. He identified trees by their bark and their leaves: spruce, whose leaves looked like rosemary but lacked the distinctive smell; red oak, identifiable by the presence of acorns, especially now that the leaves had begun to fall; aspen, nearly heart-shaped but with almost razored edges. He'd put a lot of time into this.

"I used tricks like this in Chicago," Jo said, and we all stopped to listen to her, since by my count it was the first time she'd volunteered something personal about herself. I hadn't even realized she was from the Midwest. She seemed more like a New Yorker to me, though admittedly that was based on my stereotypical impression of New Yorkers. "I used Lake Michigan to orient myself. It was always east, even if it looked like a different body of water every day. The lake was east, and the airport was west, so if I couldn't find the lake I could watch for planes and check their direction against the streets, because they were mostly in grids. I guess with all that I could find north if I wanted to."

We stared at her as if she were saying the most fascinating thing in the world. Wyatt, of course, got all bouncy. "That's totally right! You'd definitely be able to find north if you had an eastern anchor like that. We can use stars for that stuff too. We should do a night hike sometime."

Personally, the idea of a night hike bordered on the terrifying, but no one else seemed all that fazed. Wyatt chattered on as we kept walking, quizzing us on what we'd just learned, showing us how bugs, like flowers, wanted to stay warm, so things like anthills also indicated south. After we'd walked long enough that I was starting to get hungry, we reached a clearing where the main path widened briefly before branching off into multiple smaller, narrower trails. Wyatt stopped walking and reached into his backpack to pull out a tightly folded roll of fabric. It turned out to be a very thin, soft blanket. He spread it on the ground and motioned for us to sit.

We formed a circle around him as if by instinct, sitting in the same order we'd walked.

Either Wyatt was an incredibly efficient packer or his backpack was bigger on the inside than on the outside, because he kept pulling things out of it until there was a pile on the blanket in front of him. "First, and most important: nutrition," he said, passing out energy bars and bottles of water. He'd packed enough for everyone, and it must have been heavy carrying all that around. He was a very thoughtful guy, I realized, as I gratefully bit into my makeshift snack.

"Second, shelter." He'd somehow brought another blanket, one that looked like aluminum foil, as well as some twine and a roll of duct tape. "These are the three things you'll want to have so you can build a really simple shelter. There are a million kinds, and they get more and more complicated depending how long you think you might have to camp and what you expect the weather to be like, but for now we just want to keep the rain off our heads overnight."

Wyatt had only asked for the day, so I felt pretty confident that we weren't actually going to be camping tonight, but I was relieved when Jo piped up. "Hey, Shaggy, I thought you said this was a day trip."

"It is," Wyatt said. "But this is still something worth knowing?" The uncertain tone had crept back into his voice. He'd been growing increasingly confident as his expertise became apparent, and I hoped that confidence would return soon.

As he showed us how to pick two trees that were the right distance apart, how to use pebbles to create weights around which to tie the cord and to weigh down the bottom of the blanket, and which kinds of knots to use to secure the blanket to the trees, his voice lost its querulous tone. "The bottom of the blanket should be at about a forty-five-degree angle from where it's tied to the trees, with the rocks keeping it from blowing around. It's even better if there are other trees so you can tie down the bottom of the blanket too, but that's not always possible. Either way, you've got some coverage so you can sleep, and if you make sure to check wind direction, you can build a fire that will keep animals from coming into the open side of the triangle."

"Animals?" I asked. The night hike grew less appealing by the minute.

"It won't stop a bear, but rabbits will probably leave you alone," Wyatt said cheerfully, as if the prospect of bears ripping through our pathetic tinfoil blankets wasn't completely terrifying.

"Please, please, please promise me we will never have an overnight game outdoors." I clasped my hands together as if in prayer, trying to sound as if I were joking when I was most definitely not joking.

"We've got you," Chloe said, and the others nodded.

Wyatt looked a little sad, but he moved on. "We're going

to talk plants now. Like, there are a ton of plants in Vermont that you could live on if worse came to worst and you ended up stuck in the woods. I'll show you some of the ones that grow out here in the summer into the fall, but there are lots more that grow in the other seasons that we can talk about later on, if you want." He explained that the most important thing was to learn how to recognize the good plants and to know the characteristics of the bad plants. The ones with milky sap, thorns, an almond scent, or a three-leaf pattern tended to be bad. "Ready to wander and start finding examples?" He looked at us hopefully, and I knew he wanted to see enthusiasm, but I was pretty sure we all wanted the same thing, which was to get on with the game.

"Sure," Hunter said. "Do we need to pack up here first?"

"No, we're coming back," Wyatt said, and began once again walking backward down one of the paths. He showed us patches of clover and dandelions. "Late summer and early fall are all about the green plants. And I know dandelions have a terrible reputation but they're really pretty great for survival food. They've just gotten a bum rap."

Chloe wrinkled her nose, but Wyatt convinced her to try a small dandelion leaf. "The big ones can be bitter if you don't mix them with other stuff, but the flowers are kind of sweet. The roots taste gross, but some people boil them with tea."

"Only because I trust you," Chloe said, and popped a tiny

leaf into her mouth. She chewed thoughtfully, then spit it out. "I'm sure I could keep it down after doomsday, but there's a whole dining hall of food I'd rather eat."

"Let's come back to that," Wyatt said. "First we're going to talk about mushrooms. They're around from spring through fall, though different varieties show up at different times. We missed morel season, which is a bummer because morels are ridiculously good. But there's also lobster mushrooms, oyster mushrooms, some kinds of chanterelles . . ."

"Which ones can get you high?" Hunter asked.

I glared at him—it was such a dude thing to say, and I hadn't expected that from him. But he looked completely sincere, and Chloe and Jo seemed curious too.

Wyatt was with me, though. "None of them," he said. "But if you identify them wrong, they might kill you." It was the first time I heard his voice have an edge.

Hunter held his hands in front of him. "Whoa, I was just asking. I wasn't going to try to find any of those for myself, I swear."

"I was just saying, it's really easy to eat the wrong plants out here and get sick, and if things are really bad and there's no doctors or medicine, we have to be really careful." Wyatt went on to explain how mushrooms that looked like they had pores (like morels) were better than those that looked like they had gills (like portabellas, though those were edible). As we walked around he found some examples to show us, and

I was grateful we didn't have to do any more taste tests—I'd never been a fan of mushrooms, poisonous or not.

Just when I was about to interrupt Wyatt and ask if we were ever going to play, I saw that we'd circled back to where he'd left the blanket. "It's time to get started with the game, everyone," he said. "Have a seat."

We obediently sat back down in the same order we'd chosen before. Wyatt reached into his magical backpack and this time took out a handful of plastic grocery bags. "Here's how this is going to work," he said. "You have one hour to hunt for edible plants. You don't even have to guess whether they're edible or not—you can just grab whatever you find and I'll check it when you come back. Whoever finds the best stuff wins. I'll use what you find to put together a late lunch and we can see how it tastes."

If I were a nicer person I'd have found some way to keep my face from scrunching in disgust, but I wasn't, and I wasn't alone, either. Hunter looked horrified, Chloe curious; only Jo seemed intrigued. I raised my hand. "Are you sure we won't die?"

Wyatt laughed. "I've been doing this forever, and I promise I know all the plants here cold. I won't take any risks with anyone's health. But if our goal is to learn how to survive out here, we'll have to know how to eat. Besides, we're not far from the infirmary."

"Not funny, Davy Crockett," Jo said.

Wyatt, to his credit, was learning to ignore her. "Does one of you have a phone I can borrow?" After what he'd told us about the commune, none of us were shocked he didn't have a phone of his own.

Hunter handed his over without question, and Wyatt set a countdown timer for one hour and showed it to us. "You've got one hour to bring back whatever you can find. Winner is the one who brings back the best edible stuff. I'll be the judge. You ready?" We nodded.

"On your mark . . . get set . . . go!" Wyatt threw his arm up and down like he was starting a race, and maybe that made us feel like it was one—we all ran to choose our own path away from the clearing, into the woods.

I'd already decided my strategy would be to only bring back edible plants—Wyatt had said the best plants would win, not the most, so there was no point in just throwing as much as I could find into my bag. I would be methodical, strategic. I figured Jo would bring back a whole mess of stuff just to see what everything was; Hunter would find a lot of one thing and overload himself with it, thinking quantity mattered; and while I wasn't sure what Chloe would do, I figured she'd either go with the most aesthetically pleasing collection, in which case I could totally take her, or she'd be strategic like me, in which case she was my competition. Of course, I could be wrong about any of them—it's not like I knew them all so well yet—but I felt pretty good at the top of the hour.

After forty-five minutes in I felt less certain of my approach. Perhaps I'd chosen a bad path, or maybe I just hadn't been paying enough attention to Wyatt, focused as I was on Hunter's closeness and whether he was watching Chloe. Either way, I hadn't found much, other than a patch of berries that was either edible or toxic, and I wasn't willing to take my chances. In my last fifteen minutes I found some green stuff that looked promising and just went for it, but my bag was only half full.

I kept searching right up until the very last minute, which meant I was the last person to arrive at the clearing. "Empty your bags in front of you," Wyatt instructed, and as soon as we did I knew I was doomed.

My pile was sad and pathetic compared to everyone else's. I hadn't even found anything all that colorful. Wyatt went through it, separating the different things. "Purslane, a little red clover. Not bad. All edible, for sure." He was trying to be nice. I'd bombed this one. At least I'd get to see whether my predictions about everyone else were correct.

I'd been totally right about Hunter. He'd found a crab-apple tree, taken a bite of one and found it acceptable, and filled up not just his bag but his pockets and his T-shirt, which he'd turned into a basket by holding the bottom out as far away from his body as possible. There were enough apples in front of him to make each one of us a pie, and they kept rolling away as Hunter tried to count how many he'd brought back. "The numbers don't matter," Wyatt said, but I could tell Hunter wasn't convinced.

I'd been totally wrong about Jo, though. I don't know why I'd assumed she'd be so casual and haphazard when she'd turned out to be precisely the opposite. She'd done better than I had in terms of quantity, and she'd destroyed me on variety, plus she'd somehow found the time to package all her different plants into bundles, tied up with long blades of grass and arranged on the ground in front of her in rows. In addition to everything I found, she'd tracked down burdock, dandelion greens and flowers alike, amaranth, and juniper. "These would even taste good if we were really going to eat them," Wyatt said, and I could tell he was trying not to sound surprised at what a good job she'd done.

"So no scavenger salad?" Chloe said. "Thank goodness. I was absolutely petrified."

"We all were," Hunter assured her.

I didn't know what to think about Chloe's strategy. She hadn't gone for the pretty things, as I'd thought she might, and as far as I could tell she hadn't considered whether what she'd found was edible. Instead, she'd brought back a massive amount of mushrooms, as many varieties as she could. She'd divided them into pore and gill categories with a side pile for ones she wasn't sure of; Wyatt picked up one in the side pile and practically squealed with delight. "Teeth! That's a whole other category I wasn't even going to get into."

"Mine's the most interesting, right?" Chloe said. "So I should win?"

Wyatt kept working through the mushrooms, making his own piles. "These are the ones we might consider eating," he finally said, pointing at a small pile. "And the rest are the ones that might kill us." He indicated the much larger pile.

"You said we didn't need to distinguish ourselves," Chloe reminded him. "You said we should just bring back whatever we found and sort it out from there. I've still got lots of variety."

This was interesting. She didn't just want to win; she was willing to fight for her victory. But Wyatt wasn't going to make it easy. "You're the only one who brought back anything poisonous. Hunter's got you beat for quantity, and Jo's got everyone destroyed for quality. She's the only one who found anything I'd actually want to eat."

"Hey, what about the apples?" Hunter didn't sound all that serious, though. "I'm the only one who thought about dessert!"

He had a point. But it was pretty clear how this was all playing out.

Game one to Jo.

6.

Given how competitive I knew Chloe was, I expected her to be furious at her loss, to rant and rave about the lack of clarity in Wyatt's process. But she didn't bring up the game at all, and she didn't chime in when Hunter complained about it at lunch. "You'll just have to make clearer rules when it's your turn," she told him, and that was all she had to say.

Having completely flamed out myself, I was more concerned about the upcoming election. Thank goodness it was a quiet week at school, after the study nightmare of the previous week; it meant I could focus on the campaign. Five candidates from our class had gotten enough signatures to run, including the meth chemist from Game Night (whose name was Kenneth Zhang), another guy Chloe recognized as already making a name for himself in the party crowd, and a girl who hung out on the fringes of Chloe's group of followers. "The two guys will cancel each other out," Chloe said, "and I can take care of that girl easy."

The three of us were hanging out in one of the study rooms, talking strategy. We were going to need posters and slogans, and we had to decide whether to coordinate our campaigns or run as individuals who just happened to support each other. "I say we do this together," Hunter said, and just hearing him say those words, even in the wrong context, made me melt. "We both win together, or we both go down together."

I thought of a song my parents used to sing along to in the car called "We Both Go Down Together." I could never tell whether it described a murder-suicide or a suicide pact. Either way, it was not the vibe we were going for. But I wasn't about to say that out loud. "Totally," I said. "It'll be more efficient for making posters, too."

"Speaking of which," Chloe said, "what do you think of 'Hunter and Amina for a Better Future' as a slogan?"

"Isn't that a bit much?" I asked.

"Oh, I don't know," Hunter said. "Go big or go home!"

I couldn't fight with that. We decided to use blue and yellow to match the school colors, and we brainstormed ways to incorporate the Better Future theme. "We can do some space-age graphics," Chloe said.

"Also maybe do something with how the blue and yellow are like the sun in a bright sky?" Hunter said. "To get across how a better future includes improving the environment?"

I liked it. I liked all of it.

What I liked less was finding out what Chloe meant when she'd said she would take care of the girl who was running, whose name was Stacie. Stacie invariably imitated Chloe's outfits within days of them appearing on Instagram, and one day I'd checked *Chloe's Closet* to find Chloe wearing a jumpsuit we'd just seen on a TV show called *Fleabag*. The jumpsuit was beautiful, sleek and black and way too sexy for school, and it was incredibly difficult to pull off. Chloe photographed her version at the greenhouse, as had become her habit, this time in front of a display of unusual roses: maroon rather than red, with black edges, one of the roses braided into her hair.

Needless to say, not all the imitations of this outfit were nearly as successful, and Stacie did not pull it off. "Jumpsuits aren't for everyone," I heard Chloe say, and though she claimed she wasn't responsible for the hashtag #fleabagfail trending, along with pics of Stacie, I had no doubt she'd made it happen. "This is huge," Chloe said. "Look how many people are posting about it! There's no way she can win after this."

I didn't like that she'd gone after another girl. I felt bad for Stacie, really, though not so bad I wasn't secretly relieved that Chloe might be right, that one candidate might have been neutralized. Ken and the other boy had already started campaigning on similar platforms about how to make school more fun; Chloe claimed this confirmed they'd been kicked out of other, better schools, whether for drinking or drugs or other kinds of misbehavior. They were all but running as a team as well, but Chloe was sure their strategy would backfire. "People might want one fun person, but they won't want two. Two fun people doesn't even equal one effective person. Worst-case scenario one of them could squeeze past you or Hunter, but realistically, they'll just split the votes and leave the rest for the two of you."

I wasn't feeling nearly as certain. She and I were in my dorm room, having our weekly meeting but without Hunter—he was in charge of the next game, so we decided to let him off the hook, and besides, there wasn't all that much left to do. We'd put up all the posters and created online graphics that were all over everyone's social media. Chloe, who considered marketing both an art and a science, had it down. We'd made campaign promises hand-tailored to appeal to the people she perceived as her fellow influencers, placing posters advocating for vegetarian and vegan options near the dorm room of the SPCA president even as we swore, on the poster next to the football quarterback's room, to keep the vending machines stocked with Cokes and candy rather than the gluten-free energy bars and antioxidant drinks the administration had suggested. I'd worried about being hypocritical, but Chloe insisted it was strategic.

"There is one more thing that would help," Chloe said, taking hold of a lock of my hair and twirling it around her finger.

"If you say makeover, this meeting is over." I wasn't stupid—Chloe had made the occasional comment about my "remarkably consistent" wardrobe, the "natural resources" she felt I was neglecting in the form of my long, unruly hair and reasonably clear skin.

"How about this: we'll just tweak your normal look, and I'll put you on the site. I promise I'll keep it low key, nothing radical. But, you know"—and here she was doing her best to feign modesty, I was sure—"my site does have a lot of followers, even at this school."

As if I didn't know that already. She'd won over nearly the whole female population of Gardner before the #fleabagfail incident, and it wasn't long before everyone started imitating her again, especially since she'd made a point of wearing more user-friendly outfits after that. I groaned, knowing that I was going to give in and knowing that she knew I was going to give in, enraging as it was. "Fine."

Chloe clapped her hands together with glee. "Excellent! Relocation time."

I trudged behind Chloe as we walked to her dorm room. I'd never been there—we'd gotten used to being in mine because Brianna was so rarely around, and Chloe's roommate struck me as someone I would definitely not like. She was the one whose brother had gone to Gardner, who'd given Chloe the download on how things worked around here, and she'd pretty much barnacled herself to Chloe. "Will Lauren be there?" Bad enough to have to subject myself to Chloe's makeover, but to have Lauren watch would be too much.

"Unlikely." Chloe opened the door and we went inside. No Lauren in sight. But being in their room was like being in a new place: the two of them had teamed up to make their dorm feel like anything other than a dorm. The walls were painted in shades of pastel—beige, mint green, peach—that I recognized as backgrounds from some of Chloe's photos, though it had never occurred to me she'd taken some of the pictures in her own room. They'd hung strings of fairy lights just below the ceiling and airy curtains on the windows, and all the bedding matched the walls.

"Did you hire a decorator or something?" I plopped into a peachy-pink armchair. "This place is fantastic."

"It's what I do," Chloe said smoothly, opening the closet to reveal a rainbow of clothes, as well as a full-length mirror she'd attached to the door. "Outfit first, then face. Acceptable?"

"Depends on the outfit," I said.

"Do you trust me?" she asked.

That was the real question, wasn't it? But the fact was, she was doing this for me. There was nothing in it for her other than the fact that I'd let her be in charge of the campaign; there wouldn't be enough influence in my role for her to exert any behind-the-scenes leverage, despite her joke about being the power behind the throne. I might not know why she'd decided to do this for me, but my doubt wasn't about trust. "I suppose."

"Good," she said. "Because it's possible I've been planning this day for longer than you know." She wasn't flipping through what appeared to be an endless wardrobe looking for something for me to wear; she was digging through bags on the floor as if she had something very specific in mind, which, it turned out, she did.

Chloe emerged from the closet with a triumphant expression and a cardboard box. "So here's what I was thinking. You've got your whole plaid-shirt-black-leggings-red-Converse thing pretty much down."

I didn't even have to look to know she'd described my clothes perfectly. Truth be told, I clashed radically with her dorm room. "It's easy," I said. "I don't have to decide what I'm wearing in the morning, and I know I'm going to be comfortable."

"I respect that, really, I do." She was not at all convincing. "I was thinking we'd just go with a dressier version of your everyday look, you know, just a little more polish. That way you'll read more style icon and less . . ." She passed her hand over my outfit. ". . . grunge-era throwback."

I bit the inside of my cheek to keep from laughing. "And you have a plan for this?"

"Of course I do!" Too bad she wasn't president, I thought.

"And it's not even going to hurt." She started emptying the box, tossing items of clothing at me so fast I could barely see what she was throwing. "Try them on."

"Now?" I'd assumed we were strategizing the makeover, not actually engaging in it. I hoped I wasn't wearing a bra with holes.

"Enough messing around," she said. "Snap to it."

I'd gotten myself into this, so I was stuck. But as soon as I looked at the clothes I recognized just how skillful Chloe was, and I knew it would be okay. She'd picked out a red plaid shirt but in a kind of silky, tailored fabric; a pair of slim black pants that fit me like leggings but looked fancy (ponte, Chloe explained), and a narrow black blazer that nipped in just a little bit at my waist and made me look more like a girl and less like a fire hydrant.

Once I was dressed she handed me a pair of red flats that had some sort of padding in the soles. "These are even more comfortable than my sneakers!" I couldn't believe it.

"Now give me your face," she said, and I tried not to panic. Makeup wasn't really my thing. Hair care wasn't either. But all she did was brush my eyebrows with some weird clear gel, dab a little mascara on my lashes so my eyes stood out behind my red-framed glasses, and hand me a tube of reddish lip balm. "You can do that part yourself." While I applied the lip balm she braided my hair into two pigtails and then pinned them up, pulling out a few tendrils that curled around my face. One dangly pair of silver earrings and we were done. It hadn't even taken fifteen minutes.

"That's it?" I asked.

"That's it," she said. "Go look."

I almost didn't need to bother. I felt pretty much the same, which was the last thing I'd expected after a Chloe makeover. I was as comfy as usual, maybe even more so with the new shoes and my hair out of my face, and it's not like I hadn't worn mascara or lip balm before. The only thing that felt really new was the stuff on my eyebrows. Still, she'd done the work, so I went over to the mirror and glanced at my new look.

I had no idea how she'd done it, but I somehow looked exactly the same and completely different, simultaneously. Better, because that was Chloe, but I still felt like myself. "You are, like, shockingly good at this." It all fit perfectly. It was ridiculous. "Except . . ." I was embarrassed to bring it up, but I couldn't not. "You know I can't afford any of this, right?" Everything was expensive, I was sure of it, even if I didn't recognize the brand names.

Chloe made a "pfft" sound. "It's all from companies I work with. We just need to mark the post as sponsored by them."

"Sponsored?" I'd wondered what that meant early on.

"They send me the clothes, they pay me for the post. You get the free stuff. But remember, there's no such thing as a free lunch." She pulled out one more tendril from my braids. "Now let's take some pictures."

For some reason the thought of the sponsored post was far more terrifying than just the idea of being on Chloe's Instagram, which should have been scary enough. It took hours for us to get the shots right, during which time Chloe literally wallpapered part of her room (I hadn't realized that was even possible, but apparently there was temporary wallpaper she used for her shoots) and took what felt like thousands of pictures with hundreds of cameras. "I'm a professional," she'd say, when I whined to ask whether we were done yet. "We won't be done until this is perfect. You're just lucky we're doing this here and not at the greenhouse. Between the temperature controls and the lighting issues we'd have to take like a thousand more pictures."

"You're going to make Hunter do this next, right?" I was only sort of kidding. It didn't seem fair I'd have to go through this agony when he didn't, even if she'd minimized the pain.

"No one comes to my feed to look for boys," Chloe said, as she finally put the last camera away. "But you both have interviews with the school paper, so he'll share that pain."

That helped a little. "I wonder what he's going to make us do this weekend," I said, collapsing back into the armchair. I was so comfortable I didn't even change back into my regular clothes. She was a genius, Chloe.

"There's only one way to find out. Let's get him over here!" She got out her phone and started texting furiously.

"He'll never come to the girls' dorm," I said. "He could get thrown out. Besides, I thought he was all busy planning for his game."

"He was supposed to be, but then there was a soccer thing." She knew an awful lot about his schedule. I wondered again how often they talked when I wasn't around. We'd now been at Gardner for over a month, and hookup rumors had already started flying around. But there was nothing about anyone I knew, and that included Chloe and Hunter. I'd thought Jo might be in the mix as well; she was so intriguing, and I imagined both boys and girls would want to make a play for her.

Chloe's phone buzzed. "He's on his way," she said. "Any last things we need to discuss before he gets here?"

So he knew where her dorm room was, too. Unless she'd sent him directions. I had no shot. "Do you think we're in good shape? I'm not going to die if we lose, but I don't want to get crushed—it would be so humiliating."

"You won't get crushed," she said, and curled up on her bed across from where I sat. "You're both going to win, and I'll tell you why." She started ticking reasons off on her fingers. "You're both brainy but you aren't obnoxious about it. Hunter's got the good-looking jock thing going for him, and you'd be shocked at how many people will find that to be enough. And you've got this kind of dark mysterious thing going on—you don't care what anyone thinks of you, and yet you're putting yourself out there to help them. They won't be able to resist it."

Her description of me was so far from how I saw myself as to be unrecognizable. "You really think so?"

"Trust me," she said. "You'll win, and then you'll become their dorm mama, making sure everyone's got enough to eat, no matter what they want. Get a later curfew and earlier quiet hours and you'll win every year."

We were interrupted by a quiet knock on the door, and Chloe got up to let Hunter in. He was carrying the remains of a sheet cake that looked like it had been mostly devoured by hand. "I come bearing dessert and a list of new demands from the soccer team," he announced. "Starting with extended curfew."

Chloe had been right. She raised an eyebrow at me and I started laughing so hard I wasn't sure I'd be able to stop. "What's so funny?" Hunter asked, putting the cake on Chloe's desk and looking around the room. "I like what you've done with the place."

So he hadn't been here before. Relief. "I know, right?" I said.

He was peering at me closely now. "Did you do something different? Is it your hair?"

"Hair, clothes, makeup, the whole bit," Chloe said. "Isn't she gorgeous?"

Well, that was awkward. She hadn't exactly left him a lot of options. "Totally," he agreed. "Now you just have to decide whose heart to break. What's your poison?"

"My poison?" All that mattered was that he clearly wasn't talking about himself.

"You know, girls, boys, whoever." He snuck a glance at Chloe. I wondered if he was hoping she'd answer the question as well. I'd caught her looking at Jo once in a while, though I couldn't tell whether she was evaluating her for a makeover like mine or whether she could possibly be interested in something else.

"We're here to talk survival, not romance," Chloe said. "Leave the poor girl alone and tell us what to expect this weekend."

Hunter sat at Chloe's desk and started eating bits of cake with his hands. "Not a chance," he said, mouth full.

"You are so gross," I said. "Let me get a bite of that before you destroy it." I stood up and scraped at some frosting with my pinkie.

"Match made in heaven, the two of you," Chloe said, with no idea how much I wanted it to be true. "I wouldn't touch that cake with someone else's fingers."

"Hey, did you hear about Wyatt?" Hunter asked.

"What about him?" Chloe asked, while I continued working on the frosting.

"The weirdest thing. He got this package and had to open

it in the office, you know?" That was the cause of Chloe's followers' complaints: any time one of us got a package, we had to open it in the main office in front of an administrator, just to be sure no one had sent us anything we weren't supposed to have. It was the price we paid for attending a school like Gardner. It meant some other student was almost always there to see what you got. "Anyway, it was this stack of books about racism and slavery and stuff. He hadn't ordered them, and he didn't know where they came from. It freaked him out."

"That's so bizarre," Chloe said.

"Who would send him that?" I asked, wondering whether I'd be upset if someone sent me a bunch of books. If they were books about Judaism and the Holocaust I'd be offended they assumed I hadn't read them already, at a minimum.

Hunter shrugged. "I guess there was a note that said, *You've got a lot to learn.* Not signed, of course. He was all, why would people think he didn't know his own history? And I have to admit, I felt like a jerk, because I didn't even realize he was Black, you know?"

Exactly what I'd been thinking, but I was glad I hadn't said it. I'd assumed he wasn't white, but he could have told us he was Latinx or Southeast Asian and I wouldn't have been surprised. I'd never have asked, because it was none of my business.

"I guess his mom's Black and his dad's Mormon, if you can imagine that," Hunter said.

"Why wouldn't we be able to imagine that?" Chloe asked.

"It just seemed like a strange pairing to me is all," he said. "I didn't mean anything by it. I'm just telling you what he told me."

"Is he okay?" I asked. I felt this odd protectiveness toward Wyatt. He seemed so sheltered, so much younger than the rest of us, even though he wasn't. Chloe was right about me being everyone's mama, apparently. So strange that she already knew me better than I knew myself. And definitely better than I knew her.

"I don't know," Hunter said. "I guess we'll find out this weekend."

"After Amina becomes famous!" Chloe shouted.

"Famous for what?" Hunter asked.

"I'm putting her on my Insta. She's going to blow up. Everyone at school will want to know who she is."

I hoped she was kidding.

7.

Hunter let us know that he'd be claiming all of Saturday for his game, so we met in the bunker that morning. I scanned Wyatt's face, trying to get a sense of how he was feeling, but either he wasn't showing much or I didn't know him well enough to tell. I supposed that meant I could focus on the game. We all sprawled on the floor, with Hunter sitting in one of the folding chairs before us.

"I told Wyatt I'd be up for going next," Hunter began, "but I have to say, deciding what to do and how to do it was way harder than I thought. He gave me some really helpful advice, so if this works, it's thanks to him."

Wyatt blushed. "You did all the hard stuff," he said.

"Anyway," Hunter went on, "I think you all know that my biggest fears are about the environment. Which is a really big thing to be afraid of, between the climate crisis and natural disasters and all the problems with water and drilling and fracking, not to mention that whole thing about how the world is going to exhaust its resources by the time we're middle-aged. It just gets so overwhelming sometimes."

No kidding—it was overwhelming just hearing him talk about it.

"So for my game, I thought a lot about what we could do that would really illustrate the scope of the problem. But sitting in a sauna to get used to living in extreme heat or pretending to get ready for some big flood didn't seem like enough, you know? There isn't really one thing we can do that will make us feel prepared. That's why I decided it might be better for us to just help." He paused and cleared his throat, but his voice still cracked at the next part. "I haven't told y'all much about my brother, but his name's Caleb. He's the one who started me thinking about the environment and the ways people are making it worse. Caleb got involved with this organization called the Earth Liberation Movement—it's all about supporting the use of natural energy sources."

"Isn't it also about sabotage?" Chloe asked.

I was surprised to hear her speak up. She sounded a little judgmental, too. Not that she couldn't be judgmental when she wanted to be, but something about her tone was sharper than it was during our normal lunch debates.

"It's open to more aggressive action, yeah." Hunter hesitated. There was something he wasn't telling us. "Actually, my brother got into a little trouble working with them once, and I haven't seen him for a while because of that. It's how I ended up here. But we're getting sidetracked."

"Are we, though?" Jo asked.

"Maybe we should let him talk?" Wyatt asked, in his tentative way. It worked—he could somehow cut through tension just by being himself.

"All right, let me start over," Hunter said. "The Earth Liberation Movement, which goes by ELM, is coming to Vermont today to protest the Addison County gas pipeline. It's a project that local people fought in court, arguing that building it would slow the use of wind and solar energy in the state, but they lost, and Vermont Gas finished the pipeline a couple of years ago. Except it's already starting to fail, which means the company has to do repair work, which is intrusive. ELM's protest is geared toward getting the company to acknowledge the pipe isn't working."

"And to do some damage to it in the meantime, right?" Chloe asked.

Hunter was starting to get upset. The vibe now was completely different from our lunchtime debates; there, while it was clear Hunter and Chloe had different ideas about how to handle issues, they always seemed to be having a good time debating them. This was already far less fun. "Look," Hunter said, "I don't know what you've got against people taking a stand for what they believe in, but—"

"I didn't say that," Chloe said. "I just thought you were

a law-and-order guy—this pipeline went through the legal process, and your side lost. What's left to say?" She sounded downright combative. Maybe I'd been wrong that she wasn't mad about the last game; maybe she was, and she was taking it out on Hunter.

"I think we're all just worried about getting in trouble," I said. Wyatt shouldn't be the only one trying to defuse the situation. Besides, I felt a tug of sympathy now that I knew about his brother. I couldn't imagine what I'd do if Shana ever went missing. "You haven't told us about the game yet—you're not going to have us blow up the pipeline or something, right?"

"I would never ask you to do that." Hunter's face had fallen. I didn't really think he wanted us to do that either, but whatever his plan was, it was time for him to spell it out. "Look, it's mostly just a protest. It's going to be totally safe. There'll be some other organizations there too, along with the National Lawyers Guild, just to make sure things don't get out of hand. You can stay as far away from the actual pipeline itself as you want. I understand if you don't want to go, but I'm going to."

He looked so dejected I couldn't help but want to make things better. "I'm in. It sounds kind of exciting."

"What's the game, though?" Jo asked. Of course she'd be the one to ask straight out, though she was right. I wanted to know too. We hadn't even decided on a prize for our games, but it almost didn't matter—the only one of us who never gave off a particularly cutthroat vibe was Wyatt. Maybe he was just hiding his dark side.

"I thought we could make this about putting together the best go-bag. The protest doesn't start until later this afternoon, so everyone would have a couple of hours to put theirs together." Hunter briefly explained the concept of go-bags: they were meant to contain everything we'd need to make it after a catastrophe, tweaked depending on what the catastrophe actually was.

"How will you evaluate?" I asked.

"I'll look at what you bring and what you actually use," he said.

"Sounds good to me," Wyatt said. "That work for everyone else?"

We all turned to look at Chloe, given that she seemed to be the most opposed to this particular game. But she just tossed her perfect hair. "Who am I to resist the opportunity to win a game based on accessorizing?"

She had a point. We were all in trouble.

"Okay, then, let's meet by the Jacob Hawthorne Gardner statue at noon," Hunter said.

"How are we getting there?" Wyatt asked.

Hunter assured him he had it covered, and we all went back to our rooms to put our bags together. I knew Chloe thought she had this one locked down, but I planned to give her a run for her money. I threw as much as I could into my backpack, checking the weather before I left and adding an umbrella in case it rained, which I hoped would give me an edge.

It was drizzling by the time I got to the statue, and Chloe was already complaining about her hair, which she'd pinned into some kind of elaborate bun. Hunter was obviously feeling sensitive about how miserable we all were, because he volunteered to buy everyone hot chocolate.

"Just tell me we're not walking," Chloe said. "This weather is a total downer."

She'd barely finished speaking when a black SUV pulled up right in front of us, a middle-aged white guy in flannel driving. "You found a Lyft? Here?" Jo asked.

"Something like that," Hunter said. "It's ours for the day."

I stared at him with the realization that Hunter was definitely not a scholarship kid. It wasn't exactly that I'd assumed he was—he gave off an air of entitlement sometimes, but I thought the combination of being male, white, good-looking, and athletic pretty much explained it. He cared so much about his education I'd figured he was more like me than not.

"What?" he asked.

Now I looked at everyone else. No one seemed quite as surprised as I was. "Nice ride, Prince Harry," Jo said. "And now the princess doesn't have to walk."

I'd never put together that Jo's occasional nicknames for

Hunter and Chloe were connected. Did she know something I didn't?

We piled into the enormous SUV—it had three rows!—and, true to his word, Hunter made the driver stop for hot chocolate. The sugar cheered everyone up. "The site's about an hour away," he said, "so maybe we should check out everyone's go-bags on the way, just to get this party started?"

"I'll take notes," I said, getting out my phone. We arranged the contents of our bags next to us and started comparing, with Chloe in charge of going through the items. Lots of us had brought umbrellas, so no competitive advantage for me there; Hunter was the only one who'd thought to bring a rain poncho as well, but he couldn't win so it didn't matter. We'd all remembered water bottles and snacks, mostly Kind bars stolen from the dining hall, but only Chloe had thought to bring a first-aid kit. She really was going to win this thing. I'd brought a Sharpie so we could write each other's phone numbers on our arms, in case we didn't have access to our own phones for some reason. Jo had brought pepper spray and a bandanna for her face, which made me realize she was ready to get into it for real. I hadn't quite decided what I was going to do yet, whether I'd hang back with the National Lawyers Guild or what, but my mind was quickly made up when I saw the rest of Hunter's bag.

"What's this stuff for?" I asked, as Chloe held up a hammer and a pair of handcuffs.

"Got a little kink in you, Red," Jo said. "I like it."

"Put those back," Hunter said. "I thought I—"

"Hid them in a special pocket so we wouldn't see?" Chloe asked. "Yeah, no, we're not stupid. So much for not getting arrested."

"Look, you don't have to come with me," he said. "But I'm in this for real. I'm willing to go as far as I need to."

"You're really willing to get arrested?" I asked. "They'll never let you be a member of the bar after that."

"You'd be surprised what you can get away with and still be a member of the bar."

How would he know? It probably had something to do with having money. The rich knew how to get out of anything. "I don't know about this."

"You don't have to come with me for that part," he said.

"I'm not going to, if you don't mind," Wyatt said. "I don't think it's a good idea for me to get involved with the police."

He seemed nervous—had those mysterious books he'd been sent made him anxious about being a biracial person in one of the whitest states in the country? Or had he always been cautious? Brooksby was a pretty white town, but even I knew Wyatt was being sensible here, not overly careful. I wished he didn't have to worry, but then again, wasn't that why we were here? To learn how to make the world better?

"I'll stay back with Wyatt, then," I said. "He shouldn't

have to be on his own." Guess I wouldn't be winning this game either. So much for my competitive spirit.

"I totally get it," Hunter said, though he did look a little disappointed. I was too.

"I got you, Red," Jo said. "If we're going to do this, let's do it right. You got another hammer hidden away somewhere?"

"Just the one," he said, already sounding happier. "But ELM will have extra stuff, I'm sure."

"You don't know this is going to work," Chloe said.

"You don't know it won't, Princess," Jo said. "Come on, join the fun."

"Well, I am the only one who brought a first-aid kit," she said. "You might need me."

I wasn't entirely shocked she'd changed her mind, though I had to admit I'd hoped she would stay behind with me and Wyatt. Hunter directed the driver to drop us off at the barrier near the site, though we'd still had a little ways to go before we got to the good stuff. He explained how things were likely to play out as we walked. "As we get closer, you're going to see different groups of protestors, though sometimes it won't be obvious who's who. The group the farthest out will be the people who are upset about the pipeline and who show up because they know other people will be here. It's fine to stay with them if you want—it's too far to see what's really going on, but it's safe." He inclined his head toward me and Wyatt.

I wasn't sure we needed to be quite that safe, but we could decide after we knew more.

"If you're looking to be a little closer to the action without getting too hands-on yourself, your best bet is to hang with Greenpeace—they've got a big group coming. They'll give you signs to carry and they'll have an area roped off, with lawyers at the perimeter." Wyatt was nodding now, and I was relieved.

"Those of us who want to get close to the pipeline are going to find ELM," Hunter continued. We were now on a dirty road leading to the protest site, which looked like a random stretch of grass and trees just off the main road. The rain was still just a sprinkle, not heavy enough to get out the umbrellas but strong enough to be annoying. "They'll have one group blocking access to the pipe so the repair workers can't get in, and then there's another group digging down to a section of pipe to get access. They'll try to damage it. Destroy it, if possible."

"How long will this go on?" I asked. "Should we pick a place to meet up?"

"I have no idea," Hunter said. "It'll probably go on until it gets broken up." He meant "by the cops" but I appreciated him not saying it. "Check your phones in two hours? We'll see where we are then?"

We all gave the okay. Hunter led the push through the crowd as we entered the protest area, and he stopped at the

Greenpeace section, where Wyatt and I planned to stay. I watched as he, Chloe, and Jo pushed through the throng, and it wasn't until they were out of my line of sight that I turned to the Greenpeace protestor who was handing out the signs.

"You okay, staying here with me?" Wyatt asked. "Really? Because if you want—"

"This is what I want," I told him, but it was only sort of true, and I could tell he knew it. Now that we were here, I thought maybe I understood what Hunter felt and the urge to help. Making change seemed possible here in a way that it didn't in our day-to-day lives, and I found myself wanting to take out all my frustrations on an object that could stand in for everything that enraged me about the world. Holding a sign was nice and all, but it wasn't the same. Honestly, it was boring.

At least I had Wyatt to talk to. We chatted for a while about regular stuff—school, classes, the basics—but it wasn't long before we started talking about Eucalyptus and what had made Wyatt want to start it. "We've already played your game, but you never told us what you're really afraid of," I said.

"Do you want the real reason or the serious reason?" he asked.

"Those are different?"

He nodded, his shaggy hair flying all over the place. The rain made his curls tighter even as it made my hair a frizzy mess. "Okay, don't laugh, but I've always been obsessed with zombies. I know they aren't real, I know they're like scientifically impossible, but I've read a ton of comic books and novels about them and as soon as I got here I started catching up on the movies, and there is some amazing stuff out there, you have no idea." He was bouncing now. I loved how excited he got, how unembarrassed he was by his own enthusiasm.

"Zombies," I said, as deadpan as I could.

He giggled. "Let's try the serious version, then. I'm afraid of disease. I'm not a germophobe or anything; it's more like the realistic version of the zombie fear, you know? I'm afraid of biological warfare, of people not immunizing their kids so we all die of German measles or something stupid, or some superflu wiping out humanity. We could all get sick and almost everyone would die and the rest of us wouldn't know what to do."

That explained his Game Night question. It also explained his course load, which was almost all science and math. It was why we didn't have any classes together. "Do you want to be a doctor, then?"

"It's the only way I can think of to help," he said. "I've always liked science but there was no way to do hard-core lab work on the commune. I already love being at a real school."

I couldn't even begin to imagine what his life had been like before Gardner. Given his background, he was way less socially catastrophic than I'd have been. I wanted to ask him about what it was like for him here, and about the books, but it seemed intrusive, and I didn't want to ruin the easy conversation between us.

"How about you?" he asked. "I know you'll tell us more when it's your turn to set up the game, but I'm curious—what are you afraid of?"

"Maybe I should just go next and you can find out," I joked. I did not want to go next.

The words had barely escaped from my mouth before Wyatt pounced on them. "It's so great of you to volunteer!" He started bouncing again. "I can be patient, I promise."

I hadn't meant to make him wait; I was fine with telling him whatever he wanted to know. But I didn't want to dampen his enthusiasm. What had I gotten myself into?

The buzz of my phone distracted me. Hunter had sent a group text. How's everybody doing?

I took that to mean he'd gotten separated from Chloe and Jo, and sure enough, Chloe wrote back that they were heading to find us at Greenpeace. Still hammering away?

Hunter sent a thumbs-up emoji. "You should go find him," Wyatt said, after reading the texts over my shoulder. "It sounds like he could use the help."

"I don't want to leave you here by yourself." But he was right that I was itching to go.

"I'll be fine," he said. "I'll keep an eye out for Chloe and Jo and we'll see you soon."

I didn't wait to ask whether he was sure; I just started walking, texting Hunter as I went. Where are you?

There's a guy with a clipboard ordering people around, he wrote. Go stand by him.

It took me a while to figure out who he was talking about; the throng of people had gotten a lot bigger since we'd arrived, and more and more of them were moving up toward the pipeline. From the snippets of conversation I could overhear it sounded like the shoveling had gone slower than expected because of the rain but there was finally a big enough piece of pipe unearthed for ELM to start trying to do some damage. I had to ask a couple of people for help before someone was able to point me to the clipboard guy.

All the ELM people were wearing bright yellow T-shirts with pictures of a monkey holding an enormous wrench. The clipboard guy stood in the middle of a cluster of them, which was why he'd been so hard to see, but I made my way to where he stood and hoped Hunter would get there before the guy started asking me any questions.

I waited there for five or ten minutes, feeling awkward and impatient but relieved no one seemed to think it was strange for me to be there. Then there was a tap on my shoulder, and I turned to see Hunter, smiling as broadly as I'd ever seen him smile, hair wet and matted to his head, clothes covered in mud. "You've been busy," I said.

"Isn't this amazing? I'm so glad you decided to come see it up close. Wyatt's okay?"

"Yeah, he's going to meet the others," I said. "I take it you've been shoveling?"

He looked down at his muddy jeans, his dirt-crusted hands. Blisters had formed on his palms. "What gave me away?"

"And yet you're ready to go back in and start hammering? Aren't you exhausted?"

"Actually, I was thinking maybe now that you're here we could work on a little side project," he said. "It'll have the added benefit of keeping you out of trouble if the police shut things down, which I'm thinking will happen pretty soon now that the pipeline's exposed."

"Sure," I said. "What's the project?"

"We're going to try and find my brother," he said. "Remember when I said I hadn't seen him in a while? I'm hoping the ELM people might know where he is."

Hunter led me over to the clipboard guy and waited until the crowd around him thinned. "Hey, do you mind if I ask you a couple of questions?"

Clipboard Guy held up a finger as he jotted down some notes, then turned his attention to us, looking us up and down. "Oh, no way," he said, shaking his head. "What are you two, twelve?"

I opened my mouth to tell him not to be a jerk, but Hunter stepped in. "We're not looking to get close to the pipeline." Apparently he was going to pretend he hadn't just spent an hour right next to it even if it was obvious just from looking at him. "I wanted to see if you could help me out with something."

"Look, I don't know if you've noticed, but we're pretty freaking busy," Clipboard Guy said. I wanted to punch him.

"It'll only take a second. I'm looking for someone."

"Aren't we all." Clipboard Guy was bored with us already.

"No, I mean my brother works with y'all. With ELM. I'm trying to find him. His name is Caleb Fredericks."

Now we had his attention. "You're Caleb's brother?"

"Yup. He took me to a couple of these things with him."

"You were at Standing Rock?" Clipboard Guy seemed impressed.

"Nothing that big," Hunter admitted. "But I was there when he got arrested, and I haven't seen him since. Family stuff, you know. I was hoping maybe he'd be here."

Clipboard Guy shook his head. "Nah, he's gone off the grid. Bad stuff went down a few months ago at a protest in Louisiana and a bunch of people got arrested. They almost got Caleb but he took off. There's a warrant out and he's been ducking it. But he checks in from time to time. He's doing all right."

Hunter exhaled beside me. "Thanks, man." His

disappointment was so palpable I could practically touch it, but he also seemed relieved.

"You must have been really worried," I said as we headed away from Clipboard Guy, away from the pipeline.

"You have no idea. Caleb's been in trouble before, but he usually keeps in touch. I just needed to know he was okay."

"How about we round everyone up and get out of here?" I asked. "I'll text them."

"Can we just—maybe we could wait a minute?" His face was pale under the dirt and freckles.

"Do you need to sit down?" I asked. He looked like he was about to pass out, so before he could answer I dragged him over to a tree. "Give me your rain poncho."

He frowned, confused, so I grabbed his backpack and went through it myself. The rain had stayed light enough most of the day that he hadn't bothered with it, and now the sun was starting to come out, though the ground was still soaked. I spread the poncho on the ground and pulled Hunter down to sit next to me. I felt the cold, wet dirt underneath, but it wasn't seeping through the poncho, so that would have to do. From my own backpack I retrieved two Kind bars and a bottle of water, and I waited until Hunter had eaten one bar and drunk half the water before I asked how he was feeling.

"Better, I think." His skin was less pasty, so that was something. "I just—I really thought he'd be here, you know? The game was an excuse, a way to come here and have y'all with me when I found him. I wanted you all to meet him. I wanted him to know I was willing to do everything he was, despite what happened before."

I wasn't sure what he meant, but I wasn't about to interrupt.

He started talking again, and it was like he'd been saving up all these words for so long they were spilling out in whatever order he could remember them. "We haven't talked much about our families, have we? Like I know about you and the dad jokes, and that Wyatt's parents split up and Jo's are gone, but that's about it. And it's been okay so far, because I came to Gardner to get away from my parents, and maybe everyone else did too, and so we don't have to say anything. But sometimes I want to say things, you know? Sometimes I want to tell someone how awful it is to actually hate my parents, to know that my dad is a genuinely bad person and my mother chooses him over us every single time. I'm here because they would pay any amount of money to separate me from my brother, who is the only person in the world I want to be like. And I miss him so much I can't even stand it."

The tears had started when he said he hated his parents, but they didn't turn into real sobs until he started talking about Caleb. "Come here," I said, and wrapped my arms around him, pulling him close so he could cry into my shoulder. Somehow I knew he wouldn't want to look at me while he was this upset; I'd be the same way, and in that sense we were a lot alike. It was why we were friends.

I held Hunter until he stopped shaking and then gave him a Kleenex from my bag. "You've got everything covered," he said, wiping his nose. "Maybe it'll be enough to win the game for you."

"Unlikely," I said. "But I'm glad to help anyway."

Once Hunter was all cleaned up I texted the group. Chloe wrote back immediately. *We're out of Kind bars and water but we're all bonding. Come find us! Greenpeace has a tent now.*

We headed toward the tent until we saw Jo's bleached-blond hair right up next to Chloe's honey-and-caramel bun, Wyatt's curls not far off. "Hello, everyone," Hunter said, his voice all chipper and fake.

"Welcome back, Red," Jo said. "Or should I say Rusty? The dirt has dimmed your hair's auburn glow."

Hunter shook his head back and forth, causing drops of dirt to flick onto us. "Gross," Chloe said. "Sometimes you're such a dude, Hunter. And that is not a compliment."

"Clearly," he said, but he sounded genuinely happy now. "Come on, let's just call this one an apocalyptic failure and get out of here."

"What are you talking about?" Jo asked. "This was great. Princess here was a hero of the revolution. The cops tried to breach the people barrier but one of them fell and cut his forehead and she got him all cleaned up with her little first-aid kit. Totally distracted him and gave me time to squirrel our boy Shaggy right out of there. Then the guy with the clipboard promised the police we'd get out of here in an hour and they left. Can you believe it?"

"Sounds like we have our winner," I said.

Hunter glanced over at me. "You think?"

"No question," I said, and everyone else agreed.

Game two to Chloe.

8.

I don't know what I was thinking, agreeing to go next and plan a game when the election was happening in a week and first-quarter finals would be starting soon. I had only the vaguest hint of what I might want to do, and it was way more elaborate and time-consuming than what Hunter and Wyatt had done so far. "Seriously, the tension is coming off you in waves," Chloe said. "You need some sort of outlet. What do you do for exercise?"

"Exercise?" With everything else I had going on, exercise was the last thing on my mind. Not to mention that I was a slug anyway—I hated to sweat. The most I'd ever done was take some long walks, just to clear my head. Maybe that's what she had in mind. I couldn't remember if I'd even brought sneakers with me other than Converse. "Um, nothing?"

"We'll just have to change that." She was getting excited, but I knew I had to shut it down.

"There's no way," I said. "There's no time."

"We're going to make time," she said. "I get that you're busy, but you really need something to take your mind off everything. Trust me, you'll feel better. What kind of stuff do you like to do? I know you're not into group sports and all, but how about running, or yoga, or tennis?"

They all sounded awful. "I'm not into any of that."

"Well, I've got some ideas. No Eucalyptus meeting this week, right?"

"Right." I'd bought myself a little time—we wouldn't be playing my game until after finals, just as second quarter started.

"You're mine Saturday morning, then. And I still get Tuesday night. We're going to find something you like if it kills us."

I was worried it might, but I knew not to get in the way of Chloe and her plans. "Fine."

I had more important things to worry about anyway, like making sure I aced my finals and figuring out my own game. For finals I had a plan: Hunter and I were now studying together at least twice a week, and it was helping both of us. At first I hadn't been sure us working together was a good idea. I tended to be better prepared, and he needed more help, not to mention that being around him made me so nervous I left the study room each night thinking I might barf. But over time, the swarming insects in my gut flew away, and we developed a rhythm that made sense. We ran our study sessions almost like a class, with me as the teacher and Hunter as the student, and that way I got at least as much out of them as he did. As I got less nervous we grew more natural with one another, and by the time finals came around I realized we really had become good friends. I still thought we'd make a good couple too, and I still hoped maybe it would happen, but I also knew it would be okay if it didn't. We'd work well together on student council, and I told myself that was what mattered the most.

"Are you worried at all? About the election, I mean?" I asked. It was our last session before the election, which would take place the following Thursday. Chloe had strategized our meetings well, I realized; she'd picked the times I was most likely to be freaking out.

"Not really," Hunter said. "I'm too busy worrying about Caleb. I thought getting more information would make me feel better, but it's not working."

That didn't surprise me. Hunter's search for his brother had made me think about Shana, and I was now talking to her on the Sunday family calls even more than my parents. But no matter how much I missed her, I was starting to realize I didn't want to come home anymore. I'd found my people here, and even if I was still fixated on how terrible the world was, I didn't have nightmares about the temple anymore, or anything else. I was happy here, or as happy as I was going to be anywhere. Though perhaps that would change if we lost the election. Or if I lost—there was always the chance one of us would win and not the other, and if that were the case, the winner would be Hunter.

Ugh, I was stressed out, more than I wanted to admit, so much so that I was actually looking forward to Chloe dragging me off to do who knew what, just to get out of my own head for a while. When Saturday morning rolled around I scraped together as much of a workout outfit as I could find (my normal leggings and sneakers with a ratty T-shirt usually reserved for sleeping and my hair pulled into a ponytail), and I went to meet Chloe at the campus bus stop, as per her instructions.

To my surprise, she wasn't there alone; she'd brought Wyatt with her. He was wearing baggy basketball shorts and a T-shirt with the logo of Gardner's cross-country team and his last name, Christiansen, on the back. I hadn't realized he was a runner. Chloe, of course, was wearing a perfectly matching raspberry-colored workout ensemble. "Good job following directions, you two!" She'd timed our arrival perfectly, and we got on the bus and sat in the back row together.

"Are you going to tell us where we're going?" I asked.

Chloe ignored me. "You may be wondering why I dragged the two of you out with me, and I'll tell you, but before I do, I have a question: Has either one of you ever thrown a punch?" She looked at Wyatt, then at me, then back at Wyatt, who practically shrank into himself.

"No, I've never hit anyone," he said.

"No siblings? Other kids who got on your nerves? Didn't you live in some kind of cult camp?"

Wyatt seemed unfazed by Chloe calling the commune a cult, which fed my suspicion. "Well, the commune was all about peace and nonviolent resistance and stuff? Like, we talked a lot about the world ending but also how that would end war. And we had to share everything."

I found it hard to believe a bunch of little kids never got into fights, but then again, my sister and I hadn't done a lot of fighting either, other than yelling. "I've never hit anyone," I said. "I might have wanted to, but I've never done it."

"Are either of you opposed? Wyatt, are you going to get all pacifist on me?" She sounded almost flirty, but Wyatt looked terrified.

"What are you going to make me do?"

Chloe laughed. "Nothing terrible, I promise."

We'd reached downtown, such as it was. The town consisted of a general store, a bar that had seen better days, an ice-cream parlor, a post office, an independent coffee shop, and a small gym. Chloe led us over to the front window of the gym, where we could see women in outfits like Chloe's punching and kicking tall red bags. The bags barely moved. "Those look really heavy," Wyatt said.

"They are," Chloe said. "It's harder than it looks."

"It" turned out to be kickboxing. Chloe had arranged for us to take a self-defense kickboxing class. "You both need to let off some steam, I think, and besides, learning self-defense is good prep for the end of the world. Are you with me?"

Wyatt nodded enthusiastically, as he always did. I was already here, so what did I have to lose?

The self-defense class wasn't nearly as well attended as the one we'd watched through the window, but Chloe explained that it was because the class was a one-off—most classes depended on repeat customers who came in at the same time every week, or even every day. The self-defense class was only on the schedule once a month, and you didn't need any previous experience to take it. As we waited, the room half filled with a mix of younger and older women, most of whom were wearing workout clothes that looked more like mine and Wyatt's than Chloe's. "This class is more for our people, huh?" he asked.

"It's for people new to boxing, sure, and people who are more into the self-defense aspect than fitness."

Wyatt looked as relieved as I felt. He wasn't the only one who thought those bags looked heavy.

At precisely eleven o'clock, the instructor began speaking. "Welcome to Kickboxing for Self-Defense, everyone. My name is Candace and I'll be showing you some easy techniques today. You'll each be in front of a bag, but we're not going to use them for a bit—the early lessons will just be to show you form. First off, everyone should pick a partner."

That would be awkward, given that there were three of us. But Chloe immediately attached herself to a woman standing nearby who she had met in another class, leaving me with Wyatt. That was fine. We were both clueless, so we'd be clueless together.

Candace ran us through some warm-up exercises and taught us a few basic punching and kicking techniques: jabs, hooks, cross-punches, uppercuts; front kicks, side kicks, roundhouses. Wyatt was giving it his all, going at it with so much goofy energy he got himself turned around doing a roundhouse kick and ended up falling on the mat.

"You okay?" I asked, extending my hand to help him.

He bounded up, smiling. "I'm great!"

There was the Wyatt I knew, bounding and smiling and not caring how obvious it was he was excited about what he was doing. I had no idea how he'd managed to stay this carefree, and I wanted desperately for it to last forever.

"All these punches and kicks are well and good if you have the right opportunity to use them on a potential attacker," Candace said, after we'd run through each move several times. "But the key in self-defense is making the most use of whatever opportunities your attacker provides you, and using whatever advantages you have to save yourself. It's not about being able to injure your attacker, though if injuring him is what it takes, that's what you'll do. Sometimes your best move is just to yell, if you think there are people around who might hear you. Let's try it."

Silence.

"I mean it," Candace said. "We're not used to yelling, are we? We're used to being polite, to watching our tone even if we're angry. But sometimes we have to do it. Sometimes we have to scream. So scream!"

Someone had to get this started, but no one wanted to. Until I saw Chloe take a deep breath. Of course she'd be first. She opened wide and let out a high-pitched noise, between a yelp and a bleat. It was the sound I imagined I made in dreams, when I wanted to shout but found I couldn't make a sound; the frustration of that feeling was infuriating, and remembering it gave me the incentive to yell myself. I began screaming too, as did everyone else in the class, Wyatt included. Pretty soon the sound in the room started to hurt my ears, at which point Candace signaled for us to settle down.

"That felt pretty good, didn't it?" Everyone nodded. "But it was harder than you thought?" More nods. "Remember there's power in your voice. If it makes sense to use that first, do it—you might find it's the safest way out of a bad situation."

We all nodded again. Candace seemed aware the class wasn't one hundred percent female: when she discussed what body parts to target (eyes, nose, ears, neck, groin, knees, legs) she made sure to use gender-neutral language. After an hour of learning to gouge, poke, scratch, slap, and kick, and then practicing on each other, Wyatt and I were both red-faced with exertion and damp with sweat. We collapsed on the mat and waited for Chloe to say goodbye to her friend and join us.

"So?" she asked, when she finally sat down. "What did you think?"

"That was so great!" Wyatt yelled.

"It was pretty great," I said reluctantly.

"And you feel more powerful than when you came in?" She was looking at me now.

"So powerful!" Wyatt yelled.

"How about it, Amina?" she asked. She wasn't about to let me off the hook.

"Okay, fine, yeah, I feel more powerful," I said. "You happy?"

She beamed. "You have no idea."

Chloe and I decided to go to the dining hall for lunch after we got back to campus; we asked Wyatt to come with us, but he said he had food in his room and he needed to go study. Chloe linked her arm in mine as we walked. "That was fun, wasn't it?"

I grudgingly agreed.

"And Wyatt's really growing on me," she said. "Kind of like a little brother."

"Do you have siblings?" I asked, realizing she'd never actually told me.

"Sisters," she said. "We don't get along. Not like you and Shana."

I talked about my family way more than she talked about hers, I knew. "How come?"

She flicked her fingers, as if swatting away a bug. "Not important. So, it was good to get to hang out with Wyatt outside of the group, right?"

What was she getting at? "Sure, I guess."

"I was thinking on Tuesday we'd see if we can get Jo to come with us." She picked at her salad all casual, but there was a strange note in her voice. I wondered whether she shared my fascination with Jo. We'd spent some time with her now, but I felt like I could still count the things I knew about her on one hand.

"Sure," I said. "It would be nice to try and get to know her better. Will she be into this, though?"

"Oh, I don't imagine this would be her thing," Chloe said. "But I've got something in mind."

I was curious what she was up to, but I'd have to wait until Tuesday to find out. In the meantime, I studied. I'd gotten over my panic about my Chinese class; between the flash cards, the study aids I'd found online, and the fact that my teacher had all but told us what would be on the test, I felt pretty good. Poli sci was pretty much a snap, too—the reading was fun, and I knew the exam would be all essay, which was my favorite. I was more worried about the history classes, and math; my hatred of numbers extended beyond calculations to memorization of dates. I really liked my math teacher, though. She was a newer hire, and while I knew that meant she probably had a failed stint somewhere else under her belt, she'd stepped up her game. I hated studying for her class, but I wanted to do well, just to show her I was trying.

By the time Monday morning rolled around my eyes were burning from reading all weekend, even with my glasses. The last thing I wanted to do over breakfast was read the school paper, but the pre-election profiles would be out today, and I was curious to see what the girl who'd interviewed us had to say. She was a junior and on the student council herself, so I imagined she'd have opinions.

It quickly became clear as I read that opinions were the least of our concerns. The article about me was inoffensive enough; it included basically what I'd told the interviewer, plus a few other facts she probably found on the internet. The emphasis on my hard work and interest in politics had the benefit of coming across as an endorsement, even as it outed me as a scholarship kid. But as I read through the rest of the profiles, it started to feel like the interviewer had an agenda, and that agenda was to embarrass the candidates as much as possible. I'd been let off easy, unless she'd thought I minded people knowing my family didn't have much money; her ammo was reserved for everyone else.

Jo had been right about Ken Zhang. His profile revealed

he'd been kicked out of his last private school for selling his mother's prescription oxycodone to fund his cocaine habit. The profile hinted strongly that he hadn't stayed clean, though the interviewer steered just shy of saying it. The implication overall was that he'd be a terrible candidate for class rep. The other party boy didn't fare much better. His secret turned out to be that he'd cheated on the entrance exam to his previous private school; it wasn't hard to see how that might disqualify him as well. Stacie's #fleabagfail made it into her story, presented as a personality flaw: a candidate who would blindly follow someone into that kind of fashion victimhood could hardly stand up for her fellow classmates.

But the worst of the vitriol was for Hunter. The profile started out positive, talking about his athleticism, his friendliness, his desire to make the world better, but it devolved quickly. "Does anyone really believe the son of the most powerful oil magnate in Houston is the best advocate for the environment? Maybe if Hunter Fredericks found a way to separate himself from C&H Energy then he'd be credible, but as long as Daddy's paying the bills, we're not buying it. Hypocrisy is not a stellar quality in a class rep."

I finished reading with a pounding headache and a lot of feelings. First there was anger—at the interviewer for taking advantage of us and writing such hit jobs; for whoever had helped her do her research, since she couldn't possibly have gotten all this dirt from just talking to us. Then I felt horrible for everyone who was running—if these profiles had taken all the joy out of the elections for me, how must everyone else feel?

Then, underneath, there was something else. A small, ugly feeling, one that reddened my face even though no one I knew was in the dining hall to see me. A sad feeling, too, because I knew it applied to all the profiles of the other candidates.

I agreed with them.

And I was really angry at Hunter.

Sure, he'd dropped some hints. He didn't get along with his parents; his dad was on the wrong side of the issues; he'd been sent here so he wouldn't become an activist like his brother. But there were light-years between those things and being the heir apparent to the biggest oil company in the world, one so big even I'd heard of it, though it never would have occurred to me that C&H stood for (as it must) Caleb and Hunter. C&H money was funding Hunter's education; C&H money had funded our trip to the protest site. It had even funded the hot chocolates that cheered us up in the bad weather. And he'd never told us. It felt dirty.

I went to class not knowing what I'd say to him, but it turned out I didn't have to worry—he didn't show up for poli sci, or the class after it. "Have you seen Hunter?" Chloe asked at lunch. "Is he okay? He's not answering my texts. You saw the article, right?"

"Oh, I saw it." I fixated on my peanut butter sandwich. Chloe was the one who'd set up the interview; she was the last person I wanted to hear from about it. But she could talk about nothing else.

"Can you believe her? I talked to the editor in chief myself and she promised me she'd find someone good to write about you. She swore it would be a total puff piece, just a little something to clinch the election. I didn't even know they were going to interview everyone—I thought it would just be you two."

"That would hardly be fair, would it?" I said.

"You're mad at me!" Chloe frowned. "Don't be mad. I was only trying to help. I won't be able to stand it if you're angry and Hunter's ignoring me. I'll have to convince the girls to wear all sorts of horrible outfits so you'll have to think about me constantly."

I couldn't help but laugh. It did sound pretty awful.

"Okay, you can't hate me if you're laughing. Just promise we're still going to hang out tomorrow night. I've roped in Jo, and you know that's not easy. She's weirdly busy for someone who doesn't seem to have any friends."

"I don't get her," I admitted.

"I think that's how she likes it," Chloe said. "But we'll crack her. By the end of the night tomorrow we'll all be besties."

I wasn't even sure I wanted Jo to be my bestie, but I was still curious about her.

Now that I was annoyed at Hunter, it was nice to have someplace else to focus my energy.

Hunter skipped the rest of the day too, and though he didn't text to cancel our study session, I assumed he wasn't coming and skipped it myself. My rational self knew I wasn't being fair; it wasn't like he'd lied about his family, and it wasn't like I believed someone with his background couldn't genuinely care about the environment. I just hated feeling lied to, even if the lie was one of omission.

Tuesday rolled around with no Hunter. I was tempted to check on him, but I resisted. I'd lost a lot of study time stewing over those profiles, and I needed to focus. I did take careful notes in class with the intention of giving them to him later on, but I found myself holding them back, waiting for him to text me. I went to Chloe's room for whatever workout nightmare she had planned, but I was starting to worry. "Have you talked to Hunter at all?" I asked.

"We texted. He's kind of a mess but he'll be okay." She'd already moved on in her mind, and she started walking down the dorm hallway. "We're meeting Jo at the place. It's going to be epic. I've been trying to get her to tell me what her whole workout regimen is—she's so long and lean, like a dancer, but not super graceful, you know? She just laughed and said she did her own thing, and she was up for trying anything."

Chloe did not like people laughing at her, I knew. "What are we doing, then?"

"I wanted to find something that would be challenging for her but also interesting for you, right? Also something that fits our theme—you know, getting ready to defend ourselves if the world falls apart."

Oh no. I had a feeling I knew exactly what she had planned. "Are we doing Krav Maga?"

Chloe whipped her head around; she'd gotten a few steps ahead of me, as usual, but this time I'd caught up. "How did you know?"

"You said self-defense plus challenging plus something for me. The something for me is the Israeli part?" I was hardly in good enough shape to do the Israeli military's workout program, but maybe she and Jo would have a good time without me. I started to turn around.

Chloe grabbed my arm. "Don't go! Please! It'll be okay, I promise. There's a club here, and I talked to this guy named Avi, and he said he'll do a private lesson for us."

"Yeah, I know Avi." He'd shown up at a couple of the Hillel dinners but it was clear he was only there to hit on the first-year students. Once he got shut down enough times, he stopped coming. He'd never hit on me, though. He probably wouldn't even remember having met me. Not that I cared. He was a tool. Tamara and I made fun of him all the time.

"Look, they're already here," Chloe said.

We'd reached the exercise room, where Jo and Avi were chatting. Jo seemed way more comfortable than I felt, contemplating Krav Maga for the first time. She wore all-black workout gear and her bleached hair was cropped even shorter than usual. She was slim and muscular and a fascinating combination between boyish and feminine, and based on the look on Chloe's face, she was even more intrigued than I was. Though maybe not in the same way. I hated that I tended to assume people were straight unless they indicated otherwise; I really wanted to change that about myself.

"Hi, everyone," Chloe said.

"Hi, Princess," Jo said. "Hey, Amina, I didn't realize you were coming too."

She'd called me Amina? Was I not even interesting enough for a nickname? "Chloe didn't tell you?"

"She told me," Avi said, nodding at me with what seemed to be recognition. "You all ready to get started?" His overly prominent Adam's apple moved up and down, belying the bluster in his voice.

"I'm good," Chloe said.

"Me too," Jo said, and I nodded. So much for getting to know each other. We were diving right in.

Avi explained the basic principles of Krav Maga, which I'd heard before—how it had been developed for the Israeli Defense Force, how it borrowed some techniques from other martial arts but had its own spin, how it was more effective than any other form of self-defense because its practitioners weren't afraid to hurt their attackers. "None of that avoiding injury stuff," Avi said. "If we have to hurt people to survive, we hurt people."

It was basically the opposite of what Candace-from-kickboxing had said, but Chloe and Jo were both nodding. Apparently they were both fine with hurting people.

Avi walked us through some preliminary concepts, starting with how to hit most effectively (striking with the side of the hand, making good use of knees and elbows), moving on to things that were helpful but unfamiliar (attacking from a defensive position on the ground, getting out of chokeholds), and then going into terrifying new terrain (defending against attackers who had weapons, disarming attackers who had guns). Avi was moving really fast now, faster than I could handle. Chloe was struggling too, but Jo seemed fine.

"Ready to try some sparring?"

No, I wasn't ready for sparring. I glared at Chloe, but she looked kind of pissed off herself. She was in good shape, but not this kind of shape; she was in over her head. Beads of condensation had formed on her temples; wisps of hair had come out of her usually perfect ponytail.

"Totally ready," Jo said, cool as a Vermont fall day. She wasn't even sweating.

"I need a break," I said. Someone had to be honest around here.

"Yeah, looks like it," Avi said, and I wanted to punch him. Maybe I'd been wrong about not being ready to spar. "How about Chloe and Jo go first, and you and I can watch and evaluate?"

Now I wanted to punch him less. "Sounds good to me."

"Okay, Chloe, you go ahead and attack Jo. She'll be on the ground already. You can decide how to approach."

Chloe would have the upper hand. That should make her feel better. Yet, somehow, it seemed like Chloe had barely decided what kind of attack to attempt before she was on the ground, Jo's hands pinning her to the floor, Jo's knee on her chest, Jo's face right by hers, their lips practically touching. "That was fast," Chloe spat.

Jo grinned.

"Want to give it another shot, Chloe?" Avi asked. "You start on the ground this time, since you're there already."

He had no idea who he was dealing with. I hoped Chloe didn't ignore Jo and kill Avi. Chloe just needed to channel her rage, turn Jo's strategy around on her, attack from the defensive position, get her knee up before Jo could—

Now Chloe was on her stomach, Jo's arm across her shoulder blades, Jo's knee pinning her knees to the ground so Chloe's body looked like a lowercase *h*. How had she done that so fast? I was beyond relieved I'd gotten myself out of this.

"What was that?" Chloe asked. She was even angrier than I thought.

"Sorry, did I hurt you, Princess?" Jo asked sweetly. Or as sweetly as she could manage.

Avi started laughing. "Tell her," he said. "Come on, it's not fair anymore."

"Tell me what?" Chloe asked, but I had a feeling I knew.

Jo just smirked.

"She joined the club this fall," Avi said. "She's the best first year we have. She's probably going to replace me as president at the end of the school year. She made me swear not to tell."

"Right," Chloe said. "Well, thanks for helping out, Avi. See you around, Jo." She stormed out of the exercise room, leaving me there with the two of them.

"That went well," I said. "Jo, you want to chase her down, or should I?"

"Oh, she'll be fine," Jo said. "I'm just getting warmed up. I'll stick around and spar with Avi here."

"Whatever you say, boss," he said, and charged at her. The two of them were locked in some sort of grappling situation when I left.

Chloe was furious, I knew, and I'd never seen her that pissed off before. She'd gotten pretty far ahead of me, and I wasn't sure whether I should run after her to catch up or just walk behind and give her a chance to calm down. We could always talk once we got to her room.

But she wasn't going to her room. It took me a while to realize where she was headed, because I never went to the boys' dorms. We were only allowed in the common rooms that connected the boys' and girls' dorms together.

Getting in was hardly challenging, though; the main doors were unlocked, the dorm parents went to bed early, and Gardner wasn't a school of snitches. I stayed far enough behind Chloe that she didn't notice me, and I kept my steps light. I wasn't trying to talk to her now; I was spying on her.

When Chloe reached Hunter's room she knocked three times, gently. I hid around the corner, where I saw Hunter's roommate open the door. He barely had time to say "Hey, Chloe" before she told him to get out. Thankfully he left the other way so he didn't see me. She'd been here before, then.

Hunter came to the door next, wearing boxers and nothing else. My dream of seeing him shirtless was coming true, but this wasn't how I'd wanted it to go. "I came to check on you," she said.

"I'm fine," he said. "I'm over it. Mostly. Still haven't heard from Amina, though."

He wanted to hear from me? This was news.

"I'll talk to her," Chloe said.

"How'd the Krav Maga go?" he asked. She'd told him what we were doing, then. Now I was confused. I'd only just started thinking that maybe Chloe wanted Jo, but here she was, in Hunter's room, at night, and not for the first time.

"Not bad," she said. "Here, I'll show you. How would you resist me, if I were attacking you?" She gave him a shove, and they moved back into the room.

I crept out of the hallway, staying far enough away that

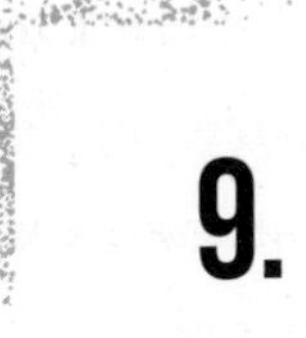

9.

I'd once heard someone describe themselves as being incandescent with rage and I remember thinking that it was somehow both a great description and an obvious exaggeration. But on the walk back from Hunter's room to my dorm I felt like I finally understood. I was having so many feelings all at once: I'd already been mad at Hunter for lying about his father, and now I had to face the fact that he really did want Chloe and not me. Not to mention that Chloe was supposedly my best friend, and yet here she was, getting together with the guy I wanted. Except she didn't know I wanted him, which meant that in some backward way this was all my fault. Incandescent was a good word: I felt like my rage could light a fire.

I walked all over campus trying to calm myself down, sticking to paths I knew by heart once curfew kicked in so I wouldn't get caught. By the time I got back to my room I had a plan: I'd do my best to fake it around Chloe and Hunter for the time being, I'd beg off my study sessions with Hunter and claim I was working on my game, and I'd vent to Tamara after services Friday. It was becoming increasingly clear I couldn't deal with all this anger by myself.

Wednesday was Hunter's first day back after the article came out, and he saved me the trouble of worrying how to interact with him by giving me a brief nod and then sitting at his desk, not talking to me or anyone else. He was equally silent in our other classes, not speaking until we were walking out of European History. "Skipping lunch to go study," he said. "I'm going to cram on my own tonight, too. Hope that's okay."

He walked off before I had a chance to say anything, and I was grateful. He'd done the hard work for me. But then I wondered whether he was still avoiding people because of the article or whether he now wanted to avoid me because of Chloe, because he'd somehow known I was into him, and I started to feel panicky. It wasn't until I relayed Hunter's plans to Chloe at lunch that I began to figure things out. "He's not eating with us today. He said he has to study."

"That's what he said?" Chloe didn't notice how much trouble I was having making eye contact with her. "He's such a liar. He's avoiding me because we've been hooking up and last night he wanted to talk about what it means and I wasn't up for it." She deepened her voice at the word "talk," as if mocking Hunter for liking her. I felt a wash of relief that I'd never talked about my crush, and I almost started feeling bad for Hunter. Almost.

I reminded myself that I was supposed to be surprised. "You've been what?"

"Oh, it's no big deal." Chloe waved her hand in what was becoming her signature move, the gesture conveying dismissiveness with a hint of disdain. "I was pissed off Jo pulled a fast one on us last night, and I decided it was my turn to blow off some steam. I figured Hunter would be up for some fun, but he got all intense about it. Given everything that's coming out about his dad I would have thought he could use the distraction, you know?"

Suddenly, somehow, I did. I could see it all, both sides: I'd been right that Hunter was falling for Chloe, and I'd been right that she had no idea, that she'd gone and treated him like a fling and might have broken his heart in the process. Now I did feel bad for him, and I was tempted to try and track him down to see if he was okay. But that was only going to make me feel worse, and I wasn't quite over learning about his family. I could take some comfort in knowing that Chloe wasn't trying to hurt me, that she'd been just as oblivious to my feelings as she'd been to Hunter's—at least there was one person among the three of us I could try not to be mad at. What did that say about her, though? What did it say about me, to have a friend who, best-case scenario, didn't notice my feelings? I couldn't even begin to wrap my brain around the answer.

With everything else going on I'd put the thought of the elections out of my head, though I'd hardly forgotten about them, especially not with the "Hunter and Amina for a Better Future" posters covering just about every surface on campus. We'd outdone our opponents in getting our names out there; now we had to wait and see how much damage the article had done, and to whom.

Voting was Thursday after classes, with the votes tallied that night. I could barely sleep wondering what I would discover Friday morning, in what ways my life at Gardner might change, if at all. But nothing could have prepared me for what the students ultimately decided: Friday morning rolled around to reveal that the two new class reps were me and Ken Zhang.

"Apparently the student body decided they wanted one rep for serious stuff and one rep for fun," Chloe announced at lunch. Hunter was nowhere to be found, and now I wondered which of the latest embarrassments was keeping him away. "It's going to mean a ton of work for you—Ken won't do anything. But at least we got you in there."

She hadn't mentioned Hunter at all. "Is he okay?" I asked, knowing I didn't have to specify who. "Did you check on him?"

This got me a sigh. "I tried, but he's still sulking. I'm sure he'll be fine."

I wasn't quite as sure. Maybe it was time for me to check in with him. I needed some advice, though, so I decided to wait until after I'd talked to Tamara. I cornered her at dinner and made her stay and talk to me in the chapel afterward. "You wouldn't believe everything that's been going on," I began, and filled her in on all the details, both hookup- and election-related. Of course she jumped on the hookup stuff.

"You actually saw them?" Tamara's eyes widened in horror, and she put her hand over her mouth. She'd painted her nails with a beehive pattern, with tiny bees scattered on each one. How did she even find the time?

"I mean, not the actual thing, but yeah, it was very clear what was going to happen. I'm over it, though. Totally."

"Uh-huh." Tamara didn't even try to be convincing. "Which part are you over, exactly? The part where you're super into him? The part where your best friend went after him? The part where he lied about his background?"

"Okay, I get it." She was saying the same things I'd been thinking, but it sounded so much worse coming from her. "I'm over having a thing for him. I never told Chloe, so it's not her fault for going after him."

"Sure." Another failed poker face from Tamara. "As if it wasn't completely obvious how you felt. I haven't even been in the same room with both of you in any real way, and I'm pretty sure I'd be able to tell. What about the other kids in your group—what's it called again?"

"Eucalyptus," I said.

"Where are they in all this? Do any of them know what's been happening?"

"Good question." I really didn't know the answer. I'd felt a vibe between Chloe and Jo but I didn't know what it was about or what direction it went in, and Wyatt tended to be clueless about interpersonal stuff. None of us had talked about Hunter's family situation, and I was pretty sure Jo and Wyatt didn't know about the hookup. "I guess I'll find out at our next meeting."

"When's that?" she asked.

Another good question. Our next meeting would be the one where we started my game. That wasn't going to happen until after finals. I didn't think I'd make it through two weeks of avoiding Hunter, not when he was in almost all my classes. Besides, I really did need to study. I was sure he did too.

Bummer about the election, I texted on my way back from services. I'm behind on studying—want to catch up this weekend?

I could see him start to type a response practically as soon as mine went out, and I felt bad all over again. He really was waiting to hear from me. Soccer away game tomorrow but Sunday yes plz!

We arranged a time, and I decided I was going to try to get over being upset about his dad. He couldn't help who his family was, and he'd taken so many steps to separate himself it didn't seem fair for me to judge him for wanting to pretend the connection didn't exist. I was lucky I had a family that not only cared about me but cared about the same things I did, even if we didn't always agree about everything. For once, I found myself looking forward to our weekly call. I'd talk to everyone this time, not just my sister.

Before I knew it, two weeks had passed. We'd made it through finals, I'd gone to my first student council meeting (with the other class rep, Ken Zhang, who to my surprise wasn't as bad a guy as I'd expected), I'd skipped the big Halloween party, and it was time for my game to begin. We assembled in the bunker, with me sitting in a chair and everyone gathered around me in a circle on the floor as if it were story time, which, given how I'd set up the game, it was.

"My game's going to be a little different than the first two," I told them. "My big fear is that the United States is going to turn out to be a failed experiment in democracy, that we're now two separate countries living under one roof, and we can't go on as we are. So in the world of my game, my worst fears have come to pass. I'll tell you the story of how it happened and then give you a character to play and tell you the rules." I'd written up a narrative explaining the world we'd all be living in, just to make sure I didn't leave anything out. "It all started with the reelection of a certain president."

I explained how the Republican Party had managed to unify itself around an unpopular leader, allowing him to pack the courts and sign off on laws that took away many of the progressive gains of years past. No more constitutional right to abortion, or even birth control; no more gay marriage; no more Voting Rights Act; no more laws against gerrymandering. Electoral districts became so skewed that Republicans took over more than three-quarters of state governments as well, which opened the door for constitutional amendments. That's when things got complicated.

First came the repeal of the Twenty-Second Amendment and its term limits on the presidency, leading to a third and fourth term for the unpopular president. The next amendment to fall was the Fourteenth, along with its guarantee of equal rights. Repealing the Fourth Amendment, against unlawful search and seizure, opened the door to a police state. If the Democrats weren't able to do something to stop it through the political process, there would soon be a military coup, and the president would officially become a dictator.

That's how the Second Civil War started.

"And we lost," I told them.

The bunker was silent. I'd managed to hold everyone's attention, so that was a good start.

"What happened next?" Hunter finally asked.

"Suspension of the Constitution and enactment of martial law," I said. "The president retreated to his vacation home and left running the country to his evangelical vice president. Women, people of color, disabled people, LGBTQ plus—no one had any protection under the law anymore, so cis white men were free to do whatever they wanted. Immigrants were either sent home or put in camps, children were separated from their parents indefinitely, naturalized citizens were denaturalized and sent back to countries where some of them had never been. And the war itself meant a smaller population, since so many people died. The economy collapsed, and we lost pretty much all relationships with other countries. We're now short on just about every resource you can imagine, but there's still some hope for a revolution."

"Sign me up for the revolution!" Wyatt yelled.

"Calm down, there, Paul Revere," Jo said. "Is that the game? To figure out the revolution?"

"That would be fun, wouldn't it?" I asked. "But no, we don't get to be the heroes here. I don't think that's what surviving the apocalypse would really be like, do you? Everyone thinks they have to save the world, but they have to save themselves first."

"How do we do that?" Hunter asked.

"The goal is simple," I said. "Survival for one week under the current regime. But it's not as easy as it sounds. We've got food shortages and rationing, along with all the legal restrictions that weren't in place before. Your task is to do the best job possible using your limited resources, given the circumstances I've placed each of you in. You won't all start out on equal footing because the world we're living in isn't fair, so the rules don't have to be fair either. I've made a bio for each of you and given you a list of sample expenses and ration coupons, and I've given you a spreadsheet template you can use to track your spending. Whoever does the best job making it through the week wins."

I gave each of them a manila folder with their biographical info and watched them start reading. I'd given a lot of thought to their characters, and I was pleased with what I'd put together.

Wyatt, I knew, hadn't grown up with much, but the people on the commune had shared what they had, so he was used to getting by and thinking collectively. This meant he was going to have to learn to be selfish, and he would need to fight for resources. I gave his character a limited number of ration coupons; to get more, he'd have to come up with a way to convince other people to give him food or coupons, and it had to be for valuable services. I knew he didn't think he had much to offer, but I bet he'd be surprised at what he could do, especially if he was hungry.

Chloe was cagey about her upbringing, but I got the sense she'd grown up under financial constraints and had managed to survive on her own terms through her social media enterprise. On the one hand, that made her one of the most fiercely self-sufficient people I'd ever met, which made challenging her difficult. On the other hand, she didn't have much taste for deprivation these days, so perhaps even making her go without some of the luxuries she'd grown accustomed to would be hard enough. I made her character extremely poor and gave her a debilitating illness that kept her from working full time and that required medication, so she didn't have enough money and coupons for both food and drugs.

I'd expected Hunter's character to be easy, now that I knew just how much privilege he'd had growing up. But while giving him a shock to the system was nearly guaranteed, I really wanted to wake him up to how hard the world was for some people, and how much worse it could get. He was so congenial that a week of living on a weird food budget might be fun for him. He'd always know safety was a few days away, and I didn't know how to remove that feeling of security, if only for a little while.

So his game had different rules. I knew it might not work; he could cry foul, and he'd be right. First, his game had a failure trigger: if he didn't follow all the rules the first week he had to keep going, and he had to live with any financial deficits he'd created for himself. Second, I made his character female. As luck would have it, she'd have her period the week of the experiment, and supplies were now catastrophically expensive. Finally, his character had a food allergy. I knew

Hunter loved his carbs, and those were often the cheapest source of nutrients, so I made his character allergic to gluten. Not just insensitive, but really, truly allergic, so he—she—couldn't eat it at all. No bread, no pasta, none of the foods he liked. I figured if he followed the latter two rules, his week would be brutal. The group might not hold him to the first rule, but perhaps he'd learn that sometimes the rules of the game were rigged against you from the start, and there was nothing you could do about it. He needed to know it not just intellectually but in his bones, especially if he was going to do the kind of work he wanted to do.

Jo was the real challenge. She was still a cipher to me; I knew she'd grown up in Chicago and that her parents were dead, but that was pretty much it. I'd finally put together that her mother was Korean and her father was white because she'd made a joke about storing homemade kimchi in the bunker and had reluctantly explained it when Chloe asked. I suspected she wasn't straight, but really that was just a combination of her shoelaces and the vibe between her and Chloe, neither of which was enough for me to draw a real conclusion. I knew we'd all assumed Jo was a scholarship student because she wore the same clothes all the time and didn't act like someone with money, but I couldn't be sure. Then there was the fact that she was scary and competitive, but I'd never seen her lose her composure. How was I supposed to make her life hard?

I decided to try to make her angry, to make her want to fight. To bring out her competitive side, as if it needed much coaxing. I had to set up obstacles that would be insurmountable for ordinary people and give Jo a chance to shine. She'd be poor like everyone else, sure, but there had to be more. I started with diabetes, which limited her food options even more than Hunter's. But that wasn't enough.

There was one thing I could do that would make Jo's situation nearly impossible, for so many reasons, but it required me to make assumptions about Jo's position on certain topics that I wasn't sure were warranted. It made Jo's life so hard it was outright mean, but I'd been mean to Hunter too. And if anyone could handle it, Jo could. So I made her sixteen years old, on her own, and pregnant.

Timing-wise, Jo had the week to decide whether to keep the baby. Abortion was now illegal in what remained of the United States, but it was legal in Canada, so it was possible, given enough money. But Jo's character had no money. The diabetes meant it might not be safe to carry the pregnancy to term if she couldn't get the right food and medication; there was a good chance she or the baby wouldn't survive. I didn't see that her character had much choice, but the logistics were nearly impossible either way. I wanted to see if Jo could find a solution.

That left only me, but I was easy, and I was only playing in solidarity, since I couldn't win my own game. My character was there for illustrative purposes, and so I could prepare for something that worried me: I'd be playing a native-born citizen whose naturalized parents had been sent away. I had access to their finances and food coupons, so I wouldn't starve, but I wanted to either go to them or bring them home, both of which required money I didn't have.

I waited until everyone had finished reading. "Any questions?"

Chloe raised her hand. "Can we pool resources?"

"Sure," I said. "And you can barter or trade, too. Although you'll find no one has much to spare."

"Any restrictions on how we can spend money, if we have it?" Jo asked.

"There's some stuff in the rules about that. You have to allocate a certain amount for housing and utilities and you have to eat enough not to die—that part's real. Meaning you're going to have to pretend-shop and then eat what you bought from the dining halls. But you get to decide the rest. Just remember that everything costs money—cell phones, toiletries, everything—and you have to account for it."

"But we don't spend money on those things now," Chloe said.

"Yes you do; you just don't realize it because it's all wrapped up in tuition," I said. "Even if you're on scholarship, the scholarship money goes toward food and housing and keeping the buildings open and lit and heated. So you have to spend money on those things because you're still going to take advantage of them during the game."

"Why can't we assume our roommate will cover at least some of those things?" Hunter asked.

"Because that's not how the world works for most people," I told him. "That's what I'm trying to get across to you here."

"What if we want more than you've given us?" Chloe asked. "Can we get another job, bring in more money?"

"You all have exactly as much job as you can handle. And I'm not trying to get in the way of anyone studying. No extra jobs, even for those of you who already have a side gig." I directed that one right at Chloe. "That means no new clothes if you can't afford to buy them, even if hypothetically someone sent them to you for free."

Chloe groaned. "This is going to be excruciating."

"Exactly," I said. I couldn't wait to get started.

10.

The game began Monday morning, the week after first-quarter finals. My nightmares had all but vanished, and I woke after a dreamless sleep with a sense of anticipation that far outstripped anything I had to do for the day, which included eating food I could afford, doing my homework, and researching my character's project. I went to the dining hall for breakfast (eggs with black beans and salsa but no tea because I couldn't swing it) and headed to class.

Hunter was already struggling. "I'm so tired," he said, yawning. "I didn't think I was that big of a coffee person, but man, that stuff is expensive. First thing to go."

By third period I was starving, and Hunter looked like he was going to fall asleep on his textbook. "I ate nothing but protein for breakfast and it's not even lunchtime and I feel like I'm going to pass out," I said. "You must be dying."

"I'll bail if you will," he said.

“Not a chance.” Maybe I couldn’t win, but I wasn’t about to go down in flames at my own game, either. I was glad, too, that the game seemed to be giving Hunter and me a way to be normal with each other. We’d made it through studying together for finals, but that was because we didn’t talk about anything but exams. It wasn’t weird, but it wasn’t exactly comfortable, either.

By lunchtime I was already rethinking my decision not to quit. I made my usual peanut-butter-and-jelly sandwich and debated whether to eat a banana or an apple—I’d budgeted enough for one each per day, though I’d have to start eating some kind of fruit in the morning. Chloe had a salad, albeit a less colorful one than usual, while Hunter plowed his way through a bread-free pile of deli meat. So far, the three of us hadn’t changed our habits all that much.

Wyatt had, though. I ran into him at dinner, where he was balancing a tray of salad, spaghetti, and an enormous fountain soda. Usually I ate dinner by myself, reading a book in the corner, skipping the dinner rush when I knew most people were there. I liked having a little alone time. But I was curious to see how Wyatt was doing, so I brought my tray of chicken over to the cross-country table and asked if I could sit.

His face lit up. “Definitely!” He gestured to the seat across from him, and his teammates made room.

I sat down and pointed at his tray. “What’ve you got there?”

He smiled proudly. "Check it out—I did a ton of research and I found ways to get the cheapest food in the largest quantities. There are so many coupons out there! Soda is crazy cheap, and if I'm going to keep running this week it's all about inexpensive calories and carbs."

That explained the pasta. It also explained why he wasn't freaking out that I hadn't given him enough ration coupons. "I'm jealous," I told him. "I don't think I realized how much random stuff I eat during the day that's off-limits now."

Wyatt nodded, and I noticed he'd gotten a haircut. It made him look older, though I found myself missing his curls. "I'm already worried about practice tomorrow—Tuesday's our long run, and I'm not sure there's enough pasta in the world."

I evaluated the trays of his teammates. "You may be right." I'd never seen so much pasta in one place outside a buffet.

"Thanks for setting this up," he said. "It's kind of fun, even if it's going to be hard. And it's probably more practical than what we've been doing so far."

"Unless the world really ends," I said. "This will mostly be useless then."

Wyatt shrugged. "Maybe, maybe not. There's more to this lesson than just learning to deal with scarcity, isn't there?"

"But of course," I said. "I threw in some tricks."

"I can't wait to find out more," Wyatt said.

I was dying to know how everyone else was doing, but I hadn't budgeted for a phone, and I didn't have time to go to the library to email—I hadn't budgeted for a computer, either. If I learned nothing else this week, it would be to not take my easy access to technology for granted. It felt so strange not being able to reach out whenever I wanted; I wished we'd all agreed on a regular meeting place, if only to check in.

I wasn't alone in wanting to check in, because Chloe came by my dorm the next night. "This is already brutal!" She flopped down on my absentee roommate's bed. "Look at me! I'm death personified!" She pointed at her face, which looked pretty much like her face always looked.

I squinted. "Not getting a Grim Reaper vibe at all."

"Where do I even start?" Chloe really did know how to bring the drama. "I can't afford a single one of my own skin care products, let alone makeup. I decided it was better to wear absolutely nothing than to spend part of my pittance on drugstore crap, so I'm completely naked."

"You look entirely clothed to me," I said.

Chloe groaned. "Face naked! I don't even have moisturizer! Or mascara! I look like I'm asleep. For the record, it's totally unfair not to let me use the stuff people send me for free. I don't see how I'm going to make it through the week."

"You'll make it through the week because if you don't you'll lose, and you hate to lose," I said. "Not to mention you're smart enough to know that if it's hard it's worth trying. It means there's something you can learn. You can pretend all you want, but you're probably the smartest person here. You know you want to learn everything you can. Just buy some Cetaphil and that Maybelline mascara in the pink-and-green tube like normal people do and you'll be fine."

Chloe eyed me with an expression I hadn't seen from her before. It was as if the Chloe I knew disappeared for a minute, replaced by someone who wasn't always exaggerating and flirting and vamping, someone who just evaluated the situation around her impartially and then made a calculated decision how to act. Or maybe I was reading too much into the absence of makeup. But I barely caught the expression before it was gone. "Ugh, you're right, I'm totally competitive," she said, flipping over on the bed and propping herself up on her elbows. "And it's true I've already gotten a little creative."

"Have you now?" I asked. "How so?"

She laughed. "That's for me to know and you to learn all about at the end of the week."

"How's Hunter doing?" I tried to sound casual and failed.

"Fine so far," she said. "I figured I'm going to need help with this game, so I went and begged forgiveness, promised not to try and hook up with him anymore. Though I'm not sure that's what he really wants." She winked at me. "Boys, you know how they get."

I had no idea how boys got.

"Are you two okay?" Chloe asked. "It finally feels like lunch is getting back to normal."

"It's been a little weird since the election," I admitted. "It never occurred to me that I'd win and he wouldn't."

"You know he doesn't really care, right? And that he's genuinely happy for you?"

"I wasn't sure." For some reason I didn't want to get into how thrown I'd been by learning about his family. I was trying to get over it. "Sounds like you've been talking a lot, though. You sure you're not going to get together? Maybe you even like him, a little bit?" I tilted my head at her, and she tilted hers back at me, and then we both started cracking up. I'd missed her, I realized. We hadn't hung out properly for a while.

"Well, it's possible I might cave on the fooling around," she said. "But I've been a teeny bit fixated on someone else."

"Jo?" I asked, before I had time to think about it.

Chloe sat up. "See, this is what I get for wanting to be friends with a smart person. You miss nothing. Yes, I've definitely been flirting with both of them. Hunter went for it, of course, because he's a guy"—I didn't point out to her that for most of us it wasn't a given that the person we wanted would want us back, whether that person was a guy or not—"but I just cannot get a read on Jo. She's so mysterious! She could be ace, or into someone else, or not just into me, and I can't tell the difference. It's infuriating."

"Why not just go for it with Hunter, then? If you know he likes you back." I couldn't believe I was pushing her toward the person I wanted, though I was starting to see that it might be possible to stop wanting him, to be okay with just being friends.

"He's like a puppy," she said. "It's all right there, on the surface. Look at my big brown eyes, pet me, love me. I think I need something more complicated, you know?"

You like the drama, I wanted to say, but I didn't. In some ways I wished I hadn't asked. It was hard to see Hunter as she did, simple and cute and needy. I was just worried she was going to hurt him, and badly. "Have you tried talking to Jo about any of this?"

"You try and pin her down. I have no idea what she does with herself. Except Krav Maga, apparently."

"Well, I should check in with her about the game," I said. "I'll let you know if I find out anything new."

Her face brightened. "Would you? That would be so amazing."

How strange, the thought of me helping Chloe with anything. I wasn't at all convinced I'd learn more about Jo than Chloe had, but it was worth a try. Especially if it might save Hunter from heartbreak by getting Chloe to move on sooner rather than later.

Without my phone I couldn't reach out to Jo, and I wasn't sure if she was checking her email, so I decided to track her down at dinner. I had no idea when she normally ate, so I showed up with a book when the dining hall opened, sat near the entrance, and waited, scanning the tables occasionally to see if I could find her.

Finally I saw her in line for the salad bar. I put together yet another sad chicken dinner for myself and followed her to a table in the back, where she also had brought a book, clearly planning to sit by herself. "May I join you?" I asked.

Jo cocked her head, then indicated the seat across from her. "Come to check up on me? You wouldn't be the first."

What was that supposed to mean? She made it so hard to ask even the most basic questions. "I wanted to see how things were going."

Her tray held an enormous salad loaded with garbanzo beans and about a million different vegetables. It looked more like a Chloe special from before the Second Civil War, but better. "I decided to go vegan—animal proteins are really expensive unless you get the cheap cuts."

I took a bite of chicken drowned in ketchup, the cheapest condiment I could find. "Tell me about it."

"I ended up with lots of beans, and digestive issues aside, it's not too bad so far," she said. "Keeps the blood sugar in check, too. Theoretically, of course." She held up her book, which was a library copy of a book about meal planning for diabetics. She'd done her homework.

"I gave you a lot to deal with," I acknowledged. "How are you doing with all the other stuff?"

Jo shrugged. "Still working on it. There are no rules, right? Other than the ones you gave us?"

I had to think about that. "I mean, I didn't say don't do anything illegal, but I hope that was implied? Although I guess it's not clear what's legal under the circumstances."

"We didn't discuss gray areas," Jo said.

"No, we didn't." This was the second person hinting at creative approaches to my game. I'd have to wait until the end of the week to find out what everyone was up to. "I guess whatever you figure out will be a good lesson for us."

The way Jo looked at me made me understand, just for a second, how she and Chloe might work as a couple. There was something about both of them I'd never understand, that perhaps I never could, and maybe they'd find it in one another. Complexity, for sure. Poor Hunter. I found myself pitying him more than wanting him, now. Chloe's description of him had crept into my psyche, and I didn't like it.

I was supposed to be doing some scouting of Jo for Chloe, but I wasn't sure what Chloe wanted to know, or how I was supposed to find it out. "Has the game affected your life in any other ways? Like, can you still do Krav Maga on the diet?"

Jo eyed me, trying to figure out what I was really asking. How did she even know to do that? "Working out isn't a problem," she said.

"Has it been awkward, like, around other people? I feel like I'd be getting a lot of questions about what I've been eating if I weren't spending so much time with Hunter and Chloe."

"You trying to figure out who I'm hanging out with?" she asked. "Why, are you interested?"

I hadn't been subtle in my quest to get information for Chloe, and now I'd stepped in it. "No, I'm just trying to help. Forget it. If you have questions you know where to find me." I started to get up from the table, trying not to knock over my tray.

"Aw, I didn't mean to make you feel bad," she said. "Just tell your friend if she wants to know anything about me she should ask me herself."

No one could hide anything from Jo. She and Chloe really would make a good match. Hunter was doomed.

Seeing him in person the next day felt the same as it always had, except now my stomach was twisting from hunger, not longing. "How are you doing so far?" I asked him in between classes, when we were alone. "Because I have to be honest—I know this was my idea, but I'm kind of dying. If I have to eat one more chicken leg I might kill someone."

"Please don't," he said. "I won't make it through econ without you."

I noticed he hadn't answered my question. "What's it like being a woman? Any observations you want to share?"

He grinned. "It's all I've ever dreamed of. I'll tell you all about it when the game's over."

"In it to win it, are we?" As soon as I said it, I felt bad, like I'd made a dig about the election. We still hadn't talked about it, other than that text I'd sent. "Listen, Hunter, I've been meaning to—"

He held up his hand. "If you're going to say something about the election, don't. I knew it was over as soon as I saw that article. It's fine. I was just doing it to go along with you two anyway."

"Still, it wasn't cool of me to just not bring it up," I said. "I'm sorry."

"It's no big deal," he said. "I was more upset that everyone had to find out about my family like that. It's not like I was trying to hide it, but they're what I wanted to get away from, you know? To have it all out there like that—it made being here feel pointless, for a while. But Chloe helped me remember I've got a life here that has nothing to do with them. And friends, too." He punched me in the arm. "We're good, right?"

"All good," I said, relieved.

I couldn't remember a week going by this slowly that wasn't Passover. At least now I could have bread, though for the first time I was actually getting sick of peanut-butter-and-jelly sandwiches. By Thursday night I was ready to eat my own arm, just for variety. I decided to go to the library and work on the research project I'd assigned myself. I buried myself in websites researching how to cross borders, how to earn money without getting yet another job, how to save more of what you were earning, anything that might help my character make some progress in reuniting with her family. I was practically falling asleep at the computer when someone tapped on my shoulder, nearly making me jump out of my chair.

"Sorry, didn't mean to scare you." I turned to see Wyatt. He wore his usual T-shirt and jeans but they looked different somehow. Was his shirt tucked in? I saw little nicks in his skin where he'd cut himself shaving, and while my first thought was that I hoped he'd budgeted for razors, my second thought was that he was trying to look nice. He'd succeeded, too. He even looked taller than I remembered. "I just wanted to say hi and see how the research was going. You said you wouldn't be using your own computer."

"You're right," I said stupidly. "You found me." Why did I feel so confused? Maybe it was the lack of sugar. "The research is going well, but it's incredibly depressing."

"Want to tell me about it? Can I sit?" He gestured at the chair next to me.

"Of course." I told him all about how hard it was now, getting families together who were having immigration struggles, even if they had money. It would be exponentially more difficult in the world I'd imagined. "There's just no way for a character in my position to make the kind of money she'd need, other than selling her eggs."

Wyatt looked horrified. There was a good chance he didn't know that was a thing women did regularly.

"It's not like selling a kidney," I assured him. "Though given the new world order, maybe she'd be allowed to do that now. Who knows?" I threw up my hands, ready to be done with my research and the game, both.

"Are you still hungry?" Wyatt asked.

I looked at him, confused—I hadn't said anything about being hungry.

"At dinner, earlier this week, you were saying how hungry you were. You were worried you hadn't spent your budget the right way?" He reached into his backpack and took out a box of generic granola bars. "I had some extra. Is this allowed?"

He'd listened to me, and now he wanted to share his food, during a week when we barely had the resources to feed ourselves. And he was all dressed up, sort of. Had he tried to look nice for me?

"Why are you looking at me like that?" Now he was blushing. "Was I cheating? I didn't mean to cheat."

"You weren't cheating," I said. "You were being wonderful." I put my hand on his just for a moment. "But I can't take these. It's not technically against the rules, but I need to try and do this on my own."

Wyatt swallowed, his Adam's apple just barely visible, moving up and down his neck. "If you can't take them now, then maybe when this is all over we could go out for something else? Like ice cream?"

Ice cream, at Gardner, was code for a date. There was

a place in town that was so good people went there even in the middle of snowstorms. Usually people took the campus bus there and then walked back, straying off the road to find places to hook up. I'd only been there for ice cream in the literal sense, and maybe that's what Wyatt was offering, but I didn't think so.

"I'd like that," I said, and he smiled so hard a normal person would be embarrassed. But not Wyatt. That's what made him Wyatt.

I ran home from dinner and got out my journal. Lately all I'd written about was how hungry I was, though as I flipped back through it and read some of my earlier entries I realized not only could I track the rise and fall of my crush on Hunter as if it were a parabola, but there were way more references to Wyatt than I'd realized. I'd written about his hair, the fact that he was somehow managing to get through the week without help, how glad I was he'd started Eucalyptus . . . had I been developing a crush on Wyatt this whole time?

Or maybe I was just having hunger-induced delusions. If I ever did anything like this again, I'd have to remember to get more snacks. Drinking nothing but water had been good for my skin but I was dying for a cup of tea or even a Diet Coke, and I hadn't planned well for other things I needed so I'd spent all my leftover money on toothpaste and soap. I was definitely learning to be grateful for what I had.

I'd failed in my side task, though—after all my research

I'd come up with nothing. "I wouldn't win this game even if I were eligible," I told everyone, when we met in the bunker Sunday night. I'd snuck a bagful of cookies and brownies out of the dining hall after dinner, and I spread them on paper towels on the floor in front of me as everyone gathered around. "I'm calling the experiment over right now because I'm starving."

We all ate as much sugar as we could stomach, and in between bites I told them about my character and how hard I'd found the week in every way. "I don't know how much you all talked to each other about the roles I gave you to play, but you all had special challenges. And your budgets weren't the same—you might have figured that out too. I wanted it to be clear that while a lot of people would have it hard, some would have it a whole lot harder than others. That's true even now."

"What did you miss most?" Chloe asked.

The answer, for me, wasn't hard. "Food variety," I said. "I bought bulk amounts of stuff I liked that was inexpensive and ate it every day. I was bored within forty-eight hours."

"Does that mean you might actually eat something for lunch besides PB and J?" Hunter said. "Because just so you know, if you ever do, Chloe owes me five bucks."

"Then Chloe might want to hit the ATM," I said, and she laughed.

"I had food problems too," Wyatt said. "I need a lot of calories to run the kinds of distances I've gotten used to, so

I ate a lot of packaged ramen. It had calories plus carbs, and salt, too. It was gross."

"You weren't supposed to be able to make it on the ration coupons you had," I told him. "Part of your game was about letting other people help you—I thought you'd have to trade."

"He's turned into a master shopper," Chloe said. "How horrifying to think we're not even in college yet and you're already subsisting on ramen."

"Yeah, I saved you from that," Hunter said, and it didn't sound like he was joking. "You're welcome."

"What do you mean?" I asked.

"We got creative," he said. "Me and Chloe. We pooled our funds so we could save money, and that got us more variety in our food."

So far that didn't sound bad. "Good idea," I said.

"And since we were both playing women characters . . ." Hunter went red.

"That's how you dealt with buying tampons," I said. "Smart. Though you can say the word 'tampon' out loud, Hunter. It's fine." I had a feeling their little collaboration went further, though. "Chloe, your character had some serious medical issues. Did Hunter help you with medicine, too?"

"He did, but this is where we got a little extra creative, you might say," Chloe replied. "You didn't say we had to do everything on the up-and-up, so I found an online pharmacy and ordered what I needed for way less money than it would have cost here. Overall I'd say we did pretty great."

"Setting aside that you did something totally illegal, and that you might have gotten fake medicine and died, sure," I said.

"If the government's going to set up a situation where poor people have to choose between food and medicine, what are we supposed to do? Isn't that what the internet is for?"

"No," Hunter and I said at the same time. I held back, knowing Hunter's law-and-order side was about to come out. "You didn't tell me what you were doing about the meds," he said. "You just told me you'd take care of the budget. And what about—?"

Chloe cut him off. "Let's hear from the others. I'm sure we're not the only ones who cut some corners."

Something strange was happening in the room, but I wasn't sure exactly what. I glanced at Jo, whose lips were pressed together, arms crossed over her chest, one rainbow-laced Doc Marten perched on her knee. She seemed stoic, but there was something else. Anger? Amusement? I'd wanted the game to get a rise out of her; had I succeeded? I was curious what she had to say. "Jo?"

She planted both feet on the ground as if she were about to stand, then seemed to think better of it. "The food was hardest for me, too—my character was diabetic, so I had to make harder choices than usual, but I figured out ways to do it. I ended up going vegan, and I'd been thinking about becoming a vegetarian anyway, so thanks to Miss Apocalypse over there for helping us imagine the worst." She gave me a fake hat-tip, and I saluted back.

"You did give me a pretty tough challenge, though," Jo said. "My character was a pregnant teenager, and I'm guessing you've all figured out by now that the odds of me getting knocked up are pretty slim. Not impossible, but not likely, either. Maybe that's why you gave me this character? I don't know."

Hunter's mouth had fallen open as Jo was talking. I wondered why—was it really so hard to picture Jo getting pregnant? Maybe he'd assumed she was gay because of how palpable the connection was between her and Chloe, but she could be bi, or pan, or ace, or some other thing all her own. She was Jo. Regular labels didn't necessarily apply.

"Anyway," Jo continued, "I had a lot of constraints. Health stuff, timing, my age. It was hard. If I were as savvy as Princess here I'd probably have found a cheap place to order the abortion pill on the internet, but I don't know, that didn't seem like the safest option. I wanted to do this on the up-and-up. So I did some research and decided that even under your scenario there would be a way to get it here. I guessed at what it would cost, and I figured out there was no way I could do it alone." She went quiet for a minute. I held my breath.

"I'm pretty sure I won't be winning this challenge," Jo said, after what felt like forever. I wasn't the only one holding my breath now, I was sure of it. "I have to admit, knowing that really sucked. I'm competitive, and I hate to lose. But I know Amina wanted us to learn things from this game, and I thought I'd have it in the bag—you all don't know my whole history, but let's just say eating on a budget isn't exactly new to me. Relying on other people is. I couldn't have made this character's situation work without help, and that was a real eye-opener for me. So thank you, Amina, for that."

I expected her to then tell us who else she had to thank, but Hunter spoke first. "Anything to win, huh, Chloe?"

"I didn't break any rules," she said.

"What is it, Hunter?" I asked.

"Oh, whatever. I just got played is all." He glared at Chloe.

I scanned the room. Wyatt looked confused, Jo was smirking, and Chloe's eyes were wide with fake innocence. "What?" she asked, when my gaze landed on her. "It's not like you all didn't know I was competitive. I'm not a survivalist like some of you—I just want to play. And win."

"Well, I'm sure you will," Jo said. "Maybe we should let Amina work her magic and tell us who won."

That sounded like as good a plan as any. I had no idea what had happened in the game, but I had a sneaking suspicion that whatever I learned would explain what was happening in real life. "Go eat the rest of the snacks," I told the group, gathering up everyone's spreadsheets and reports. "I'll be over here in the corner." I tried to get a little privacy as best as I could and started reading, and it didn't take me long to figure out what was going on.

Wyatt, of course, had followed my rules to the letter. He'd largely subsisted on spaghetti, ramen, and soda, just as he'd said, and while he'd budgeted well, his sodium numbers would probably kill him before he turned thirty. Efficient use of resources, yes. Responsible? Not really. I added some points for him offering me food when I was hungry, but it wouldn't be enough for a win.

My own situation wasn't all that different, I had to admit. I'd done fine, had learned some things about food budgets, but my approach to food was boring at best and I hadn't taken much time to think about nutrition. I'd failed to address my hypothetical family situation. I was last.

Hunter hadn't bothered to do a spreadsheet; he'd just written a cursory report directing me to look at what Chloe had done. It was annoying, but it was also very Hunter, assuming that other people would be willing to work to put the pieces together, and not realizing how much extra work they'd have to do.

Chloe had made things easy for me, in a sense. She'd used the spreadsheet template I provided and laid out all the data perfectly, including an extra page that aggregated hers and Hunter's. I felt warmly toward her until I remembered she was the reason everyone seemed so annoyed.

But even with her clear spreadsheets I couldn't make sense

of the numbers I was seeing. Not, at least, until I reviewed Jo's data. Then I finally got it. Chloe was so good, better than I could have imagined.

Chloe had played my poverty game and made a profit.

I saw how she'd done it, though I had no way of knowing exactly what she'd said to either Hunter or Jo during the process. I hadn't prohibited lying, so technically Chloe might not have done anything wrong. But as best as I could piece together, Chloe had convinced Hunter to pool resources by telling him about her medical issues but not disclosing that she'd found cheap places to buy medicine, so their splitting the bill wasn't equitable—he'd put in more than she had. She'd then convinced him it was her character who was pregnant and that she needed an abortion for health reasons, and even though it wasn't Hunter's character's responsibility (given that he was playing a woman), she'd gotten him to help fund her abortion. I had a feeling she'd played on his real-life feelings for her to help her in the game, which was probably at least part of why he was irritated with her. Learning she'd helped Jo couldn't have made things better, especially if he suspected Chloe had feelings for her too, which at this point I was pretty sure he did.

It hadn't been enough for Chloe to fleece Hunter; she'd gotten Jo as well. She must have told her she'd help out and they'd split the cost, because Jo, instead of arranging an abortion herself, had given her money to Chloe, who'd told Jo she'd obtained the pill legally but had of course bought it from the same online pharmacy where she'd gotten everything else, for a fraction of what she'd told Jo it cost.

And she'd pocketed the difference.

I grudgingly admired the ingenuity that went into Chloe's plan, but I wasn't about to let her win that way. She'd taken advantage of just about everyone: me for setting up a system with loopholes; Jo for learning to trust someone—something that was difficult for her; Hunter for being willing to do anything for Chloe, rules or no rules. Only guileless Wyatt had escaped, and that was just because he was blissfully running his cross-country miles and then bathing in sodium.

No, Chloe wouldn't be winning this one. The only question was who would be, and that wasn't so hard. Wyatt was out because of his poor food choices; Hunter was out because he'd shirked his responsibilities and learned nothing in the process. Only Jo had played by the rules as best as she could and gotten something valuable out of the experience as well. She'd done the best job with food, and she'd learned the hardest lessons—she'd had to trust someone, and then she'd had that trust broken. I didn't want that to be her takeaway. Not to mention that it would make Chloe furious to lose to her.

"We have a winner," I called out.

Game three to Jo.

11.

This time I knew Chloe would be angry she hadn't won, and in some ways she'd be in the right—she hadn't technically broken any rules, since I'd barely laid out any. But I was sick of living in a world where bad people got to manipulate the rules and win and good people colored in the lines and lost. If Chloe thought winning meant doing whatever she needed to do, I wanted her to learn that there were consequences when she did things other people considered untenable.

The question was how her anger would manifest. The only time I'd really seen her upset was when Jo showed her up at Krav Maga, and she'd given little indication of how pissed off she was in front of us; she'd just gone to Hunter. Given that she'd used him to pull off her scam, and given that he didn't seem too happy about it, I had a feeling she'd take a different approach.

But once again I was wrong. Monday rolled around, and

the three of us ended up back at the lunch table as if the game had been no big deal. Hunter's sandwich monstrosity had reached epic status, Chloe's salad was back to its full-on rainbow, and I, as promised, was not eating PB&J.

"Where's my five bucks?" Hunter held his hand over Chloe's salad until she rolled her eyes and got some money out of her pink mini crocodile purse.

"I didn't do this for you," I said. It had taken me nearly fifteen minutes to decide what to eat, and while I'd settled on a noodle stir-fry, we all knew I'd be back to my normal sandwich soon.

Though Chloe and Hunter seemed to be getting along just fine, it became clear as the week went on that it was surface-level fine. Hunter and I were back on our study schedule, and he wasn't one for gossip; all I could get him to tell me during our Tuesday-night session was that he'd learned a lot about Chloe during the game, and also outside of it. He didn't say what he'd learned, or whether it was good or bad, but Chloe filled in the gaps for me.

"He assumed me helping Jo by ripping him off in the game was some sort of metaphor for what was happening with us in real life," she told me as we sat on the shuttle downtown. The kickboxing bug had bitten me, and we'd agreed to start going once a week. I'd asked Wyatt if he wanted to come, but he said once was plenty and he would stick with running. His loss.

"Why would he think that?" I asked, although at this point no one could miss the energy between Chloe and Jo.

"We've started hanging out a little bit," she said. "Me and Jo. Not, like, in any official way. Just once in a while."

I had no idea what Chloe meant by "hanging out," but if it was enough to upset Hunter, it meant that, at a minimum, she was spending more time with Jo than with him. Beyond that, I figured it was none of my business. "How's that going? Does she talk to you? Have you learned more about her?" I'd tried as best as I could, or I thought I had, but sometimes it felt like Jo had a force-field around her. I was impressed Chloe had managed to get past it.

"She tells me some stuff, but not a lot," Chloe admitted. "She is not the easiest person to get to know. It makes for a fun challenge, though."

I didn't doubt it. I felt bad for Hunter, but if Chloe and Jo were happy, then I was happy for them. And I was still waiting for Wyatt to follow up about us going out for ice cream. Maybe I'd misunderstood and he wasn't really asking me out. Maybe he really did just want ice cream. I'd written the words "ice cream" in my journal so many times they were starting to lose their meaning. I hoped he made his move soon, before the next game.

But that wasn't going to happen.

If the text hadn't arrived in the middle of the night we'd all have been deafened by the sound of nearly every cell phone in school receiving it at the same time. By Thursday morning, it had become clear that just about everyone had gotten the pictures. Pictures of Chloe, pictures that were not exactly Instagram-worthy, pictures she would not want the whole school to see.

I didn't even bother calling. I ran to Chloe's dorm room and knocked on her door softly, not sure if she'd want to let me in, or if she'd be hysterically crying. But she answered me right away, her face dry of tears. "Chloe, I—" I didn't even know what to say. "Are you okay?"

Her face was completely locked down. I couldn't see anything. "I'm fine," she said. "You don't need to worry about me. Come on, let's get out of here so we don't wake up Lauren." She walked out into the hall and toward the lounge.

I followed her and sat in an overstuffed chair. "Doesn't mean I'm not going to worry," I said. "Tell me what I can do."

"Nothing right now," she said. "But maybe after I come up with a plan."

"A plan?"

"Someone is going to pay for this," she said, and I realized I was finally hearing what it sounded like when Chloe got angry. Her voice was low and knife-sharp, every word articulated precisely. I would not want to be the person she was angry with right now, that was for sure.

"How are you going to find out who?"

"I'll figure it out," she said. "It's about to get ugly."

I wanted to ask more questions, to know how she planned to find the person who'd sent the pictures around, or even who she'd been with, but it felt invasive to ask. "Have you talked to . . ." I let my voice trail off, hoping she'd fill in the blanks for me. ". . . whoever took them?" Chloe might be an expert photographer of herself, but even I knew she hadn't taken those pictures. They were amateurish, badly lit, even occasionally unflattering. The opposite of Chloe's curated approach.

"I don't want to talk about that," she said. "I don't want to talk about any of this. I want to deal with it myself."

I'd spent so much time wondering what it would be like for Chloe's rage to explode that it never occurred to me that it might implode instead. Chloe was keeping her anger private. Kind of like how I'd kept my crushing on Hunter private. It made me feel like we had more in common than I thought, despite the fact that she was way less freaked out at the thought of the whole school seeing her naked than I would be. I couldn't help imagining how I'd feel if Hunter or Wyatt saw pictures like that of me.

"What is going on inside that head of yours?" Chloe asked. "You look like you just peeled a lime and ate it like an orange."

I hadn't realized I'd pursed my lips and scrunched up my whole face until she said that. I made myself relax but I could feel myself turning red at the same time.

Chloe inspected me more closely. "Are you blushing right now? Is there something you want to tell me?"

I wasn't sure I was ready to talk about Wyatt yet. I wasn't even sure what was happening, if anything. But she knew a lot more about boys and dates and relationships than I did; it was tempting to ask for advice, even if I had no idea what I wanted to know. But now wasn't the time. "You're trying to change the subject," I said. "And no. But maybe soon."

Sooner than I thought, given that Wyatt messaged me from his computer later that night, after Chloe reassured me a million times that she was okay and that she'd come up with a plan on her own. Ice cream this weekend? No Eucalyptus—Jo's up next but she needs more time.

Sure, I wrote back. Saturday?

That meant I just needed to get through one more day of trying not to stress about what I was pretty sure was my first date. And probably Wyatt's too. I needed distraction.

Chloe had already warned me she'd be lying low for the rest of the week, and Hunter had skipped lunch the day the pictures came out, which convinced me he'd taken them, though I was sure he hadn't been the one to send them around, even if he was upset with her. But did I only think that because I wanted so much for it to be true? There was no way. I decided my best option for distraction was to do a little detective work. Chloe might have wanted to handle this herself, but she shouldn't have to.

I grabbed Hunter before class Friday morning. I might have convinced myself he wouldn't do something to hurt

Chloe that badly, but that didn't mean he didn't know who did. "Lunch today. You and me. No skipping out, okay?"

"With Chloe?" he asked.

"Just me." We went to the dining hall but stayed away from our normal table, just in case; Hunter made one of his gargantuan awful subs, while I had a grilled cheese with tomato soup.

"I can't believe I'm not getting more money for this," Hunter said. "Another new lunch!"

"Shut it," I told him, but secretly I was pleased. I enjoyed his teasing. "Now tell me how you're doing, and don't lie to me. I know you took those photos."

Watching a freckled person blush was fascinating—the pink kind of crept around the tiny brown spots until it subsumed them. "Did Chloe tell you that? You don't think I sent them, do you?"

I was glad he'd decided to be honest. "She didn't tell me, and no, I don't think you sent them. And she said she wants to deal with this herself, but I thought if you took them then maybe you'd know who sent them to everyone else."

"No idea," he said. "I was all up night thinking about it, hoping it wasn't my fault, but then I looked at what got sent around and what was on my phone, and I didn't take all the pictures. Whoever sent the text didn't get the pictures from me."

That complicated matters—I'd been thinking one of Hunter's soccer friends had gotten hold of his phone and stolen the pictures and then sent them out, maybe as some sort of terrible joke. But if Hunter didn't have all the pictures, that theory didn't hold up.

"How's Chloe doing?" Hunter asked. "She's not answering my texts."

"She's on a quest for revenge, and I don't doubt she'll get it."

"Neither do I," Hunter said. "I hope she brought two shovels."

I for one was hoping no graves would need digging. Given that Hunter seemed okay, I decided to bring up my other pressing concern. "So can I ask you a random question?"

"Anything." He wiped a smear of mustard off his face with a brown paper napkin, and it occurred to me that I really must be over him, if he was the person I most wanted advice from right now.

"Have you and Wyatt become friends through all this Eucalyptus stuff? I know you do different sports and have different groups of friends, but do you talk? Like, about guy stuff?"

"You mean like about how into you he is?"

"What?" I almost spilled my tomato soup. How did he know?

"Oh, come on, his whole nervous twitchy asking-questions thing gets a thousand times worse around you. How have you not seen that?"

"Um, because I'm always there when he's around me?"

Hunter tilted his head. "You have a point. Okay, Wyatt is way more twitchy around you than he is when you're not there. He's totally into you. You should think about it."

Now I was the one turning red.

Hunter pointed at me and laughed. "Ha, you've got a thing for him too! It is so on!"

"I do not!" I protested, except why was I doing that? I'd wanted Hunter to confirm that Wyatt and I were really going on a date, and that was exactly what he was doing. "Okay, we might be going out for ice cream tomorrow."

Hunter reached out for a high five. "That's my girl! Best news I've had all day. All week. All month, really."

"My love life is your best news? After you nailed first-quarter finals?" I had too. Grades had just come out, and I could not have been more relieved to find that our hard work had paid off.

"Sad but true," he said. "I just wish my grades felt more important right now."

"Do you want to talk about it?" I asked. We both knew I was asking about Chloe, and not just the pictures.

He shook his head. "I'll get over it. There are lots of great girls at this school. I'll just have to find one who likes me as much as Wyatt likes you."

"You don't know that for sure," I said. But it still felt good to hear him say it.

Wyatt and I met at the bus on Saturday afternoon. Thankfully it was sunny, though we were heading into mid-November and the weather was getting chillier by the day. Wyatt was more accustomed to being outside in the cold than I was, given that the cross-country team ran year round, so I felt pathetic when I saw he was wearing a fleece when I had on my puffer coat. "I'm such a wimp," I said as we got on the shuttle.

"Not at all." He rolled up his coat sleeve to show me the sweater he was wearing underneath, then rolled up the sweater sleeve to show me a flannel shirt, then rolled up the flannel sleeve to show me a long-sleeved T-shirt that looked like it was made of nylon. "It's long underwear for outdoor runs," he explained. "I bet I'm warmer than you are in that coat. It's a nice coat, by the way."

It wasn't, but I appreciated him saying so. I would have to get me some of that long underwear too. "I can't believe we're getting ice cream when it's this cold."

"We don't have to," he said. "I just wanted to hang out, and I didn't know what would be fun for us to do." His eyes went to the floor. I'd made him feel bad, and I hadn't meant to.

"No, ice cream is a great idea!" I said. "I just think it's funny, that's all."

Not many people agreed that ice cream was a great idea; the ice-cream place was empty when we arrived, which was nice. I had time to examine all the flavors—Ben & Jerry's, of course, since we were in Vermont, after all. "Want to sit here while we eat?" Wyatt asked. "It's warm and quiet and we can talk."

"That's perfect." I was glad he'd suggested it, since I wasn't excited about being outside, and all I knew about other people's post–ice cream dates was where they'd stopped to make out. I was enjoying hanging out with Wyatt, but that didn't mean I was ready to jump to the kissing part. "So what did you think of the game?" I asked him.

He smiled, flashing me a glimpse of those crooked teeth that I was starting to find way more charming than I would have expected. "It was great! I knew you'd come up with something creative."

"Don't you think it got kind of . . ." I wasn't even sure what phrase to use. ". . . weird?"

Now I got a laugh. "Sure, it got weird. But in a good way, mostly? We got to see Jo be vulnerable, we got to see just how competitive Chloe is, and we found out Hunter's not completely her lap dog."

I hadn't realized Wyatt saw Hunter that way, the same way Chloe did. Was I destined to constantly be reading people wrong? "He'll get over being annoyed at her, won't he? I thought Chloe would be mad about losing, but she wasn't."

He thought about that one for a minute. "I think he will. And Chloe being mad could have gone either way. But it seems like Chloe always does that hyperintense thing and then moves on. I'd be curious to know what Jo thinks of all this."

"You and me both. I've tried to get to know her a little, but she's such a closed book."

"Yeah, I'm only starting to be less scared of her," Wyatt admitted. "She's pretty intimidating. But I think deep down she likes us, and she wants us to like her."

"I can't imagine what her game will be like." It was terrifying to think about.

We spent the rest of the afternoon talking, staying at the ice-cream place so long we ended up getting seconds just so the staff wouldn't be annoyed. I learned more about Wyatt's crazy family situation; he'd recently met his dad's parents for the first time and found out they were full-on preppers.

"Dad joined this group called Another Voice of Warning. He said it was just a Mormon prepper group, but they have this awful Facebook page that makes them look like white nationalists, you know? That's not what the Mormons I know are like." Now he was the one sounding sad. "I didn't want to point out to him that he has a Black kid, even if I was raised in a 'colorblind' household."

"Seriously?" I asked.

"Yeah, it was my mom's idea," he said. "Which she has since come to regret, big time. But she had this idea of us all growing up in a post-racial environment, as if we didn't notice ourselves that not everyone on the commune looked the same, as if my brother and sister and I weren't treated differently at the library or when we went shopping. There's no way to pretend race doesn't exist in this country, though someone here thinks I need even more lessons."

He'd never mentioned the mysterious book deliveries to me directly before, and I'd never felt it appropriate to ask. "What's going on with that?"

"There's been a bunch of messed up stuff." He told me about the books, a shipment of literature and essays from Black writers that included James Baldwin, bell hooks, Ta Nehisi-Coates, Roxane Gay, and Ibram X. Kendi. "There was a gift card, and all it said was 'Those who don't understand the past are doomed to repeat it.'"

The hairs on the back of my neck stood up. "The real quote is 'Those who cannot remember the past are condemned to repeat it,'" I said. "It wasn't a Jewish person who said it, but Jewish people talk about it a lot."

"I know," Wyatt said. "I have to admit, I wondered at first if maybe you'd sent the books. You're the only Jewish person I know here."

That might explain why he'd never mentioned the books at Eucalyptus meetings. "You know I didn't, right?"

He kicked me under the table, but not hard. "Of course you didn't! I never really thought so. I was running through possibilities, you know? And besides, you'd never have done the rest of it."

"There's more?" This was starting to sound scary.

"Just a little. I don't know if it's the same person, but right around when the books showed up I noticed I was starting to get a lot of what I thought was spam. I've had an email address for a long time but I've barely used it, so at first I thought it was because the account was getting more exercise, you know? But it wasn't regular spam—someone had signed me up for a bunch of websites and mailing lists. Some of them are actually pretty good and I stayed subscribed—there's a website called Very Smart Brothas that's great—but some of them are awful. Have you ever heard of 4chan?"

Oh, I'd heard of 4chan.

"I started getting notifications of threads from white supremacist message boards. I'd assume that the person who signed me up was just super racist, but combined with all this other stuff?"

"It's like someone's trying to give you an education," I said. "By exposing you to the best and worst of what the world has to offer."

He nodded grimly. "As if I didn't already know about those books. And yeah, maybe I'm not up on the latest online trolling platforms and all that, but why would anyone care? Why would they want me to have to deal with so much hate?"

"I'm so sorry, Wyatt." I reached over and placed my hand over his, like I had so briefly back in the library, but this time I left it there.

"It's no big deal," he said. "I blocked the worst of it, kept the good stuff, and tried to look at the books as a harmless prank."

"It's good that you can do that," I said. "Chloe's trying too, though Hunter's having a harder time."

Wyatt looked puzzled. "Did something happen to Chloe and Hunter?"

"There was that article about Hunter in the school paper, and now there's the pictures." When his face didn't change, I realized he'd never seen them. Which made some sense, since he didn't have a phone, and he barely checked his messages.

"Someone sent out a text with pictures of Chloe attached. The kind of pictures she wouldn't want the whole school seeing."

He frowned. "Was she doing something bad? Drinking at a party?"

Sweet, innocent Wyatt. "Nothing bad. Just . . . private pictures."

His face reddened. It was cute, really. He was cute. "Right, that. Right. There were pictures?"

"They went out to everyone at the whole school, as far as I can tell. Chloe's furious."

"I can't even imagine," Wyatt said. "Does she have any idea who could have done this? Do you?"

"I got nothing," I said. "Someone would have needed access to her phone to get the pictures. Maybe her roommate? But I can't imagine why Lauren would do something like that."

"What about the person she sent the pictures to?"

Wyatt had gone to the same place I had, but I didn't think it was appropriate to tell him about Hunter. And suggesting that she might have sent pictures to more than one person didn't seem like a good friend move, so I just shrugged.

"It's strange that three of us in Eucalyptus are being pranked. Or whatever you call what's happening," Wyatt said. "It almost feels like someone's out to get us."

I was starting to feel the same way. "I can't imagine who, though." Though I felt a prickling in the back of my neck. There was someone else Chloe might have sent pictures to, after all. Someone who was cryptic and strange and upset with Chloe at the moment. But I didn't want to say her name out loud. I didn't want my suspicions to be real.

"Well, it definitely can't be someone in the group," he said. "There's just no way. So it would have to be someone who knew all of us and held a grudge."

We sat quietly for a little while, trying to imagine who might resent the group this much. "Could it be someone you invited who didn't find us? Maybe they feel bad about it now?" I couldn't think of who might fit in that category, but then again, I didn't know who Wyatt had invited.

"Maybe. I did invite a lot of the people from that first Game Night—just about everyone I could track down. But you people were the only ones who came, and I thought that meant you were the only ones who tried. It's possible someone couldn't crack the code and got frustrated."

Game Night—that was when Jo had gotten into it with Ken. Ken, who was now on student council with me because Hunter had been effectively eliminated by that article revealing his background. I'd much rather the bad person be Ken than Jo. I asked Wyatt what he thought, but he didn't seem convinced. "If he was upset about Game Night, wouldn't he have gone after Jo? She's the one who embarrassed him."

He had a point. "If it's not him I've got nothing," I said. "I guess we'll have to see what Chloe finds out."

"Guess so," Wyatt said. "Should we head back?"

It was a little chilly to walk back to campus, which would have been when normal first-date kissing stuff might have happened, and I found myself relieved. Not that I didn't want to kiss Wyatt, because at this point I was pretty sure I did. But there was something so lovely and innocent and non-stressful about our simple ice-cream date. I wanted to save the stressful parts for later, when I had some time to get ready. Wyatt seemed to get that; he walked me back to my dorm and then asked if I might want to hang out again sometime soon, and when I said yes he gave me a quick hug and then went back to his room.

It was perfect. And for once, I didn't let myself feel guilty for being happy when the world around me was less than perfect.

12.

Thanksgiving break came at the best and worst time. I needed to get away desperately. I'd let the combination of daydreaming about Wyatt and worrying about my friends derail me from getting real work done. Second-quarter finals would be upon us soon enough, and I'd only survived first quarter by working as hard as I'd ever worked in my life.

But Wyatt was also an issue. We hadn't yet had our second date, which meant we hadn't yet had our first kiss, and given that I was pretty sure it would be the first kiss for both of us, I could not have been more nervous. I almost wanted us to just smash our faces together to get it over with, but then we'd remember the horror of it forever, even if we learned to do a better job later on. Best to wait.

Going home did mean having to deal with my family in person. Much as I hated to admit it, I'd missed them terribly; the weekly phone calls kept me up to date on what they were all up to (Mom and Dad were mostly working, as usual, while Shana was becoming obsessed with softball), but I'd never been willing to get into detail about Gardner, even though I was long over being angry they'd sent me there. I hadn't realized how far from home I felt until I got off the bus at South Station. My dad came to pick me up, and I was shocked to find my eyes stinging with tears when I saw him. I blinked them away before he could see.

I don't know why I bothered—I broke out into full-on sobs when we got home and the whole family started hugging me. "Oh, honey, is everything okay?" Mom asked, her arms squeezing me even tighter. "If we thought you'd be this miserable at school we'd never have sent you."

"I'm not miserable," I said, though my nose was so plugged from crying all my *m*'s sounded like *b*'s. "I love it there." It was true, too. I really did love Gardner.

"Then what's wrong?" Dad asked, smoothing down my hair.

"I just missed everyone. I'm sorry I've been so awful." I had the best relationship with my family of any of my new friends—Jo had no parents, Wyatt struggled with his parents' divorce, Hunter hated his dad and resented his mom, and Chloe barely acknowledged the existence of hers. And here I was, resenting my own parents wanting to help me through a bad patch. All this time we spent in Eucalyptus worried about the end of the world, and I'd barely considered the fact that my world really would end without my family. Maybe I'd been wrong about being Team Survival.

"You've got nothing to worry about," Mom said. "We love you no matter what."

"As long as you keep making those grades," Dad said, only half joking.

"I will need to study this weekend, but not until Saturday," I said. "Let me help cook."

Mom looked surprised—I'd never offered before—but we went into the kitchen and she showed me her to-do list. I'd had no idea how intense Thanksgiving was, especially since we had my aunt and her family over, along with my grandparents on my mom's side. Dad's family was still in Israel, and we'd only met his parents and brothers a few times—Dad had resolved not to go back until the political situation changed, though he'd said he wouldn't stop me from visiting if I wanted to.

Mom set me up peeling potatoes over the sink while she chopped up celery and carrots for stuffing. We worked quietly for a while, companionably more than awkwardly, until finally Mom broke the silence. "So, anything you want to tell me about school?"

"We talk every week," I reminded her. "You know all about school."

"I know all about your classes," she corrected. "I know almost nothing about your life there. I'm assuming you have one, given that you seem so happy there."

I'd already admitted they were right to send me; I wasn't about to do it again. Still, Mom was right—I'd told her almost nothing about Gardner outside of academics. But where to start? "I went on a date last week," I said.

Mom put her knife down. "You did what?"

"His name is Wyatt." After we established that he wasn't Jewish but wasn't otherwise religious, as far as I knew, I told her about our ice-cream date, and then about Eucalyptus and my other friends. I didn't get into the drama; my mother was worried enough about the club.

"You joined a survivalist group?" She'd been excited about Wyatt, but now she frowned.

"It's not that, exactly," I said. "It's more a group for people who care about what's going on in the world, you know? Like climate change and immigration and stuff. And we play games. It's fun."

Mom looked skeptical. "Well, I'm glad you're having a good time. Are you still doing your research?" She was referring to all the obsessive reading I'd done after the temple fire, the books about white supremacy and World War II and governmental collapse.

"No, there isn't as much time, with schoolwork and everything." I didn't tell her I'd talked Hunter into doing our team project in European History on fascism or that I was writing a term paper on genocide.

"I have to admit that's a relief." Mom went back to chopping and told me to peel apples when the potatoes were done, and we went back to working in silence.

The holiday weekend flew by in a blur. Thanksgiving was a raucous affair, as always, my family lining up to inhale turkey, potatoes, stuffing, gravy, cranberry sauce, and a million desserts. We ate until we were stuffed, watched the Patriots game, napped, ate leftovers. On Black Friday I wanted to do nothing but sleep and finish digesting, but Shana insisted on dragging my mom and me to the mall for all the sales. She already had better style than I did, though she talked me into some sweaters and boots for the Vermont winter, along with a new pair of Converse that had zebra stripes, just to mix things up. I spent the rest of the time studying, as planned, and actively avoiding thinking about how Hunter and Chloe and Jo were doing. We still had two games left, and I didn't want the club to break up just because everyone's romantic lives had gotten so complicated, including mine.

I found myself anxious about going back to school. Wyatt and I had messaged back and forth all weekend, so I was less worried about him than everyone else. I knew Hunter had gotten roped into a vacation with his parents; his mother wasn't much of a cook, and, as he put it, "They're not thankful for much, other than their money." Chloe and

Jo were both staying on campus, but it wasn't clear to me what their status was. It was entirely possible I could come back and find Eucalyptus in shambles.

It was a relief to show up at lunch and find Hunter and Chloe in our usual seats, complete with their customary trays of horrific sub and colorful salad, respectively. "Hi, you two," I said, setting my tray down. After a few weeks away from PB&J I'd returned to form, and there was something comforting about being with my friends, all of us eating our usual lunches. "How were your holidays?"

"Complete disaster," Hunter said, but cheerfully. "My parents booked us on a four-day cruise to the Caribbean. Can you imagine? They even got me my own room and there was still no way to avoid them. Thankfully I found other ways to keep busy." He didn't say what they were, but he was blushing a little, and I took that to mean he'd met someone on the boat. I checked to see Chloe's reaction, but she seemed unfazed. I hoped that meant they were going to get back to normal, but I wondered whether Chloe had ever found out who sent the pictures.

"At least you got to go somewhere warm," Chloe said. "They barely keep the heat on around here. And you wouldn't believe the sad, dry turkey they served in the dining hall."

"I heard there were good parties, though," Hunter said. "Not many dorm parents, lots of kids with free time and money."

"Sounds like an opportunity for scandal," I said. "Did you end up hanging out with Jo at all? She's doing the next game this weekend, right?" According to Wyatt, she'd said she would, but who knew, given everything that had been going on?

Chloe gave me the side-eye. "She was here, yes. And we hung out. No scandal, as far as I know. I think it's still game on."

That didn't completely clarify things, but I supposed it meant they were on good terms, which was a start. I wanted to know more, but I wasn't about to ask in front of Hunter.

"How was home, Amina?" Hunter asked. "Did you pine away, missing Wyatt?"

"Missing who?" Chloe turned toward me so fast her hair practically hit me in the face. "Amina, did we not just have a conversation about how you would tell me if you had boy-related news to report? And you shared it with that one?" She jerked her thumb over at Hunter.

"It wasn't on purpose," I said. "He just busted me is all."

"Whatever," she said. "Spill."

I sighed, and then I told them about the ice-cream date and messaging over Thanksgiving weekend (Wyatt was visiting his dad in Utah, and I was learning more than I ever expected about Mormon preppers). I did not bring up kissing or the lack thereof, and if Chloe did I was going to kill her.

"Have you seen him since you got back?" she asked.

I shook my head. "No, but we talked about doing something over the weekend."

"I love it!" Chloe said. "Don't you love it, Hunter? Isn't it just the best news ever?"

"Totally," he agreed.

I, for one, thought they were both happy to have another couple in the group to take the attention away from their nonstarter of a relationship, but that was fine with me. I was just looking forward to the weekend. Jo emailed later that day calling a Eucalyptus meeting for Saturday afternoon, and Wyatt and I agreed to do something afterward.

I got to the bunker early, eager to find out what Jo had planned for us but even more eager to see Wyatt. I could have tracked him down at dinner at the cross-country table, but I didn't want to be around him with other people; I wanted him all to myself. Otherwise I was afraid I'd do something awkward and horrible and I didn't want this thing to end before it started. Seeing him in the bunker with everyone else wasn't nearly as nervous making.

I wasn't the only one with plans to get started quickly, though. When I opened the door it became clear someone had beat me there; the room was mostly dark, with a row of candles flickering along one of the shelves.

"Don't turn the lights on," Jo said. "I'm not done here."

In the dark I couldn't see her face, and it took me a while to get used to the darkness enough to notice there were candles set up everywhere. Jo was in the process of lighting them, flicking a lighter in her hand on and off. "Ouch! This thing gets hot really fast."

"Let me help," I said, taking one of the lit candles and using it to light the others.

With more light, I could see her looking at me with surprise. "I don't know why I didn't think of that."

"You don't have years of lighting menorahs behind you," I said.

"That's a Hanukkah thing, right?"

I nodded, though Hanukkah was only one of the many holidays that involved lighting candles. I especially loved the braided candle lit for Havdalah, the service signaling the end of Shabbat. But usually we used matches or lighters for that. The candles Jo had chosen looked more like traditional Shabbat candles but thicker: white, unscented pillars that tapered at the top. Their flickering lights made the room somehow feel both festive and calm. I had a feeling Jo's game was going to be good, whatever it was.

The others arrived not long after we were done lighting up the room, and I almost broke my face smiling when I saw Wyatt. His smile was just as wide when he saw me. Funny how different it felt, having a crush versus liking someone who liked you back. I'd had butterflies with Hunter, but they'd made me feel a little bit sick. Wyatt made me feel nothing but happy.

"All right, let's get this party started." Jo sat in a chair, and we all gathered at her feet, as had become our habit. "You'll notice I've done a little work to our bunker here, and that's designed to help me explain what we're going to be doing. Most of you don't know this about me, and I don't like to admit it out loud, but I've got a thing about the dark."

"A thing like you love it?" Hunter asked.

Even in the faint light I could see Jo glare at him. "A thing like I'm scared of it, okay, Red? There are reasons, some rational, some not. But we're not here to talk about those. We're just going to talk about how the odds are the power grid isn't likely to survive the apocalypse, even if we do. That's what my game is about."

I started to panic. I could handle the dark just fine, but she was talking about more than just lighting.

"My game goes like this," she went on. "An asteroid has just hit the power grid in Vermont. The state government has informed us it will take at least a week to get it back up, if not longer. No power, no internet. It's getting pretty cold and I'm not a terrible person, so we're going to pretend the school's using radiant heat and the plumbing runs on well water, because I don't want to have to deal with not using the toilets or showers. But other than that, starting tonight, we'll need to live as if we have no power."

Chloe's hand shot up in the air.

"Slow down, Princess," Jo said. "I'm sure you have a

million questions, but let me finish the rules and we'll see if I've covered them, okay?"

Chloe groaned but nodded. I swallowed a giggle. This game was Chloe's only chance of even getting a tie—she'd only won one and Jo had won two. But Jo was no idiot—she'd designed the game to drive Chloe insane. Makeup by candlelight? This was going to be fun.

Jo laid out the plan. She hadn't picked the completely worst time; exams didn't officially start until just before break and I had no papers due until then, so technically I could probably get by without my computer for schoolwork. She'd tracked down our roommates and suggested they might want to sleep elsewhere for the week, if they were willing (and she'd either convinced them or terrified them), so there was nothing to keep us from getting started. "You can assume the school is using backup generators for classes and stuff, but that doesn't extend to the dining hall—you can't eat anything that requires refrigeration or cooking. You can't use power in your rooms at all, so you'll have to figure out something else. And it all needs to be stuff you already have or stuff you can track down on campus. No shopping for this one."

I could practically hear the air whooshing out of people's lungs. I had to tamp down another laugh, because there was no way Jo hadn't done all this on purpose. She'd designed a game that Chloe would almost certainly lose. It would be hilarious watching this go down. Maybe this was my chance to show I could be a competitor too. "We're starting right now?" I asked.

"Yup," Jo said. "Sometimes things take us by surprise, and we've got to make do with what we've got."

Wyatt and I exchanged a glance. We could still hang out after the meeting, but that meant we'd miss the last few hours of daylight to prep for the game, and that was not a good idea. I made a face at him and he nodded. He got it. "This is exactly what we need to practice," he said. "It's going to be hard."

"I'm going to make it a little harder, too," Jo said. "No sharing of resources for this one. No teamwork. Everyone for themselves."

Chloe frowned, but Hunter asked the question. "Why?"

"Testing different skills," Jo said. "Remember Wyatt's original question, back at the beginning? It wasn't about whether we wanted to survive in general; it was about whether we were willing to survive alone. We've been doing all our lessons and games in a group, but that's not really what this is about. It's about time to test whether we can make it solo."

It seemed to me that this game was skewed in Jo's favor, which was funny given that she couldn't win. I wondered, too, whether she'd missed the point of Wyatt's question. It wasn't really about surviving alone; it was about surviving without the people you loved, about your willingness to start over and learn to be with new people, and maybe to love them too.

Still, she had a point. We'd need to survive alone for a while, anyway, and why not start here, now, where it was safe?

"We can still talk, though, right?" I asked. "Hunter and I need to study."

Chloe snorted. She knew Wyatt and I were supposed to hang out after the meeting.

"You can talk all you want during the day, in class or at the dining hall or wherever, but as soon as you're responsible for your own light you're on your own. Unless you're comfortable together in the dark." I'd have expected her to look at Chloe for that one, but her gaze was fixed on me. How did she know about me and Wyatt? Had Chloe told her? Or was Hunter right and everyone else had always known, except me?

"Afternoon study sessions, I guess," Hunter said.

Chloe stuck her hand in the air again. "You still have questions, Princess?" Jo asked.

"Just the obvious one," Chloe said. "How do we win?"

"Outplay, outwit, outlast," Jo said. "Last person standing."

"So this isn't just a week," I said.

Jo laughed. "One week is the qualifier. If you all crap out in under a week then no one wins. Let's see how real those internet addictions really are."

"You've got to be kidding," Chloe said. "The lack of a hair dryer alone . . ."

Chloe loved taking on the drama queen role, but we were all freaking out. One week of studying with no computer and no internet access was doable, but two weeks? Three? I felt my dream of winning the game slipping away. My only hope was that no one else was capable of going that long without power either, but I had a feeling Wyatt could be a real threat.

"Come on, let's try it," he said. I bet he knew he could win, too. I'd have to tease him about it later. "How will we ever know we can make it if we don't practice? Isn't that why we agreed to do this?"

"So how's it going to work?" Hunter asked. "And will you play, even if you can't win?"

"Of course," Jo said. "Someone has to show you wimps how it's done. Game's over when we're down to one person, and you have to come find me to tap out. Then I'll call a meeting and announce the winner." Like one of the survival shows I'd watched on TV, where people got dropped off somewhere in the wilds of Canada to live alone. Each season ended with one scrawny, haunted-looking winner having trouble remembering why he'd gotten involved in the game in the first place. "Is everyone in?"

"The sacrifices I make for you people," Chloe said. "Yeah, I'm in."

Jo looked surprised—she must have expected more resistance from Chloe. "I'm in too," I said, and Hunter and Wyatt agreed.

"Excellent, team," Jo said. "I'll look forward to seeing who falls first."

We all split up to go back to the dorm and scrounge. I had no doubt Chloe had a giant pile of scented candles she'd gotten from her site, but I knew where Hillel stored the Shabbat candles, and I pilfered a couple of boxes as my first order of business. Wyatt probably already had a battery-powered lamp or something. My money was definitely on him. It was definitely not on Hunter, who I imagined would be the first to drop out.

And I was right. We were only a few days in when Hunter dropped his tray across from me and my eyes widened at what I saw.

"Hot dogs?" I asked. "Tater tots? Please do let me know how you're going to justify this to Jo."

"I'm not." He stuffed an entire hot dog into his mouth.

"I'm not going to save you if you choke, you know. It serves you right."

He chugged a fountain Coke and got the rest of the hot dog down, then let out a long, low belch.

"Gross," I said.

By then Chloe had arrived. "Hunter's tapping out," I said. "And he swapped a hot dog and tots for his nasty sub."

"I needed something cooked," he said. "It wasn't enough of a celebration to just eat something refrigerated."

"Guess it's down to you, me, and Wyatt, then," Chloe said. She'd been eating these weird bean salads since the game started, all stuff you could get in cans. Not very appetizing, but whatever got her through the day, I supposed. "Just so you know, I have to win this one. It's a pride thing."

As if she were the only one who had any pride. "Well, we're going to make it as hard for you as possible."

"Oh, look, they're a 'we' now." Chloe chucked me under the chin. "So adorable!"

"Don't even," I said, and she knew enough to stop.

"I feel like a total loser, but honestly, I cannot believe how hard this has been already." Hunter launched into his tale of woe, which included indoor soccer practices all week at night and accidentally cheating the very first night by chugging an energy drink from his mini fridge, which of course he'd forgotten to unplug. "I've been a disaster from the minute we started." He bit into another hot dog, squirting mustard and relish onto his tater tots. "Quitting might be worth it just for this."

"This is tragic," I said, but I couldn't help laughing. He didn't care, and that was fine. "You okay with afternoon studying still, so I can try to win this thing?"

"Of course. Take her down!"

Chloe glared at him.

"Oh, come on, you've already won one," I said. "It's not like whoever wins the most games wins an even better prize—we never even came up with prizes for the individual games. Give the rest of us a chance."

"Throw a game?" She sniffed. "Never. But you're welcome to try and beat me fair and square."

I didn't mention how she'd hardly been fair and square during my game. "Challenge accepted," I said. "And good luck to you."

Unlike Hunter, I was finding everything pretty easy so far. It took me a couple of days to get used to not having a computer or a phone, not being able to look anything up as soon as a question popped into my head. But it wasn't long before I got used to the idea that I'd have to be patient, that my questions would be answered in good time or not at all, and if I really wanted to know something, I'd have to look it up in an actual book. Since I didn't have any papers due, I didn't need the computer for much else. I was shocked to realize how much time I spent on it now that I couldn't use it at all, and I was even more shocked at how much other stuff I could get done in its absence.

I had more time to think than I knew what to do with, though. At first being alone in my own head was so disconcerting that all I could do was try to remember the plots of books and movies I loved, or make a bucket list in my journal of everything I wanted to do before I kicked it, or write down my dreams for the future. I thought about my friends, and Wyatt, and everything that had happened at home, and everything that was happening here. Hunter was getting over the takedown interview, Chloe hadn't found out who sent the pictures but I knew she was still upset about them, and Wyatt never learned who sent the books or signed him up for all those emails. Three of my closest friends hurt; three people who were in the same club. The only Eucalyptus members who hadn't had anything bad happen to them were me and Jo, and I while I knew I wasn't responsible, Jo seemed capable of anything, including some degree of cruelty. But every time she let us scrape past her surface, even with something so simple as admitting she was afraid of the dark, it felt more like she trusted us, and that she cared about Eucalyptus. She might be the only one of us left, but I was having trouble making myself believe it could be her.

I debated whether to run my theory past Wyatt. On Friday afternoon I went to try and find him to see if he wanted to take a walk; I knew the cross-country team didn't have practice, the weather was unseasonably less-than-freezing, I was going to miss my first Shabbat dinner because I couldn't eat the food, and I wanted to keep busy. His face brightened when he saw me, which made me happy.

Wyatt picked out one of his favorite paths through the woods, and at first we walked quietly, with him pointing things out on occasion—markers to keep track of the path, evidence of animal burrows, different kinds of trees. It was like he knew about an entirely different world. All I taught him was stupid stuff, like how to find (and use) the emoji keyboard on his Mac and who certain pop stars were.

As I suspected, his week was going great. He didn't mind eating the few kinds of food available as long as he could carbo-load for cross-country, and having limited access to technology was something he was used to. He'd probably be able to continue forever, which meant he was almost certain to win.

I wasn't really struggling yet, but I could see it coming. I'd been starting to play with the rules in my head: Was tea really off-limits, if I could theoretically boil water over a fire? Did that mean I could cook certain things, too? Jo had said no cooking, but she meant no cooking with electricity, right? I hadn't crossed the line yet, but the fact that I was even thinking about it told me this wouldn't be the game where I showed my true competitive spirit.

"Want to sit for a while?" Wyatt asked. "I brought a blanket."

Seriously, he was the most thoughtful person I'd ever met. He spread out the blanket next to an enormous tree with a thick enough trunk that we could both lean against it. At first we both sat stiffly, our backs as flush with the tree bark as we could make them, legs stretched out in front of us (his jean-clad, mine covered in black leggings, as usual). But I fidgeted to avoid the knots in the tree trunk, and he wiggled his legs as if they hurt, which maybe they did—he seemed to be getting taller by the day—and before either of us knew it we'd rearranged ourselves so his arm was around me and I was curled into his chest, his legs crossed, mine making a sideways *V*, my thighs pressed into his. It felt comfortable and natural and it was strange to me how we could be so easily entangled together when we hadn't even kissed yet.

"This is nice," Wyatt said, and I nodded into his armpit.

All I wanted to do was stay here, nestled into him, moving only for what felt like the inevitable moment when he would finally kiss me. Or when I would take the plunge and kiss him; why was I so intent on making this his responsibility? He'd done all the hard work up to now. I'd done nothing but be receptive. That was unfair, I decided. I had to be brave.

I lifted my head from his chest and started to scoot up a little so our faces were closer together, but at the same time Wyatt turned toward me and bent his head down. Great minds think alike, I thought, as our noses banged into each other. It was so fantastically awkward that all I could do was laugh, and Wyatt laughed too. I was still smiling when he finally leaned in and kissed me, his mouth fitting right where the corners of my lips turned up. Suddenly it wasn't so funny anymore, and I stopped smiling, but only so we could kiss properly, forever.

I gave up the following Wednesday. Wyatt and I had spent the daylight hours of the weekend making out, which left me somewhat behind in my schoolwork, and once my English teacher assigned us a paper, I knew I was done for. I celebrated by making so many cups of tea I barely got a good night's sleep because I had to get up to pee so many times, but it was worth it.

"You've got this in the bag," I told Wyatt on Thursday. We were taking another walk. Somehow I didn't care about the cold anymore.

"Maybe," he said. "But Chloe's stubborn. This could go on forever. And I don't know that I want to follow Jo's rules anymore if it means I can't see you at night." I understood. There was something different about being together only during the day, something missing. We'd spent some of the time over the weekend talking about what we'd do when we weren't restricted anymore, making a list of the movies we wanted to watch together, even if that just meant lying together on a rec room couch, snuggled under a blanket.

"Give it until Saturday," I said. "I've got Shabbat dinner Friday night anyway—I skipped last week because I couldn't eat, and I've been dreaming of roast chicken ever since. Then you can go tell Jo you're out, if you want."

"Will you come with me? She's still kind of scary."

"Do you think she means to be scary? I've been wanting to ask you about her." I'd never managed to bring up the topic of Jo the other day in the woods; once the kissing started, there was no room for anything else. Now I explained to him what I'd been thinking. "In some ways she's the only person who makes sense, and yet I can't really picture her doing any of this. She's nothing if not straightforward about how she's feeling. If she wanted us to know she knew these things about us, I think she'd just say it."

Wyatt nodded slowly. "Yeah, she scares me because she's so in your face, not because I think she's a bad person. I'm so used to everyone around me being nonstop positive because of the commune and all—it's hard for me to get used to her. But I don't think she's the one who sent me those emails or did any of the other stuff."

"So who do you think did?"

"No idea," he said. "I don't know that it's worth trying to figure it out, especially not if there isn't any more bad stuff happening."

He was probably right. Better to just focus on the game.

With no word from Chloe on Friday, Wyatt and I set out for Jo's dorm on Saturday morning so she could call an afternoon meeting and we'd have Saturday night to ourselves. Neither of us had ever been there before; she lived in the same building as Chloe but on a different floor, and Wyatt had never ventured into the forbidden part of the girls' dorm. I held Wyatt's left hand as he knocked on the door with his right.

A girl I didn't recognize opened the door, wearing a long fleecy nightgown that looked like something someone's mother would wear. "What do you want?" she asked, yawning. I supposed we'd woken her up, but it was ten o'clock, so I didn't feel that bad about it.

"We're looking for Jo," I said, peering around her into the

room. I'd have expected Jo to stake out her space, for half the room to be all black or something, but their dorm looked a lot like everyone else's, desks piled with books, floor piled with clothes. One of the beds had a rainbow-striped duvet covering a lump that I presumed was Jo.

"I got this, Grandma," the lump said, and then Jo emerged from under the duvet.

"Seriously, can you stop calling me that?" the girl said, and flounced back to the other bed.

"When you stop dressing like a grandma, I'll stop." Jo came out into the hall, in pajamas herself, though really it just looked like she'd kept on one of her myriad white T-shirts and swapped out her jeans for men's boxer shorts. "You crapping out on me, Survivor?" she asked Wyatt.

Wyatt squeezed my hand, but I couldn't answer for him. "I decided I was wrong," he said. That wasn't what I was expecting.

It wasn't what Jo expected either. "Wrong about what?" she asked, and she forgot to add a nickname.

"About my question. That first night. Even if we had to survive without anyone we knew, that didn't mean we wouldn't come to know other people too, later on. It didn't mean we had to be completely alone."

Funny, that's what I'd been thinking about too, when Jo proposed the game. How similar Wyatt and I had turned out to be.

"Anyway," he continued, "I don't think I could survive if I had to be really alone. I don't think I'd want to. I don't need to win more than I need people in my life."

Jo looked at me even as she asked Wyatt the question. "Guess you're not talking about your roommate, are you?"

Wyatt was so cute when he blushed. "No, but now that you mention it, he is getting sick of sleeping on the rec room couch."

I'd met his roommate, who I knew had been more than happy to spend the past two weeks sneaking into his girlfriend's dorm room. Wyatt was just drawing Jo's attention away from me, which was sweet.

"Okay, I'll call the meeting," Jo said. "See you in the bunker after lunch, okay?"

"We'll be there," I said.

At the dining hall I watched Wyatt eat a truly shocking amount of pasta, and then we headed to the bunker so Jo could give Chloe her victory. I couldn't imagine Jo would enjoy it; they were tied now, with only Chloe's game to come, and I was sure Chloe would try as hard as Jo had to make her game impossible for Jo to win. She handled it well, though.

"We all know why we're here," Jo said, once we'd all settled in. I sat between Wyatt's legs, his arms wrapped around me. Everyone knew about us by now, and I hated missing an opportunity to be close to him. "You all fought bravely—well, most of you." She narrowed her eyes at Hunter, but she smiled at the same time. "Only one person didn't last the week, and two people made it to the very end, but there's only one winner. Before I announce—"

"Oh, come on, just give it to me!" Chloe shouted out from her pile of pillows on the floor. "Can you imagine how much I've suffered without a curling iron? Although I have to say that I look even better in candlelight, so this was educational."

I was never sure, with Chloe, whether to be horrified or entertained. We all knew she didn't mean half the things that came out of her mouth, but she got such a kick out of being willing to say them it was hard to be offended.

"I don't know, Princess, it seems like the people here might want to know how you pulled off such a heroic feat," Jo said. "Anything to say to your subjects?" I couldn't tell whether she sounded sarcastic or flirty.

"Okay, fine, you want the method to the madness, I can do that." As if she hadn't wanted to spill anyway. "I've got a monster stash of tea lights for photos, so I knew lighting wasn't going to be an issue. Not to mention, like, thousands of candles people have sent me. And you didn't say we couldn't use that stuff this time."

"You're right," Jo said. "It was all fair game."

"So while all of you were running around figuring out how you were going to manage at night, I set up two weeks' worth of automatic posts for *Chloe's Closet.* Can't have the site going dark just so I can win. I made an updo hair challenge so no one would expect me to have a proper blowout, my clothes steamer is battery-operated, I'd been meaning to try a raw food diet for a while, and there you have it. Best two weeks ever." She dropped her eyes then, not looking at Jo, and I had a feeling they'd still been hanging out, even if it was only in the dark. "So is that enough? Can I have my victory now?"

"All right, it's yours," Jo said. "You earned it." She looked at Chloe with an expression I hadn't seen from her before. Softness, maybe? It was hard to use the word "soft" in relation to Jo.

"Don't you worry, you've still got a chance to win it all," Chloe said. "My turn next, right, Wyatt?"

"You're the only one left," he said.

"I'm not going to make it easy for you, Jo, but then again, I won't make it easy for anyone," Chloe said.

"You never do," Hunter muttered.

"What's that?" she asked.

He didn't respond. He wasn't quite over her, then. Interesting that Jo seemed to have moved past Chloe's shady behavior more quickly than Hunter had. It just proved I didn't know anyone nearly as well as I thought.

Wyatt leaned in to whisper in my ear. "You pick the movie, I'll microwave the popcorn."

Then again, maybe there was at least one person I knew, for real.

13.

Chloe had just one request for us in anticipation of her game: she wanted it to take place after finals, before everyone left for break. There was a gap of just under a week in between exams and Christmas, and it was apparently a Gardner custom to hang out on campus for parties, since we got almost a whole month off. Jo and Chloe were planning to stay on campus for break, so for her it was no big deal; Hunter and Wyatt were happy to delay going home as long as possible. I'd been planning on leaving right away, but it didn't take much convincing to get me to stay. Not if it meant more time with Wyatt.

We were hanging out as much as we could, but between studying for finals and taking care of end-of-quarter student council stuff I barely got to see him. I'd started bringing him to Friday-night dinners, since he had a lot of questions about Judaism and what it meant to me. Some things

I could explain, like how it felt to be one of the only Jewish kids growing up; how I'd both resented and enjoyed spending afternoons in Hebrew school, learning how to read another language and hearing stories repeated over and over again; how certain tastes and smells made me think of specific holidays, like apples and honey at Rosh Hashanah and potato latkes at Hanukkah and cinnamon-scented kugel to break the fast on Yom Kippur. But I couldn't describe to him the feeling of sitting down to a table lit with matched pairs of plain white candles and eggy loaves of challah and roasted chicken and how it helped me take stock of my week, ease into a weekend where I made sure to regenerate myself for the week to come, and take comfort in being surrounded by people who'd grown up with some of the same traditions and pressures I had, for good and for bad. I wanted him to see that for himself, if only to understand me better.

He, in turn, taught me about the woods. Anytime we could get away, when the weather wasn't so cold that a parka and gloves was enough, we went for walks. I loved getting to know Wyatt in his happy place, and it was great to see how confident and calm he was when in his own surroundings. His habit of making statements into questions was already fading—maybe Hunter had been right that I made him nervous—but in the woods it was gone entirely, and though he still bounced with excitement on occasion, I liked it, and I liked learning about what he loved. Though what I liked best were the breaks we took to sit together under the big tree that had become our spot, blanket laid out on the ground, kissing until my hair was tangled up with bark and leaves and sometimes snow. We had complete privacy outside, and I felt like I was alone with Wyatt but also together with the whole world. I never thought I'd be someone who could be happy just sitting wrapped up with another person, whispering inanities about how blue the sky was or how purple the sunset or how twinkly the stars when it got dark, but that was me, now.

Until one day I went and knocked on Wyatt's door and he didn't answer, though I was sure he was in there. We'd talked earlier in the day about watching a movie in the dorm lounge after I finished studying, though our plans had been tentative. But he hadn't planned to leave his room, and I could see light coming through a crack in the doorjamb.

I kept knocking and knocking until finally the door opened. Only it wasn't Wyatt; it was his roommate, who I'd only met in passing. "He doesn't want to see you," the roommate said. "Okay? No more knocking."

"Wait, what?" I asked. "What did he say?"

"Above my pay grade," the roommate said, and closed the door in my face, before I could look in the room and catch Wyatt's eye. If he was even there. I felt the burn of tears and shook my head to make them stop. What could have happened between this morning and now to make him not want to see me?

It didn't make sense. I ducked into the lounge and texted his computer a bunch of times before I remembered Wyatt would only be able to check his texts from the computer lab, and he was in his room. I tried to track down his roommate's cell, which kept me distracted for a while, but finding it only made things worse. I called what felt like a hundred times before his roommate finally answered. "What part of Wyatt-doesn't-want-to-talk-to-you is unclear?" he asked. "Don't call anymore or I'll block your number."

"Please," I said. "Don't hang up. Just tell me something. Anything."

There was quiet for a moment, and I worried that he'd hung up, but he'd just put the phone on mute while he checked in with Wyatt. "He just needs a little time alone," the roommate said. "He said give him a couple of days so he can think."

I didn't see what else I could do. I hung up the phone and then ran to my dorm room. I needed to be alone, especially since I was about to start bawling. I hated feeling so frustrated, and I hated that I wanted to talk to Wyatt about it except that he was the one making me feel this way. I managed to flop on my bed before the crying started in earnest; it was a relief to be by myself.

Except I wasn't. "What's wrong with you?" Brianna asked. She didn't even sound mean; it was almost like she thought that was a legitimate question to ask when one's roommate started hysterically sobbing.

"Why do you care?" I snapped back, burying my face in my pillow.

"You seem sad," Brianna said. "And you're my roommate. Why wouldn't I ask?"

Now I was confused. "You have wanted nothing to do with me since the very first day we moved in, and just because I'm crying you're interested in my life all of a sudden?"

"Oh, that's how you see it?" She sounded almost amused, but then her voice cracked. "Because in my world, you said hi to me on the first day, asked if I wanted to go out when I was so depressed and homesick I could barely talk, and then you made some friends and never spoke to me again."

Brianna's description of our relationship was so radically at odds with mine that it had the unanticipated effect of stopping me from crying. I sat up in bed and leaned back against the wall. "That's what you think happened?"

"That's exactly what happened," she said. "When you left for Game Night, I spent the whole night crying. I had the worst time getting to sleep, and when I finally did you woke me up screaming but wouldn't tell me why. It took like a month for the night-screaming to stop, but at least I'd made some other friends by then, and I could stay with them if I was desperate. Like when your scary friend kicked me out of my own room so you all could play a game without me."

I gaped at Brianna while I tried to process what she

was saying. The events lined up perfectly, but my memory of them was so different. Yet it didn't mean she was wrong. It just meant maybe I didn't understand what was going on around me as well as I thought I did. This feeling was becoming familiar. After a silence a few minutes past comfortable, I decided there was only one thing to do. "I'm sorry, Brianna," I said. "I really am."

"Whatever," she said. "I'm fine now. I've got my people. Just didn't like seeing you so sad, that's all."

"That's not all," I said. "You're being nice to me when you thought I'd been awful to you, and even if I didn't mean to make you feel that way, I'm sorry I did. Could we maybe start over?"

"You did give me the extra closet space," she said, with a half smile. "You want to tell me what's going on, or are you all done with the crying?"

I didn't want to talk about it, but I felt like I owed Brianna a gesture. "I'm good on the crying, but I could use some advice." I told her about Wyatt, how we hadn't been together that long but how his roommate had sent me away and then told me to leave Wyatt alone. "It doesn't make any sense."

"This kind of thing doesn't come out of nowhere," she said. "Are you sure nothing happened today? Is it possible something happened while you weren't around?"

I couldn't imagine anything that would make him react

that way, and I said so. "Not that I'm so perfect or anything. It's just that things have been going so well. What could possibly have changed in only a few hours?"

"Well, it sounds like your job is to answer that question," she said. "Sorry not to be more helpful, but . . ."

"No, this was incredibly helpful." I got up and got a Kleenex from the box on my desk so I could blow my nose. "Thank you."

"No problem." Brianna stood up. "You came in here wanting to be alone, so I'm going to split. I'll see you around, though?"

"Definitely," I said.

She paused before leaving the room. "You can call me Bri, you know," she said. "All my friends do."

Months of living here, and I hadn't known. "Thanks."

After Brianna—Bri—left I just sat on my bed for a while, thinking about how completely I'd misread her. It didn't seem possible, and yet her description of things made total sense when I looked at it from her point of view. I'd always thought I was a pretty understanding person, thinking about other people and not just myself—how had I managed to hurt someone so badly and not realize it? What did that mean for the relationships I thought I understood?

Bri was right—I needed to find out why Wyatt had stopped talking to me. I'd have to get him to explain.

If he wouldn't answer the door, maybe he'd eventually check his email and see that I was still writing to him. I got out my computer and started typing. Email this time, because it felt more formal. Dear Wyatt, I wrote,

> I don't know what happened that made you stop talking to me—I keep hoping it's some sort of mistake and you'll write back or come to my dorm and everything will be fine. But if it's not a mistake, please tell me what happened. Even if you think I won't like it. It can't be worse than not knowing. I miss you.
>
> Love,
>
> Amina

I debated signing it "Love," but I was pretty sure I did love him, even if it was way too soon to tell him that for real. I hit Send, and then I waited. And waited and waited and waited. I skipped dinner and tried to study, but I couldn't focus. I kept clicking the message window over and over again, hoping something would change.

"Did you find out anything?" Bri asked, when she got back from dinner.

"Nothing so far," I said.

She placed a sandwich wrapped in a brown paper napkin on my desk. "I had a feeling you'd bail on dinner, and I thought you might be hungry." She'd brought me a PB&J, a bag of chips, and a brownie.

"How did you know?" I asked. "What to bring?"

"I ran into Chloe at dinner." She saw my face and laughed. "Don't worry, I didn't tell her about Wyatt. Figured if you wanted her to know you'd tell her yourself. I just said you fell asleep studying and I didn't want to wake you up."

"Thanks, Bri." I felt a wave of guilt, thinking about how much I'd missed, not getting to know her earlier. At least it was still early in our time at Gardner, even if it didn't feel like it right now.

Just when I'd finally given up and gotten into bed with a book, well after Bri had fallen asleep, my phone buzzed. I had a new message from Wyatt, and it looked like a long one. I got up and sat at my desk to look at the message on my laptop. At first I had trouble understanding—all I could see were chunks of text that looked cut-and-pasted from somewhere else, all about Hunter and his red hair and adorable freckles and how much more appealing that was than Wyatt's awkwardness and enthusiasm, and then I realized that some of the words looked familiar and some of them didn't and I got this sick feeling deep in my stomach. The last thing I read was the worst: Maybe if I get together with Wyatt it will make Hunter jealous and he'll realize we should be together. It's not like Wyatt would ever figure it out.

I couldn't make sense of the individual words and phrases I'd thought before, combined into sentences I would never, ever write. Not even just to myself. Not even in my journal.

Oh no: my journal. That's why so many of the phrases looked familiar—they weren't just things I would say; they were things I'd written down. I tore open my desk drawer, forgetting to be quiet, hoping against hope that it would be there. And somehow, it was.

But someone had clearly read it, and they'd mixed things I'd said with things I would never say in an effort to hurt me, or Wyatt, or both of us. And it was working. My mind started scrolling through the events of the last couple of months, thinking about all the random bad things that had happened—Wyatt's books and emails, the pictures of Chloe, and now this. The only person in Eucalyptus who hadn't been targeted was Jo. Given that she and Chloe had started hanging out, it was entirely possible she'd have access to Chloe's pictures. Maybe Chloe had even sent them to Jo herself. Was it really that simple? I wasn't sure, but right now I didn't care. Right now all that mattered was making Wyatt understand that I hadn't said those things about him.

I started another message, typing furiously to try and make him understand, but every time I read back over what I'd written it seemed either insufficient or way over the top.

There was only one way to fix this, and it meant making myself as vulnerable and exposed as I'd ever been to anyone in my entire life. Was I ready to do this? Did I trust Wyatt enough? I thought for a while, and then decided the answer was yes.

> Dear Wyatt,
>
> I can't imagine how hurt you're feeling right now. I don't know if it will make it better or worse to tell you I didn't write those things, at least not all of them, and not in that way. If you're willing to give me a chance to explain, go to the package office tomorrow after lunch. I'll have left something for you.
>
> Love,
>
> Amina

"You're giving him your journal?" Chloe literally dropped her fork when I explained to her and to Hunter why I was late for lunch. There was no reason for them not to know, especially since I was hoping they'd have some ideas about why all these things had been happening, whether it was possible that they'd been done by one person, and whether that person might be Jo. "That is madness."

"Oh, I don't know," Hunter said. "Under the circumstances, it seems like the easiest way to fix things, doesn't it? Especially if she trusts him?"

"Sorry, but there is not a person in the world I'd trust that much," Chloe said. "But hey, you do you. I've got bigger things to worry about."

She had effectively managed to turn the conversation back around to her, but I wasn't quite ready to give up the floor. I didn't want to talk about Wyatt anymore, but I wanted to figure out who might be behind this. As much as I didn't want it to be Jo, I was having a hard time coming up with other options. Chloe would never believe it, though.

"I'm happy to talk about your game, but can I ask one question? Have you thought at all about who's been doing all this?"

"What do you mean, 'all this'?" Chloe made air quotes with her fingers.

"Like these emails, and the pictures, and Wyatt's books and all that."

"What about the profiles, too?" Hunter asked.

"Amina didn't get nailed in hers," Chloe said. "Hers was a puff piece. A love letter."

"Not her fault," Hunter said, but Chloe didn't look so sure.

I kept going anyway. "I was just thinking that all these things—I don't even know what to call them, pranks? Whatever they are, they've happened to everyone in Eucalyptus. Except Jo."

Chloe started to look angry. "That's totally unfair. The

profiles were about more than just people in Eucalyptus, and you got let off the hook there. And who's to say this whole journal issue isn't about hurting Wyatt and not you?"

She had a point, but that didn't change the fact that nothing had happened to Jo, though neither she nor Hunter seemed convinced when I mentioned it. "Just because we don't know about anything doesn't mean nothing's happened," Hunter said. "She's not exactly all about full disclosure."

That was also true. "You're right. Maybe I'm just trying to find someone to blame and I picked the easiest person." I remembered how quick I'd been to write off Ken, though the more I got to know him through student council, the less likely it seemed that he could pull off something like this. He wasn't as bad as I'd thought he would be, but his party-boy shtick wasn't just shtick. And besides, now that he'd gotten on student council, he had what he wanted. Was there anyone else? Someone I was missing? Could Bri have been so angry at me that it spread to my friends? She did have access to my journal.

"Just because Jo's the easiest person doesn't mean we need to jump to that conclusion," Chloe said. "Besides, whoever did this had to have tons of connections, and that doesn't scream Jo to me."

"She knows more people than we realize," I pointed out. "Remember Krav Maga?"

"Sure," Chloe said. "But how would she get your journal?

How would she get in your room?"

That was a good point. It's not like she was secretly friends with Bri. I didn't think so, anyway.

"How about we put this aside for a while and start talking about what's really important?" Chloe said.

"Like your game?" I asked, and Hunter groaned.

"What could be more important than that?" She grinned. "It's going to be epic!"

I had no doubt she was right. Unless Wyatt and I still weren't talking, in which case it was going to be a complete nightmare. Either way, I'd find out soon enough.

14.

I tried not to think too much about who was behind the awful things that had happened as I powered my way through finals, but I couldn't help it. I'd designed my curriculum to learn about politics and fascism and the ways single nefarious individuals could destroy social structures, which made it impossible to use schoolwork as an escape from reality. The parallels were so obvious as to make me feel not just stupid but like a terrible person—I hadn't given the thought of Chloe's photos or Hunter's interview takedown or Wyatt's books my full attention until the bad stuff started happening to me. For someone who'd been raised on the slogan "Never Forget," I sure had forgotten a lot of lessons very quickly.

Much as I would have liked to think I was learning something from all the negativity swirling around me, I knew my second quarter would not be nearly as successful as my first. Studying felt impossible. I checked my texts constantly to see whether Wyatt had gone to pick up the journal, though I hadn't yet gone so far as to check myself, in case we ended up there at the same time and I ruined everything. Again.

It was a relief when finals ended and Chloe summoned us to the bunker Saturday morning. I knew whatever she had planned would be elaborate and encompassing and likely ridiculous in some way. As awkward as it would be to see Wyatt when I didn't know whether he'd read the journal, it was better than sitting around moping.

As usual, the game designer sat in the middle—that meant Chloe—and the rest of us sat on the floor facing her. Normally I'd have curled up with Wyatt, but he'd come early and chosen a spot backed up against a shelf, with an empty pillow next to him. As if I'd have gone over there not knowing whether he was still angry. Maybe we didn't know each other as well as I thought. I studiously avoided eye contact and sat between Hunter and Jo.

"Okay, everyone, I think you all know that I'm not nearly as worried about the end of the world as the rest of you," Chloe began. "I've indulged all your apocalyptic scary talk because I like the games, and I like all of you, but I for one have had it with the doom and gloom. Yes, there's been some crap happening, but we've got to move past it. I hope we can agree that I got the worst of it, and if I can deal, then the rest of you can too. So this game is going to be less about how to survive and more about what survival means to us. What kind of world do we want to live in, once we've gotten past the worst of it? Who are we going to be when we've started over? For this game, I'm going to give everyone a chance to show what they can do to make life worth living after the apocalypse."

I hoped Chloe would take the collective groan in the good-natured spirit I was sure we all intended it. "Please don't tell me we're going to have to make our own clothes or something," Hunter said.

Chloe made finger guns at Hunter and then laughed at the expression of panic on his face, mirrored on everyone else's. "Just kidding. No sewing, I promise. But you're on the right track. Let me do the setup first, okay?"

Hunter gave her a finger gun right back.

"All right. Where to begin?" She paused. "In the town where I grew up, it was all about steel. More than half the people worked for the same steel mill, and when it shut down, the town might as well have shut down too." This was as personal as I'd ever heard Chloe. The bunker was so quiet I could hear everyone breathing.

"Everyone said new jobs would come once there was agreement about what kind of energy to invest in—wind, solar, nuclear—but there never was a consensus, and there never were any new jobs. So my family stayed broke, and my dad kept on ranting. Wind and solar power were too expensive and weather-dependent. Nuclear power could destroy us all. I knew in some ways he was full of crap, but that didn't keep me from freaking out about nuclear plant meltdowns, and it wasn't a big leap from there to being terrified of nuclear power, and nuclear weapons.

"So: our game is about living in a post-nuclear world, and by post-nuclear, I mean post–nuclear apocalypse. We've still got power and all that, but the air quality is no good, so we can't go outside."

I glanced at Wyatt—he would be miserable. He grimaced but didn't look back at me.

Jo noticed Wyatt's look too. "The wind chill is like twenty below," she said. "Staying inside won't kill you."

"Don't worry, I'm not a stickler for rules, as you know," Chloe said. "I'm not going to make you stay inside the whole time. I just mean that all the game stuff will be taking place indoors."

"The woods are still yours, Romeo," Jo said.

So she knew about our walks, but she didn't know that we weren't speaking. Maybe Chloe and Hunter were right, and Jo had nothing to do with any of the bad stuff. But why wouldn't Chloe have told her? Could Jo be pretending not to know?

"Here's how this is going to work," Chloe said. "There are two parts to each game, but the winner is the person who does the best job overall. The first category is shelter: each person has to find an indoor space and then stock and decorate it."

"Decorate it? Seriously?" Hunter asked.

"Yup. This game is about thriving after the apocalypse, not just surviving. The best combo is what matters, so if you kill it on the stocking part and you don't bother to decorate, you lose. Are we clear?"

We nodded. I loved that Chloe had designed a game best suited to herself, even though she couldn't win. It was such a Chloe thing to do.

"Second part: a progressive party. We'll each show off our decorations and people can vote on which theme they like best."

I raised my hand. "Are we talking about a party for the five of us, or something bigger?"

"I had something bigger in mind," Chloe said, "but if you want to make it all sad and private, that's your prerogative."

"Is there going to be drinking at this party?" Jo asked. "Because if that's what we're talking about, I'm out. I don't care if other people do that, but that's not happening in my room." I had no idea Jo had such strong feelings about alcohol.

"Doesn't have to be," Chloe said. "People can do that in the other rooms, if they want."

Jo nodded. That was enough to satisfy her.

"So, are you in?" Did Chloe sound a little nervous? How odd—that wasn't like her.

"I am," Wyatt said, though with less enthusiasm than we were used to. "I've never planned a party. It'll be fun."

Hunter gave the thumbs-up, and Jo and I said we were in as well.

"Excellent!" Chloe clapped her hands. "You've got a day and a half: the party is Sunday night, because most people are taking off on Monday and Tuesday."

"You'll do the inviting, right?" I asked. If it were up to me it would be the five of us, the student council, and Hillel, and I wasn't sure how well those groups would mix. Although getting Ken and Jo back together could be entertaining.

"Working on the invite list as we speak," Chloe said.

Now I had to figure out what, exactly, I was going to do next.

The first thing that had to happen was finding an actual space. Obviously the bunker was off-limits, but I didn't imagine I'd be the only one who'd be trolling the underground tunnels for empty rooms. There was no shortage of options, both on the lowest level and the one above it, where lots of students had already figured out where to go to be alone. That basement level was a possibility, but it wasn't the best one, not if I wanted some real privacy. I dug out the map I'd drawn of the lowest level back when I'd had to track down the bunker. September seemed like such a long time ago, but we'd only just finished the first half of the year. How was it possible for so little time to have passed and yet feel like forever?

My map, I saw as soon as I looked at it more carefully,

was terrible. But then I remembered that some of the others had located the bunker by looking at blueprints they'd found online or in the library. I texted Hunter to see if he still had his and crossed my fingers that he didn't get all hyper-competitive on me and tell me to go find the blueprints myself.

He wasn't like that, though. Here you go, he wrote, with the blueprints attached.

I opened the file on my laptop and blew it up so I could read the details. There weren't a whole lot of rooms on that lowest level, which the blueprints called the subbasement, but there were a few spaces that appeared to be closets or storage rooms, and it seemed worth checking them out. That was how I found myself wandering around the dark, dusty subbasement on Saturday night, looking at blueprints on my phone and trying to find a space bigger than six square feet that could serve as both nuclear shelter and party room. How had Chloe convinced us this was a good idea?

After confirming that more than half the spaces I'd found on the map were tiny closets, I finally stumbled on a more promising room. The door was locked but it wiggled when I pushed on it, which made me think the lock was weak. I twisted the knob and thrust my shoulder at it a bunch of times as if I were a cop on some bad TV show, and to my surprise, the lock gave way. I fell into a room just a little bit smaller than the bunker. A cloud of dust swirled around me, turning my sweatshirt and leggings a uniform shade of gray and blurring my vision.

Once I was able to see, it became clear I'd have my work cut out for me to get this room both shelter- and party-ready in under a day. It was full of empty cardboard boxes that had deteriorated over the years, having been divested of their contents long ago. Some of them still had legible text that told me they'd held mostly cleaning products and paper goods; this had been some sort of central storage space, but not for decades. It smelled awful, musty with some underlying scent I didn't recognize until I discovered the bodies of several dead mice.

Other than the boxes and the rodents and the dirt, the room was empty, and it seemed perfect. It was at least as protected as the actual shelter, which I could use as a model for how to set up the space. I just had to claim it as mine and get to work, so I took out the Sharpie and Post-its I'd brought, wrote my name on a Post-it, and stuck it on the door. Then it was back to my room for the world's longest and most thorough shower before I wrote up my game plan.

Sleep was not an option, but then again, sleep had been nearly impossible lately, between finals and obsessing about Wyatt, so that was nothing new. I spent the whole night cleaning my party room, throwing everything out so the room was a blank canvas that I cleaned and then painted. I wasn't much of an artist, so I kept it simple, but I wanted the space to remind people there was an outside world, even if we weren't supposed to be part of it anymore. I painted the floor green and the walls and the ceiling blue, and I found some leftover fake turf in one of the storage rooms under the gym and decided it wasn't stealing to use it for a school project, and then convinced myself I could make the case for this being a school project. I painted clouds on the ceiling along with an enormous yellow sun, trees and flowers on three of the walls, and a sandy beach leading to an ocean on the remaining one and set out cheap beach chairs in front of it. The gym storage locker also had lots of equipment, so I liberated a volleyball and a net—I could always return them later. I got some canned goods and bottles of water so it looked like I was really trying to care about the survival side of things, and then I brought a ton of potato chips and powdered juice mix to serve at the party, figuring the enterprising degenerates could spike it and I didn't have to be in charge of finding booze.

When I was done, I did a slow turn around the center of the room to observe my handiwork. I'd done a good job, I thought; I'd found a beanbag chair that could serve as a bed if Chloe insisted on the room being truly functional, and while the artsy kids would find no competition from me, the space looked bright and reminiscent of the outdoors. I'd taken a dank, musty subbasement storage room and made it feel like spring. I might not have this game in the bag, but I was in the running.

The party was scheduled to start Sunday night at nine, after the dorm parents had shut themselves away but before our formal curfew. We'd all sent our locations to Chloe so she could put together a map for people to follow; the five of us would meet in the bunker at eight so we could do a tour first, before all the students came and trashed our hard work.

It hadn't occurred to me that we should dress up in some way that signaled what our room would be like, but as soon as I saw everyone else I sensed I'd missed an opportunity. Chloe wore a short dress made entirely out of silver sequins; she looked like a disco ball personified, which made perfect sense when she showed us her room, one of the abandoned bathrooms on the second level that had a big lounge-type area with half-length mirrors on one of the walls. She'd covered every square inch of space with silver: mirrored tiles on the floor, silver wallpaper covering the stalls so you couldn't even see there were toilets behind them, silver boxes covering the sinks to create a shelf where she arranged drinks in silver plastic cups and silver-foil-wrapped kisses in silver bowls. And of course she'd hung a disco ball from the ceiling, which made the whole room twinkle.

Chloe twirled in the center, her dress creating even more glitter, though that might also have been because she was throwing glitter around as she spun. By the time she was done we were all sparkling, and I was pretty sure she'd gotten some in my nose. "What do you think?" she asked.

Hunter peered more closely at the shelf. "I think you'll get through this party, but I don't see you surviving five minutes past it. There's no food besides chocolate. There isn't even a bed."

Chloe was having none of it. "Well, if I can't win my own contest, then I'm not really obliged to play fair, am I? Come on, admit it—this place is fabulous."

"I can admit it no problem," Wyatt said. "I've never seen anything like it!"

He was such a good sport. We all acknowledged her design acumen and how high a bar she'd set.

I was next, since my room wasn't that far from Chloe's. I had to admit the space looked kind of rookie next to the sophistication of Chloe's disco palace. "It's very . . . cheerful," Jo said. "Way to be an apocalyptic Pollyanna."

I couldn't even get offended; apocalyptic Pollyanna was what I'd been going for. I checked to see if I could get a read on Chloe, but her face was impassive; she was taking her role as judge seriously. Hunter, on the other hand, couldn't hide the fact that he was giving my volleyball setup the side-eye, which I didn't appreciate. I'd left a blanket at the foot of one of the trees, hoping Wyatt would notice I'd tried to paint our spot, but he didn't say anything. So I wasn't going to win, and I hadn't even managed to get a reaction from Wyatt. I felt like a failure.

Hunter, unshockingly, had chosen a hidden storage

space behind the locker room for the boys' soccer team. I should have known his plan the minute I saw he was wearing his soccer uniform. As soon as I walked in I understood the look he'd given my volleyball net: he'd also raided the athletic department's storage units, and had created a mini-golf course. He hadn't done much with the décor, so I had him there, but his mini-golf game looked like a lot more fun than my sad volleyball court. He'd also used the AstroTurf to create the putt-putt holes, and he'd made one of those windmills you had to shoot the ball through to try and get a hole in one, though I noted (only to myself) that it wasn't mechanized. It was cute, but he wouldn't win either.

That left Wyatt and Jo. "Who wants to go next?" Chloe asked. "I'm looking to be blown away here."

"Not sure I can do that, but I can go," Wyatt said.

I couldn't imagine what Wyatt would do. He was the most outdoorsy person I knew, and this was the most indoorsy game ever. He was screwed. His clothes didn't give much away, other than that he was wearing a lot of layers—a hoodie over a flannel over a T-shirt, which seemed like overkill.

Wyatt led us out of the gym and into the campus chapel, where the Hillel services were held. It was a beautiful building, though I hadn't thought of it that way before, with gleaming wooden pews and stained-glass windows. Hunter's and Chloe's voices echoed as they joked about Wyatt taking us to church, but to his credit he ignored them and led us to a staircase hidden behind the dais, one I'd never noticed before.

As soon as I saw the room he'd found, I knew two things: first, Wyatt wouldn't be winning this game either; and second, he'd read my journal, and he believed me. Wyatt had taken over the attic of the chapel, a room that was too small for five people, let alone a party, something he must have known when he made the decision. The attic was almost all windows, with multiple skylights and floor-to-ceiling windows along the walls. During the day I imagined it was at least as beautiful as the chapel downstairs, despite the lack of stained glass; the sunlight would sweep from one end of the room to the other as the day progressed. I understood Wyatt's outfit now; the windows didn't provide a lot of insulation, so it was freezing.

More impressive was how Wyatt had set up the place. He too had replicated our tree, but he'd gone literal and bought a big plant and then set up a blanket next to it, along with some cushions for us to lean on. He'd brought in shelving filled with some of my favorite snacks; another shelf held books I loved. In a corner was a small desk with two chairs where we could read or use our computers as long as there was power, and on the desk was my journal.

He'd made this room for us.

"Methinks someone missed the point of the assignment," Chloe said.

"Oh, I don't know," Jo said. "Methinks someone might have bigger concerns than winning this game. Right, Romeo?"

So that nickname would stick. Wyatt lifted one shoulder and then let it drop. "You asked how we would thrive after the apocalypse. This is what thriving looks like to me."

I wanted to kiss him in front of everyone, but that would be totally embarrassing and completely unnecessary. Except for how I didn't care. I walked over to him, lifted my hand to his cheek, and pulled his face down toward mine. "Thank you," I whispered afterward, though he might not have been able to hear me through all the hooting.

"Get it, Wyatt!" Hunter said.

"Ugh, sexist. Get it, Amina!" Chloe said.

"All right, all right, enough of this romantic crap," Jo said. "I'm pretty sure I've got this one locked down. Let's go confirm."

I lingered with Wyatt for one last kiss before we followed Jo out of the chapel, more relieved than I could remember being. I was almost tempted to pull him away, to skip the rest of the game and the parties so we'd have one night alone together before break. But Eucalyptus was his baby, and we had to see this last game through.

I shouldn't have been surprised when Jo led us to a place I'd never have expected, since the only consistent thing about Jo was her ability to surprise. Still, I'd never have pegged her for a drama geek, and yet not only were we in the drama building, but Jo had a key that allowed her entrance over the weekend.

"Another facet of Jo's secret life revealed," Chloe said. "Couldn't have planned this game better if I tried."

Jo glanced back at her and pushed the door open. "You know, if you people are interested in my extracurricular activities, all you have to do is ask."

"Okay, I'll start," I said, still giddy with relief and happiness. "Hey, Jo, why do you have the key to the drama building?"

"Because I'm the stage manager for next semester's show," she replied. "I was the assistant this fall, and I got promoted because I killed it."

"I don't recall getting invited to see that show," Chloe said.

"Aw, are you sad there was a party that wasn't for you, Princess? I'm sorry." Jo did not sound sorry. She did sound excited, which was rare for her. We followed her down several hallways until we reached a stretch that seemed to go on forever, with a door at the end. "Go in and hang out for a minute and then I'll do some explaining, okay? Just go with it?"

We nodded, and then she let us in and shut the door behind us. Immediately we were thrust into complete and total darkness. There was no light anywhere, and even as my eyes grew accustomed to the change in light, I could see nothing. It was completely disorienting and I started to feel dizzy; I felt behind me and took small steps backward until I found the wall so I could lean on it. This was awful. What was Jo thinking? And how could she even stand it, given how she felt about the dark?

I'd just barely found the comfort of the wall when the room filled with twinkling lights that looked like stars against the blackness. At first the lights stayed still, as if we were under the night sky; then they started swirling around the room, moving like the reflections of Chloe's disco ball. Instrumental music began to play from speakers all around us, slow and steady with a prominent but not-too-thumpy bass line, and the lights turned from sparkles to spotlights, one for each of us, but only briefly. Then each spotlight turned a rainbow color, swirling in the same pattern the stars had, making the room look like a kaleidoscope. It was beautiful and intense, and as soon as the song ended, the lights went out again and we were thrust back into darkness.

Jo turned the lights on, and I blinked a few times before I saw that we were in a large room painted entirely black. She'd dressed to match the room too, in all black from head to toe. She'd even swapped out the rainbow laces on her Docs for black ones. "This is what's called a black box theater," Jo said. "I convinced the school to let me set one up, so I have to turn it over after the party. You can stage shows here in any configuration you want; it's just a matter of where to put the chairs."

"I don't see any chairs," Hunter said.

"Turn around, wise guy," Jo said. "The walls are all closets—if you look closely you can see where they open. One wall has the chairs; the other closets have food and water and the stuff we'd need if this were really a shelter."

Chloe looked skeptical. "You're basically saying you painted the room black?"

Jo groaned. "Yes, I painted it black, and I built the closets myself, and I convinced the school to start a black box theater group so we can have smaller, weirder shows and not just the overproduced junk the drama club is doing. You asked how we'd thrive after the apocalypse; I'm bringing us post-apocalyptic art."

Now Chloe was starting to get it, as were the rest of us, and I felt stupid. Everyone but me had created the future they wanted: Jo had made a space for theater, Hunter for sports, Chloe for dancing, and Wyatt for him and me. I'd tried to please everyone else, as if a fake sun could stand in for any of the things we really wanted. Did I even know what I'd want, just for me, if the world were going to end? Why did all my friends seem to know themselves better than I did?

"That's a pretty good story," Chloe said. "It just might be enough to win. But we'll have to see what the others think, after the party. Wyatt, I'm sure you won't be offended when

I say you disqualified yourself—we can hardly have a rager in a church."

"Not a problem," he said. "I had other goals in mind."

Jo snickered but didn't say anything. That left me free to say what I suspected everyone else was thinking. "I think we should just have the party here. There's enough space, and we can go back and get our food and drinks and stuff."

Chloe frowned, but come on, she'd made a discotheque in a bathroom. People weren't going to want to actually hang out in there.

"We could get some of the decorations from your room, too," I added. "And we could all bring music."

"Works for me," Hunter said. "We can play mini-golf anytime."

"Just tell everyone to get their drink on somewhere else," Jo said. "I don't care if they come here wasted, but I'm not about to get in trouble."

"The people who require social lubricant can pre-party in my room," Chloe said. "I'll gather the troops, and we'll meet back here whenever."

Jo shut the lights just as Chloe flounced out of the room, and the music started up again, this time with some singing. The stars came back and did their dance along the walls, and I decided I'd rather hang out here with Wyatt than go get stuff I'd bought for the party. I pulled Wyatt into the middle of the black floor and we began to dance. Neither of us were very good, but the blackness made us feel like it didn't matter, and the stars glittered on our clothes, on our faces, in our hair. We got so into dancing we didn't even pause to kiss, and yet I couldn't imagine feeling any closer to him.

I don't know how much time passed before other people arrived, but it must have been late because lots of them seemed drunk already. I saw Tamara and Avi and a bunch of the Hillel kids, Ken Zhang and his party friends, lots of kids from my classes. So many people from so many different social groups, all hanging out together. The room was packed. We danced to techno, to rap, to pop music, and just when I thought I would collapse, sweaty and exhausted, someone yelled out, "Turn out the lights and slow this thing down!"

Wyatt and I looked at each other and laughed. Someone wanted to hook up, and I was happy to take advantage of the darkness. The opening chords of the music began, a strummed guitar soon joined by an electronic piano riff, and I recognized a song I must have heard on some TV show or something. It was old, like really really old, and it wasn't all that slow, and I couldn't remember the name until the chorus rang out: *"Run-run-run-run-runaway."*

"What is this crap?" The person who'd asked for a slow song was not happy with the choice, and whoever was in charge of the stereo was paying attention, because another song began. This one wasn't any slower, though, with rapid-fire synthesizers blaring right away. Once again we only just made it to the chorus, and that's when I knew something weird was happening. *"She's a little runaway."*

"THIS IS NOT BETTER!" the guy screamed over the guitars.

A slower song this time, acoustic guitar, male singer with a growly voice. *"Runaway train, never going back . . ."* Now more people were screaming for the music to change.

Fast-forward again. This time there was just the plink of a single piano note, over and over again, until after maybe fifteen times it dropped to a lower note and we got some variety. By the time the fake drum set kicked in it was clear to me there was a problem, because I knew this song. Kanye West. "Runaway." What was going on here?

We didn't make it to the chorus. The lights came on, the music stopped, and Jo's voice rang out over the crowd. "Everyone get out. Right. Now."

15.

Now I was sure Jo wasn't behind the pranks, or whatever we were calling them, but I didn't know what to do about it. I couldn't think of a single person who wasn't in Eucalyptus who knew us all well enough to know how to hurt us, and we'd all been hurt, and badly. I didn't know what about the music had set Jo off, but I could tell it had hit her hard. I felt awful I'd even considered her a suspect, and I hated to think how she must be feeling right now.

Are you okay? It was the first text I'd sent just to Jo; the day I'd tracked her down at lunch to ask how my game was going was still the only time we'd ever hung out alone. But I didn't want to just show up at her dorm, especially if she was freaked out. Who knew if she'd gone straight home? I'm around if you want to talk, whenever.

It was already past midnight, so I didn't expect to hear from her right away. But the buzzing of my phone woke me earlier than I expected; I'd planned to sleep in, since I was taking a bus home on Tuesday to avoid the Monday rush.

That would be good. Off campus? I could use some time away from here.

We agreed to meet at the campus bus. She was waiting when I arrived, wearing the same clothes she'd had on last night. Her eyes were swollen and red and her short hair was matted around her face. I wondered whether she'd slept. I wasn't sure what to do—she looked like she needed a hug, but neither one of us were huggers, and now didn't seem the time to start.

"Can we just not talk for a while?" Jo asked, as the shuttle approached. "Is that something that could happen?"

I nodded to show I was starting right away. She sounded angry but not at me, and she'd agreed to come, so whatever she needed I could do. She hadn't even called me by a nickname.

We sat in silence as the campus bus puttered its way on gravel roads and then main roads, and then we walked quietly to the coffeehouse. It was nearly empty when we got there, and the few people sitting at tables were townies, not kids from school, which was a relief. I got my usual milky tea and Jo got black coffee, and we went to the back room and sat at a corner table.

Jo didn't wait for me to ask any questions. "You want to know what happened last night, and I'm going to tell you, because you're the only one who checked in on me," she said.

That was surprising—I would have thought Chloe would be on top of it. But maybe she was scared of an angry Jo. I was too, but I was going to have to get over myself, especially if we were ever going to be real friends. We had two and a half years of school left; it wasn't too late.

"This isn't something I like to talk about," she went on, "so let me get through it, okay? No interruptions. This is the truth, just enough so you understand."

I nodded again, the living embodiment of that smiley-face emoji with a zipper across its lips. I could follow orders.

"Okay, then, here we go. The short and illustrious life so far of Josephine Reed." She let out a noise that sounded almost like a snort, and I wasn't sure if it was because of her opening or because she'd said her full name. "Everything was pretty normal at first—my parents loved each other, they loved me, we lived in a nice house in Chicago, I went to a great school and did well, and blah blah blah, drunk driver hits taxicab, and tada I'm an orphan."

Way to blow through the hardest part, I thought, but I'd promised not to speak. Or maybe this wasn't the hardest part. I shivered, though it was warm inside.

"Obviously that complicated matters." Jo sipped at her coffee. "My grandparents hadn't been in the picture up to that point—my mom's family, the Korean side, was horrified she'd married a white guy, and my father's family goes back to the *Mayflower* so they weren't having my mom either. My parents had told them all to piss off early on, but they hadn't planned on dying so young, so there was no one else to take me in. My grandparents weren't exactly thrilled to have me, either—you can probably imagine I was not exactly what they'd had in mind for their retirement."

I kept my mouth shut, holding my tea in front of my face with both hands.

"My dad's parents lived in this enormous house in a Chicago suburb called Lake Forest—it had a gate where I got locked in when I wasn't at school. They sent me to my Korean grandparents every few weekends, which was the complete opposite of being with the Reeds. They lived close to the city and didn't care what I did, so I could roam around wherever I wanted. And for a while, having that much freedom was enough to make up for feeling like I was in a giant cage most of the time."

I felt nervous. This story was not going to a good place.

"I wanted desperately to get out of there, but I'd asked my dad's parents about boarding school and they weren't having it. I dreamed about college, getting as far away from Chicago as possible, and I really thought I could make it until then. But one night I woke up in my room in Lake Forest to the sound of the knob turning. I saw my grandfather standing there, watching me in my bed."

I wasn't sure I was breathing anymore. I was starting to understand Jo's fear of the dark.

"At first he just stood there in the doorway, and I stayed quiet, staring at him as he stared at me. Then he came closer to the bed and shut the door behind him. I couldn't even see him walk across the room, but I felt him sit down, and I smelled his breath as he leaned over me. Whiskey, though I didn't know that at the time. I didn't know what to do, so I turned over and pretended he wasn't there, pretended I was still asleep, and finally he left. But I knew I'd gotten lucky. The next time he wouldn't leave."

Now I got why she hadn't wanted me to talk, and I was grateful. I had no idea what to say.

"I couldn't wait to get to my other grandparents' place, so I skipped school the next day, snuck into my grandfather's office, and stole the gate code. I got their driver to take me to an outdoor supply store and bought a backpack, a sleeping bag that rolled up to fit, a Swiss Army knife, and a case of energy bars. I went back home and got some clothes, and then I took off.

"At first it was an adventure—I slept on park benches in the suburbs until the police chased me off, and when the energy bars ran out I went freegan and got my food from dumpster diving. In the burbs, that wasn't so bad. But the cops were everywhere, and I was worried they'd start to recognize me and send me home. So I went to Chicago, where I wouldn't stand out as much, and I figured out how to make it there." She paused now, and I knew she was thinking about the things she'd had to do to survive. She wouldn't tell me the worst of it, but then again, I probably didn't want to know. That was most likely how she'd learned to identify Ken Zhang as a drug addict.

"Long story short, I made it a few months until a group of kids figured out I was stashing money and jumped me. I'd gotten my black belt in tae kwon do as a little kid, but that can't save you from a gang of five people. I woke up in a hospital room with a few broken ribs and no spleen. The nurse told me I'd fought back, that two of the others looked worse than I did, so that was something, I guess. I was in so much pain it didn't matter."

This was one of the most upsetting stories I'd ever heard. It was killing me not to talk, even if just to say how sorry I was, how glad I was she was okay now.

"The hospital let my grandparents in not long after I woke up. The Reeds, the ones I didn't want to see. My grandmother laid into me for making them worry, and I was two seconds away from telling her the whole story when my grandfather told me he'd pulled some strings and gotten me into Gardner. I had to recuperate at home, but then I got to leave, and I swore I'd never go back, and that next time I was on my own I'd be better prepared." She drank down the rest of her coffee, which must have been cold by now. "Maybe you understand now why I can be a little prickly. I get that I'm not the easiest person to have as a friend. But I'll never forget what it was like waking up in the hospital in that much pain, and what led me there. So yeah, the surprise 'runaway' playlist did not sit well with me. And that's all I'm going to say about it. Now I'm getting more coffee."

Jo got up and left the table before I could say anything, taking my empty cup with her. I felt like someone had physically extracted the air from my lungs. All I could do was focus on breathing in and out until my heart rate came down. What was I supposed to say? Should I tell her I had nightmares too, though they'd gotten better? Should I tell her I was glad she'd gotten away from her family? I couldn't think of a single thing that seemed right.

She came back with a steaming cup of black coffee for herself and more tea for me, with exactly as much milk and sugar as I liked. She'd paid attention to how I'd taken my first cup, and I found it more touching than I could have imagined. Maybe we really were friends, or maybe I was the closest thing to a real friend she had. I hoped that didn't mean things had gone south with Chloe, but now didn't seem the time to ask.

"I'm sorry all that happened to you," I said. It was basic and not nearly enough, but anything more felt wrong.

"Thanks," she said. "You don't need to feel bad for me—I'm okay. Or I will be. I do need more help than I've been letting myself get, but I'm going to fix that. I want to put all this behind me."

"What about the person who did this?" I asked the question before I could stop myself. "Don't you want to find out who it is?"

Jo's expression was hard for me to read, but I recognized it. Pity. What was going on here? "Don't you know?"

"Of course I don't know! I wouldn't ask you if I knew!"

She shook her head. "We should go back. I don't want to talk about this anymore."

Now I was getting upset, but I wasn't about to start a fight with someone who'd just shared her worst experiences with me. Fine. I'd try to stop worrying about who was responsible. Jo apparently knew and didn't think it was worth doing anything, and she'd been through far worse in her life than I had, so maybe it was time to drop it. I had Wyatt back, it seemed like Jo and I were friends, I was done with finals, and it was time to go home. I looked forward to seeing my family, even if I had no intention of filling them in on every last detail of what was going on around here.

My plan was to spend the rest of the day packing and then go see Wyatt. We were taking the same bus as many other students who were headed to Boston, whether because they lived there or because that was where they were picking up the train or taking a flight. I thought the mindlessness of putting my room in order would be a useful distraction from all the swirling thoughts in my brain, but no such luck; the rhythm of folding clothes and putting them back in my suitcase quickly allowed me to forget what my hands were doing and lose myself in thought. I could not stop thinking about everything that had happened, how close I'd come to losing Wyatt, how much pain my friends had been put through.

I had to do something.

I got out my phone and sent a group text. Meeting. Bunker. One hour. Then I emailed Wyatt to make sure he knew as well and I headed underground. I wasn't sure what I was going to say to everyone, or what I was proposing, but I couldn't go home with this burning question on my mind.

Wyatt was the first to arrive. He got there a few minutes before I did; I loved that he knew me well enough to know I'd come right away, even if I'd given everyone else some time. "Are you okay?" he asked. "Is this about what happened last night?"

"Kind of," I said, answering both questions at once without meaning to. "I think we all need to talk."

We sat quietly together, waiting for everyone else to arrive. I'd set up the chairs in a circle, and we sat next to one another, holding hands. I looked around the bunker and tried to memorize it, as if I'd somehow forget it when I went home, as if I weren't coming back in just a few weeks. We'd made a fair number of changes over the past months, and the space had come to feel more like a home than a place designed for bare-bones survival. There were Chloe's throw pillows, plus the area rug she'd brought; Hunter routinely snagged extra energy drinks from soccer practice, so many that they now had their own shelf next to the bottled water; Jo had covered the wall space with posters of old catastrophe movies; I'd made a little reading nook in the corner with some of my favorite books; and Wyatt had taken care of adding to the variety of snacks by making off with bags of chips and cookies from the dining hall. I felt more at peace in this bunker than I did in my own dorm room.

Hunter showed up next, sweaty and out of breath in track pants, an old T-shirt, and sneakers. "Pickup basketball," he said, still panting a little. "Ran over here as soon as I could. Everything all right?"

I hadn't realized how much I'd freak everyone out calling a meeting the way I had. "Yeah, I'm okay. But last night was pretty awful, and I don't think we should go home without seeing each other one last time."

"Can't argue with that," Hunter said.

Just for a minute I wondered what Wyatt was thinking. He'd had a chance to read my whole journal; he knew the history of my crush on Hunter, along with everything I'd ever thought about Wyatt up until a few days ago. I couldn't imagine having that much access into someone's brain. I wasn't sure I'd want it.

I was surprised when the next person to open the bunker door was Jo. She'd cleaned up from this morning; she was back in her usual uniform, and her face showed no signs of tears. It hadn't even been an hour, so I hadn't expected everyone to be here already, but if anyone were going to be early, I'd have thought it would be Chloe. She hadn't responded to any of my texts, which was also strange.

"Guess we're just waiting for one more," I said.

"Sure, boss," Jo said. If she was back to nicknames, she must be okay. "Might be a while, though."

"What do you mean?" Wyatt asked.

She shrugged. "Just saying. Have any of you heard from her?"

We shook our heads. "That doesn't mean she's not coming," I said. "She'll be here. I'm sure she will."

"Well, we don't need to sit here in total silence, even if you don't want to start the actual meeting without her," Hunter said. "Remind me: Who's doing what over break?"

"I saw my dad at Thanksgiving, so I'm going to see my mom," Wyatt said. "Berkeley in winter is way better than Utah. We get enough snow here in Vermont. You?"

"Home," Hunter said. "But this time I got out of the family trip, so I get to hang in Houston by myself. Well, my grandparents are staying at the house, but they let me do my own thing. I'll get to see my friends, and I'll have time to try and track down my brother."

"That sounds like a good plan," I said. "I'm just going home. I miss my family." I hadn't said that out loud to anyone here before, but it seemed like the right time.

"I'm here," Jo said. "As usual." She didn't sound bummed, just matter-of-fact, but the thought of Jo here in the dorms all by herself, surrounded by no one but kids who had nowhere else to go or who weren't wanted at home, along with dorm parents who were seriously the least parental people I'd ever encountered, made me so sad.

"Why don't you come home with me for a bit?" I asked.

Jo blinked a few times. "What?"

"I mean it," I said. "Come for a week or two. My parents won't mind. You can stay in my room with me, or if you want your own space, my sister can stay with me and you can have her room. We don't celebrate Christmas, but we have a Hanukkah party every year and we make really good food." I felt like I was selling it too hard, but I didn't know what it would take to make Jo agree. I just knew she had to.

"I hate Christmas," she said. "It would be great to get away from it. Thanks, Amina."

"No problem. It'll be fun." I meant it, too. "Now seriously, where's Chloe?" I got out my phone to see if she'd texted, but I'd forgotten that we had no service this far underground. But

Chloe was rarely late, and never when she thought there'd be drama. If everyone else came running when I said we should meet, why wouldn't Chloe do the same?

"Maybe we should just start without her?" Wyatt asked.

I didn't want to; Chloe was so smart, and maybe she'd see connections the rest of us didn't. But I also didn't want to keep everyone underground all day; they had their own packing to do. "Okay," I said. "I called everyone here because I know some of us, Chloe included, have been talking about the random bad stuff that's been going on and whether it's really random."

"I don't remember anyone talking to me," Jo said.

I immediately felt awful, though she didn't sound angry. "I know, and I'm sorry. Nothing had happened to you, and I just wasn't sure . . ."

"You thought maybe I was the one doing it." She laughed. "And last night cured you of that delusion."

How was she so calm? I'd be furious. "I really am sorry. I should have known better."

She waved me off. "It's fine, don't worry about it."

No nickname. Somehow it made me feel worse. "Anyway, I haven't been able to stop thinking about everything that's happened, and after last night I felt like maybe we should talk about it. See if we can put our heads together and find a connection so we can put a stop to it. I don't want to be worrying about this when we get back."

No one said anything for a long while. There was a lot of looking around, then looking at the floor, and then looking away. "Tell me this, Amina," Jo said finally, and more gently than I'd ever heard her speak. "Is this a question you really want answered?"

"Of course!" How could anyone not want to know?

She turned to Hunter and Wyatt. "How about you guys?"

They exchanged glances. "I thought I did," Hunter said. "But now that it's all starting to make sense, I'm not sure I want to say it out loud."

What was he talking about? I turned to Wyatt, who also looked confused. *Help,* I mouthed.

"I'm starting to think maybe not all of us in this room are on the same page?" Wyatt said. I hated that the tentativeness was back in his voice. It felt like my fault.

"I'm happy to bring us all there, if that's what everyone wants," Jo said. "I just think we should make sure first. We can't come back from this."

It sounded like she was saying it was one of us, but the only one of us I'd ever considered was her, and it didn't feel like she was about to confess. "Come on already," I said. "Just tell us what you know."

"All right, but don't shoot the messenger." She planted both feet on the floor and put her hands on her knees. "Let's be methodical here. Who do we know who has shown a willingness to hurt some people in support of others"—and here she started ticking off items on her fingers—"who is smart enough to know how to be stealthy, knows us all well enough to know how best to hurt us, has the tech and media savvy to pull off all these stunts, and isn't here right now?"

When she laid it all out like that it was obvious, and I instantly felt stupid. But I didn't want her to be right. Chloe would never do that to us. Though she was the only one of the group who spent time in my room. She knew about my journal, how important it was to me. Where I kept it. "What about the pictures of her?" I asked.

"They kept us from ever considering her," Hunter said. "Which might have been the point."

"She was so upset," I said, but I knew I didn't sound all that convincing. "What about the profile stuff? She didn't have anything to do with that."

"You don't think?" Jo said. "One of her little fan club members is the editor. Those interviews got you in and Hunter out, which I'm sure was exactly what she wanted."

I'd forgotten about the editor—Chloe had even mentioned that to me when I did the interview. "But why?" It came out almost more as a sob than a question, though I resolved I was not going to cry. "She's my best friend here. Why would she try to break Wyatt and me up? Why would she want to hurt you and Hunter?"

Jo shrugged. "Beats me. Though she flipped out when I asked her about it last night."

"You what?" Now Hunter was the one asking questions.

"She's the only person at this school who knew about my background," Jo said. "I told Amina about it today. That runaway crap was for me. As if I wouldn't know it was her. And she had the nerve to act surprised when I confronted her with it." She shook her head. "I don't know why I ever thought things might work between us."

"That's why you were so sure she wouldn't come," I said.

"She's probably in her room sulking because I won the game," Jo said. "Sometimes I think games are all she cares about, and not just of the Eucalyptus variety."

"Well, she can't just get away with this," Hunter said. "We have to do something."

"What are we supposed to do?" Wyatt asked. "Except tell her we know and hope she stops?"

"We can kick her out of Eucalyptus, to start," I said. "And then we can make her tell us why she did all this."

"If you really want to know," Jo said. "At this point, I'm not sure I care."

I couldn't stop now. Not when we were so close. "I care, and I'm going to get answers," I said. "Who's coming with me?"

16.

I didn't look behind me as I stomped my way out of the bunker and back toward the dorm, though from the sound of footsteps everyone had decided to join me. By now I knew the underground tunnels well enough that I could pop up right near my own dorm room gopher-style; I wasn't quite knowledgeable enough to locate Chloe's room underground, but Hunter and Jo both were. We giggled awkwardly when we realized why, and that broke the tension.

"Do you even know what you want to say to her?" Wyatt asked as we speed walked our way up the stairs.

"I'll think of something." I was filled with righteous rage and hoped that would be enough.

We continued our march down the hallway and stopped in front of Chloe's room. The light was on, throwing a ray of light through the crack at the bottom of the door. "You want to do the honors?" Jo asked.

I knocked, three firm raps I intended to signal that this was an important visit. I'd barely moved my hand from the door when it opened.

Lauren. "What is it? Did you find her?" Her eyes were so wide they looked round, like a cartoon character's, and she radiated a frenetic energy.

"What are you talking about?" I asked. "We're looking for Chloe."

"Well, duh," she said. "So is everyone."

I pushed past her into the room. Chloe's bed was its usual rumpled mess; Lauren's was neat and tidy, almost in rebuke, except that Lauren would never do anything to risk her friendship with Chloe. She'd turned into the queen of the followers these past few months, imitating Chloe's outfits with a rigor previously only matched by #fleabagfail Stacie. I'd checked Chloe's Instagram this morning, as I always did, and she'd put up her usual photo. "Winter is being friendly!" she'd written, along with the usual pile of hashtags I didn't care to decipher. She wore all white: white jeans, white boots with a puff of fake white fur at the top, a long white puffer coat with matching fake white fur, silvery makeup. We'd had a storm during finals that coated the ground with a thick layer of snow and the trees with glittering ice. Lauren, too, was dressed all in white, but the effect was less ethereal snow princess and more hospital staff—she clearly didn't have many winter-white clothes to work with, and white wasn't her color anyway. Her pale skin looked washed out, though it might have been from lack of sleep more than the clothes.

"You're telling me she's not here?" I asked, though it was obvious. "When did you last see her?"

"Last night, like everyone else," Lauren said. "She didn't come back, and I haven't seen her all day. I've asked everyone and no one's seen her since the party."

"I saw her," Jo said.

"Then you were the last one." A tear escaped from Lauren's eye. "Did she tell you anything? Was she planning on going somewhere? I've been freaking out but I thought maybe there was a chance she was with you guys, but if she isn't . . ."

This was unexpected. "She must have been here at some point," I said. "She posted on Instagram this morning."

Lauren snorted. "She schedules those. She could have made that post a month ago. Doesn't mean anything."

I'd forgotten about that. That didn't help, then. I turned to Jo. "When you talked to her last night, what did she say?"

Jo frowned. "I confronted her about the party, and at first she lied about it, said it had nothing to do with her. She's so convinced she can make people believe whatever she wants. But I pushed, and she started getting upset. Panicky. I don't think anyone's ever called her out for anything. She started crying, and then she split." She paused, then added, "She did say one thing before she left that I thought was bizarre, but now I'm wondering whether it was a clue."

"What was it?" I asked.

"She said, 'I'm better at survival than all of you,'" Jo said.

That gave me pause, and then it gave me an idea. "Lauren, did you come back here right after the party broke up?" I asked.

"No, a bunch of us moved the party to one of the lounges for a while," she said. "No one was ready to go to bed yet."

That meant Chloe could have come back to the room. I went to her closet and started rifling through her clothes, trying to see whether she'd packed a bag and left or whether she'd just wandered off somewhere to be alone. It was winter, after all; if she was going to go outside, she'd have to take a coat with her. But Chloe had so much stuff it was impossible to tell whether anything was gone.

"Do you know where she keeps her backpack?" Wyatt asked. "The one she brought as a go-bag, for Hunter's game?"

He was thinking the same thing I was. "I don't," I said. "It's not in the closet. Lauren?"

"She's got some storage bins for extra clothes under her bed," Lauren said. "You could check there."

Hunter reached down and started pulling out the bins. They weren't labeled, but when we opened them they were organized. One was filled with tops, another with pants, another with dresses and skirts. One was entirely for makeup, and then there was one for bags of all kinds: handbags; shoulder bags; little fancy purses in odd shapes, like cats and typewriters and piano keyboards. This was where a backpack would most likely be, but there wasn't one.

"I think she ran," I said. "I think she took her go-bag and decided to prove to us she was the best at survival."

"We have to find her," Jo said.

"Do we really?" Hunter asked. "We know what she did. Is it that important we find out why?"

Wyatt shook his head. I missed his curls. "It's not about that anymore. We have to make sure she's okay. It feels fine outside now, but the sun's already going down and tonight's supposed to get pretty cold. She may not realize how bad it will be if she's outside."

"You really think she's out there?" Lauren asked. "She's not exactly the outdoorsy type."

She had a point. Chloe could be anywhere—none of us knew where she went when she wanted to be alone, because it seemed like she never did want to be alone. "We need to think about all the options and then split up," I said. "Jo, what was your first thought when she said she was better at survival than we were?"

"I thought she meant it literally," Jo said. "I know a little more about her than you people do, and I'll just say she hasn't had it easy. I can't blame her for splitting when things got hard—I've done the same thing myself."

"Does anyone have any ideas about where she'd go?" I wanted answers.

"If she meant survival as in actual survival, then maybe she was trying to show us what she could do," Wyatt said. "That's why I think she could be outside. I think we should check the woods."

Hunter shook his head. "I'm with Lauren that she's not all about being outside in the cold. I think she'd go somewhere she'd want to be found."

"Sure, but who knows where that is?" Jo asked. "We're the ones who know her best, and we can't agree on where she might have gone."

"She's playing another game with us," I said. "She wants to see which one of us can find her." As soon as I said it I knew I was right. Chloe might have been upset, but I couldn't imagine her getting so upset she'd pass up a chance to get one more shot at messing with us. Jo was right: everything was a game to her, even the terrible things she'd done.

"You all are so messed up," Lauren said. "I'm going to get some people who are serious about finding her. Shut the door on your way out, okay?" I noticed she didn't take a coat when she left; she didn't think Chloe had gone outside either.

Now it was just the four of us, alone in Chloe's room. "We're not really going to treat this like a game, are we?" Wyatt asked. "If she's missing, shouldn't we get help? Talk to the dorm parents or something? Or the police?"

"The police won't do anything," Jo said. "And the dorm parents here are a joke. You know they've been paid off to ignore us until everyone who's going on break has left, don't you?"

Wyatt's eyes widened. I loved that he lived in a world where he still thought the people in charge were good. I wanted that feeling back, and I was afraid it would never come. That's how this had started, for me; it only made sense we'd come full circle, to a place where we needed to help ourselves because the adults weren't going to be of much use.

"I say we go with it. Four people with four different strategies for finding Chloe, plus her Insta friends searching on their own—we're more likely to find her that way." I was getting into it now. "We'll take our phones and check in every hour. Person who finds her wins, and we'll have a real prize this time: winner gets to ask the first question."

"How should I check in?" Wyatt asked. "No phone, remember?"

"Here, take mine," Jo said. "I've got a burner in my room."

We stared at her.

"What? You never know." She got out her phone, pressed the screen a bunch of times, sent a few quick text messages, and then handed it to Wyatt. "I got rid of the password. Everyone's contact info is in here, and I sent a group text that includes the burner so you all have the numbers in one place."

"Thanks," Wyatt said, holding the phone as if it were a used Kleenex. It had never occurred to me that it wasn't just that he didn't have a phone; he didn't want one. But this was the easiest way for us to stay in touch, and he knew it.

"All right, let's do this," Hunter said. "It's about three o'clock now. First check-in at four?"

We agreed, and then went our separate ways. I headed back to my room to think. If I'd thought Chloe was in real danger then maybe there would be more urgency, but I was convinced she was toying with us, playing a maddening game of hide-and-seek. I hadn't won any of the games so far, but I was determined to win this one. To do that, I'd have to be methodical.

I sat on my bed with my journal; I'd slipped it into my bag the night before, as we were leaving the chapel and heading to the black box theater. This was the first time I'd opened it, and a piece of notebook paper fell out.

Thank you for this, but I don't need it. Your secrets are safe. I'm sorry. XOXO, Wyatt.

After all that, he hadn't even read it. If it weren't for this whole Chloe situation I'd have been relieved, even happy, but now wasn't the time. I set the note aside and went back through everything I'd written about Chloe, every detail, looking for evidence that I knew her better than anyone else. Wyatt would be searching in the woods, as he'd said, but I was sure Hunter, Jo, and I would be staying indoors, and there was a time when each of us would have been convinced we knew her best. Right now wasn't it, though, and I didn't know what to do.

I read over every entry that mentioned Chloe until my eyes started to hurt, so I closed them and tried to remember, hoping details I hadn't written down would emerge. There was Game Night, of course, and the first day of school, when she and Hunter and I had started having lunch together. There was our election planning, most of which had taken place in one of the dorm lounges; there was our makeover session, but that had been in her room, although hadn't she mentioned something about going somewhere else?

I opened my eyes and sat up straight, aligning my back with the wall. This was it; I could feel it. What had she said? I should be glad we were shooting in her room because otherwise something about temperature controls and lighting and I couldn't remember what else. I got out my phone and pulled up Chloe's Instagram feed. Picture after picture with all sorts of different backgrounds thanks to the magic replaceable wallpaper in her room, but also thanks to the never-ending supply of fresh flowers she seemed to have access to.

Oh. Because Chloe loved the greenhouse.

It would be the perfect place to hide in winter, because of the temperature controls. No one would be there because it was break, and only someone who paid attention would realize that's where she set up many of her photo shoots.

Now I had a choice. I could go straight there, or I could check in with the others. Before I could decide, my phone started buzzing with texts.

Nothing yet, Jo wrote.

Ditto, from Hunter.

It took a little longer for Wyatt to reply, but that wasn't surprising. The text message notifications had probably scared the crap out of him. I smiled just thinking about it.

I sent my own message with no hint I was making progress—if I was right, I'd have something to report soon enough—and decided to go straight to the greenhouse. My heart raced with excitement. This was it, I was certain.

I knew where the greenhouse was; I'd even walked by it a bunch of times and thought about going in. But I wasn't into plants and flowers and nature, and I was getting enough of it through Eucalyptus anyway. Besides, it was Chloe's thing. I threw on my coat and walked across campus.

The building was long and rectangular, like a barn, but made entirely of panes of glass and with a sloped glass roof. There were doors at both ends, and I wasn't sure which one to use. Did I want to surprise Chloe, or did I want her to know I was there as I walked in?

I picked the door closest to me and tested it out, confirming it was unlocked. As soon as I entered the greenhouse I felt a surge of heat, as if I'd entered an entirely different climate.

Which, I supposed, I had. There were leafy green plants everywhere and evidence of a functioning sprinkler system, since everything looked wet. My coat quickly became unnecessary, so I took it off and slung it over my elbow as I scanned the aisles of plants to find Chloe.

Of course she wasn't going to make it easy. I passed by plants that looked like cacti but were labeled as succulents; Wyatt would probably know the difference. There were little trees with tiny lemons on them, and some with little oranges, too. But where were the flowers? I had a feeling if I found the flowers, I'd find Chloe.

I made my way through the rows and rows of plants until I saw there was a whole section at the far end that was blocked off, almost as if the rows were the stripes on the American flag and the blocked-off section was the rectangle containing the stars. There were glass panels enclosing the space, making it into its own room, with a glass door separating the room from the rest of the greenhouse. That's where the flowers were, with their own microclimate, in clusters rather than rows. And in the corner of that section I saw a thick white winter coat strewn on the floor like a blanket, with Chloe asleep on top of it.

I'd won my first game.

Greenhouse, I texted the group. ASAP.

17.

By the time everyone arrived it was dark, and Chloe was still asleep. I almost felt bad at the thought of waking her up for an ambush, but then I thought about what she'd done to us and I got over it quick. The greenhouse fans had turned themselves on, loud enough that I could barely hear everyone making their way through the rows of plants, and with the fans had come the greenhouse's nighttime lighting system, faint as it was.

"Amina?" Wyatt called out.

"Over here." I was sitting on the ground just outside the flower room, but I got up when I saw them coming. "She's in there. Out cold."

They peered through the windows at Chloe, conked out on her own coat, oblivious to the sound of the fans. She must have been exhausted. I almost felt bad for her. Almost.

Then, as if she could feel our presence, she began to stir.

"How do you want to play this, boss?" Jo asked.

It wasn't the time to bask in the fact that I'd finally won a game. "Let's all go over together. We can give her a minute to wake up, though."

Jo, Hunter, and Wyatt sat down next to me and we watched as Chloe woke up with a stretch and a yawn. Even in the minimal light I could see that Jo hadn't been kidding about Chloe being upset the night before; her face was puffy and streaked with makeup she hadn't taken off, displaced by tears. Her gloriously highlighted hair was tangled and knotted, and while she'd managed to change out of her disco-ball dress, she'd opted for a sweatshirt and yoga pants rather than her usual cute pajamas. She looked more human than I'd ever seen her, and I again wavered in my anger.

But I wasn't the only one who needed answers. "Let's do this," Hunter said, and we all stood up and went into the flower room together.

Chloe seemed to take a minute to realize she wasn't alone. "What—what's going on? What are you all doing here?" She rubbed her eyes and wrapped her arms around her knees, as if making herself as small as possible.

As we walked closer I saw we'd been right about her taking her go-bag; it was sitting next to her coat, and she'd used it as a pillow. But she had more stuff there—she'd set up a plastic set of drawers, full of who knew what, though I suspected it was gear for her Instagram photo shoots. She'd probably

convinced some staff person to let her store her things there.
"We came for you," I said.

For a moment a hopeful expression crossed her face, and I saw how moved she was by the idea that we'd searched for her, that we were worried, that we perhaps weren't as angry as Jo had seemed. Then she realized I'd meant something very different, and her face collapsed. Tears rolled out of her eyes, making new mascara tracks on her face. She dropped her head to her knees and shook it back and forth, and we stood in silence and watched her. I wasn't sure how to feel. It wasn't just that I'd never seen Chloe cry before; it was that I couldn't even picture her crying as a possibility, and yet here we were, watching it happen. She looked so small all curled up like that, like a little kid.

Then she picked up her head. Her face had hardened into a mask. "You've got me," she said. "Let me have it."

With that, my sympathy was gone. Brave, foolish Chloe, thinking we'd just do some yelling and then this would be over. "That's not how this is going to work," I said. "You're going to tell us everything."

"What does that even mean?" She reached up and twisted her ratty hair into a knot that stayed up all by itself. Ugh, Chloe could even make looking terrible look good.

"Come on, Princess, the game is over. You've been awful to us, and we've been good friends to you, so it's time to explain why." Jo shivered in her leather jacket, though it was plenty warm in the greenhouse.

"You're cold," Chloe said. "Maybe we should go somewhere else."

"Or you could just start talking, and the sooner you finish the sooner we can get out of here." I wasn't about to let her change the scene to suit herself, and I didn't want us to lose momentum.

"Fine, whatever," she said. "What do you want to know?"

Everyone looked at me. I wished I'd done a better job preparing, or any job at all. "We want all of it. You sent Wyatt those books and signed him up for those emails; you set up the interviews that would screw Hunter over after convincing him to run for student council; you sent around those pictures of you; you tried to break me and Wyatt up; and you tried to humiliate Jo in front of, like, the whole school. We've done nothing but be your friends, so why would you do all that to us?" By the time I finished talking I had to choke back a sob, which was enraging—I'd wanted to be calm and methodical, and angry if I had to be. I hadn't wanted to get weepy.

Chloe sighed. "You make it sound so terrible. It's not like I did any of you any real damage."

Was she kidding? "It was more than terrible," I said. "I don't know how you define damage, but you can't possibly think anything you did was okay."

"I didn't say that." She was quiet for a minute. "Okay, you

really want all of it? I'll tell you, but you have to promise you'll really listen."

"That's all any of us want," Hunter said.

"Then you're going to have to sit down, because I'm not about to have you standing over me and glaring." Chloe was starting to sound like herself now. And while I didn't like the idea of her dictating the terms of this conversation, I also wasn't about to stand the whole time if she was going to launch into a long story.

Everyone again looked at me, acknowledging I was in charge. I liked it. I gave a little nod, and we sat down.

Once we were settled in, Chloe began. "I wasn't in the greatest place when I got here. I know that's true of lots of people here, so I'm not saying it as an excuse. I'm just explaining. I know I told you all how my dad's been out of work, but I don't think you have any idea what it's like to be dirt-poor in western Pennsylvania, with four siblings all younger than you, with parents who don't care about you but expect you to be like a parent to all the kids.

"I'm not book-smart like you people. No one at school was looking out for me or telling me I was special, that I could get out of there. I had to figure everything out myself. When the site started making money I had to hide it, and I'm here at Gardner on my own dime. I had to beg the school to let me in, even though my family has way less money than most of the scholarship kids. I got myself out of a bad situation and I'm never going back. So yeah, I kind of had a chip on my shoulder when I got here. Everyone was either rich or special, and I was neither." She paused and bit her fingernail. I'd never seen her do that before.

I also hadn't considered the prospect of there being more than two categories of students at Gardner. I'd had such a simplistic mindset about it. About so many things. "Keep going," I said.

"Okay." She sat on her hands, as if that were the only way to stop biting her nails. Maybe it was. "I knew I had to change my attitude if I was going to survive here. I could either find ways to make myself feel better, or I could make friends. I knew making friends was the better plan, obviously, but I hope you're starting to see why that might not have been so easy for me. I had a bunch of friends back home, but only after the site blew up. When I was broke and wearing dirty Salvation Army clothes they were awful to me, and they somehow thought I would forget. I wasn't about to let that happen here. For once, I was going to have the upper hand. I was going to make the rules. And I would have some fun in the process, get a little of my own back."

"I'm not following," Wyatt said.

I wasn't sure I was either, but I had a sneaking suspicion I was about to get there.

"Let me get through this, okay?" Chloe said. "I'll make it make sense as best as I can, I promise."

Wyatt nodded.

"So yeah, that first night, Game Night, I was checking everyone out to see what I could learn, to think about what I wanted to do. I decided I'd find me a rich screwup and a scholarship kid and have a little fun with them. When I saw Amina and Hunter at lunch that week it was like fate, you know? Like I'd been sent my own set of toys to play with."

I felt my lips curling and tried to make my face a mask, like hers had been. This was the person I'd thought was my best friend? I was a toy for her to play with?

"Don't make that face, Amina," Chloe said. She always did have a read on me. "You asked for all of it, and I'm giving you all of it."

"Whatever," I said. "I'm listening."

"I thought I could take you both down a peg, that's all. Hunter, you were cute and fun to flirt with, but it didn't take much to figure out who your dad was and how much you didn't want people to know. Amina, you were drooling so hard for Hunter you'd do whatever I told you if it meant being close to him, so I talked you into running for student council. The plan was for both of you to lose."

Now my face was red with both embarrassment and rage. I didn't dare look at anyone, especially Hunter. "But that's not what happened," I managed to get out.

"No, because I started to actually like you." Chloe sat cross-legged now. She was getting her confidence back, and I hated it. "Hunter still needed to go down, though. Our whole situation was getting a little too complicated."

"Oh, so I was the lucky one," I said. "What changed? If we were really friends, why'd you send all those fake quotes from my journal to Wyatt? Why'd you harass him, anyway? And what about Jo?"

"Slow down," she said. "I'll get there."

"Get there faster," Hunter said. "You've wasted enough of our time already."

I wasn't the only one getting angrier and angrier as Chloe talked.

"Okay, Wyatt first," Chloe said. "At that first Eucalyptus meeting, when he told us his whole background, I was furious. He grew up with a whole community of people who loved him and who shielded him from everything hard in the world, and when one bad thing happened to him he ended up at Gardner. Boom. Still protected from everything, never had to fight for anything. It made me so angry. I wasn't trying to be a terrible person; I just wanted him to understand how easy he'd had it, how the world was a much worse place than he knew. So I sent the books and put him on a few mailing lists."

"Let me get this straight," Wyatt said. "You thought you were trying to help me?"

"I did," she said. "You seemed so oblivious. You needed to understand the full range of what's out there."

"The full range included some pretty horrible stuff," he said. "You brought the worst of it right to my door. And you're wrong that I don't know what it means to be Black in the United States. I may have been shielded from some things, but there's no getting away from it without avoiding all people everywhere. I'm not as naive as you think, and I don't see what right you'd have to wake me up even if I were."

"Way to go, Wyatt," Jo said, and it was nice to see Wyatt smile at Jo calling him by his actual name.

"I suppose you were helping me, too, Princess?" Jo said, not even trying to keep the sarcasm out of her voice. "Outing me as a runaway to everyone in the whole school, when you were the only person who knew?"

"I mean, kind of," she said. "You needed to get over it. And you needed to talk to someone about it who wasn't me. I bet Amina reached out to you immediately, didn't she? She's a good friend, and you needed one."

"Let me get this straight," Jo said. "You ruined a perfectly good party to remind me of the worst period of my life, all in the hopes I would make a friend who isn't you?"

"Well, you were about to win my game, too. Couldn't have that."

Was she serious? Is this what it was like to be inside

Chloe's brain? "You think this is all okay? That this is how people behave?" I asked.

"I'm not saying I was right," Chloe said. "I'm telling you what I was thinking. You asked."

"So let me guess. You broke up Wyatt and me because Hunter was done with you and Jo wasn't sure she wanted to be with you."

"Now you're catching on." She looked almost sad again. "Also I was mad at you. You didn't follow the rules of your own game. I should have won."

I'd been right—she was pissed off she'd lost. I thought she'd hidden it well, but I'd misunderstood.

"It's all fixed, though. You two are happy again. No harm done." What killed me was that she really believed it. I could hear it in her voice.

"Let me see if I can work out the rest," I said. "You sent out pictures of yourself to make sure none of us suspected you."

"Yes, but not just that." She turned to Jo. "Those were for you."

Jo scowled. "Why would I want to see them?"

"I wanted you to want me," she said simply. "I didn't know how to make it happen. That was just one thing I tried."

"You should have tried being a real person, Princess," Jo said. She sounded so sad. "When I felt like you were being honest, that's when it seemed like we might be getting somewhere."

"I'm being honest now," Chloe said. "Does that mean you all can forgive me?"

She couldn't be serious. "Do you even care how much you hurt us?" I asked. "I get that in some warped way you thought you were being useful some of the time, but you can't have thought there wouldn't be any fallout."

"We're going to need some time," Wyatt said. "It's getting late, anyway, and some of us have to get ready to travel tomorrow. How about we call it a night, and maybe we can talk when we get back, after break?"

Chloe looked at Jo. "You'll be here over break with me, won't you? We can talk before that?"

Jo shook her head. "Changed my mind. I'm going home with Amina."

Chloe blinked a few times, and I could see she was trying to keep herself from crying again. Maybe she did realize how wrong she'd been. "Sure, I get it." Her voice didn't crack, but it lacked her usual bravado.

Wyatt, Hunter, Jo, and I headed out of the greenhouse without saying goodbye. I didn't hear Chloe behind us; I could only assume she needed a little more time to herself. We walked back to the dorms in silence, processing what we'd just heard. I found the whole situation nearly impossible to believe. How could I have been so wrong about Chloe?

How could I have thought she was my best friend here and not realized what she was doing? How could I have seen her do terrible things to other people and thought I was safe? It was arrogant of me, in a way, to think I was somehow better than the girls who followed her on Instagram and did whatever she told them.

We stopped in front of the girls' dorm. "I guess this is it for now," Hunter said. "Wish me luck avoiding my family." We traded hugs, even Jo, in silent accord that we weren't going to talk about Chloe. "Wyatt, you coming back to the boys' dorm with me?"

Wyatt took my hand and squeezed it. "I'm going to drag Amina off for one last walk, if that's okay."

I squeezed back. "Fine by me. Jo, we'll meet tomorrow to catch the bus?"

"Bright and early," she said. "Have fun, lovebirds."

Now that was a nickname I could live with.

Wyatt and I turned back toward the woods, agreeing without saying anything to go down our usual path, to find our tree. "You warm enough?" he asked.

The air was getting colder by the minute, but I didn't care. "I'm fine. How about you? I bet you were outside the whole time."

"I was. I was sure Chloe was trying to show off her survival skills by setting herself up outside. I thought maybe she'd have built a little shelter."

"Making up for a game she didn't win," I said. "I see the logic."

"I wasn't the only one," he said. "Jo checked out all the secret rooms from last night's game—how funny, it was just last night, when it feels like years ago. She thought Chloe would have piggybacked on someone else's setup."

"And Hunter?" We'd reached the clearing now. Wyatt had his backpack and spread out a tarp on the cold ground, then layered it with towels. "You do think of everything, don't you?"

"Well, I didn't want our last night before break to go by without us spending some time together. I'm brave enough to break curfew but not brave enough to sneak into your room."

"It's not like they can send you home as punishment," I said. "You're already leaving." But it was sweet of him to think of this. I sat down on a folded-up towel, and he sat next to me. "Tell me what Hunter did. This is the first game I won, so I want details."

"Hunter, well . . ." Wyatt cleared his throat. I had a feeling I knew where this was going. Wyatt was a little shy when it came to talking about sex. "He went to places where they'd hung out together."

"Nice euphemism," I said. "Do I even want to know?"

"You can guess some," he said. "The rest? No, you probably don't. Jo definitely didn't. We were talking about it on the way to the greenhouse, and it was super awkward."

“I can’t even imagine.” I leaned my head on Wyatt’s shoulder. “What do we do now?”

“Maybe we should take some time off, give this some more thought,” he said.

I sat up straight. “What? Give what more thought?”

He laughed and pulled me back down to him. “Eucalyptus. We’ve played our games and learned a lot, but maybe we learned some things we didn’t expect. And maybe there are things we need to know that we left out.”

“Like what?” I agreed with him, but I wanted to know what he had in mind.

“Like how to work with other people, to start. How to listen, how to understand. Maybe I asked the wrong question, back at the beginning. Maybe it isn’t so much about surviving without the people we love.”

“What is the question, then?”

“I’m not sure yet, but I want to take some time and find out. It might take the rest of the school year, but we need to deal with everything that’s happened so far anyway. We need to think about forgiveness, what that means to us, when it’s possible and when it isn’t. Maybe that’s more important than planning for the end of the world. Maybe it isn’t. But we need to answer some of those questions for ourselves. Then we can decide whether we want to keep this going.”

He was right. We’d been so fixated on managing big-picture problems that we hadn’t yet learned how to deal with the day-to-day complexities of being ourselves, being part of our communities, our relationships. I was pretty sure that was what he meant. "When you say 'this' . . ." I held my breath.

"Just the group." He took my hand and then turned it over, stroking my palm. "I don't want to give you up. Not if you still want me."

"Of course I still want you." I hated the idea he'd ever doubt it, and I wanted to make sure he knew that. "Is it kissing time yet?"

I didn't wait for an answer, just reached for him so he'd know I didn't want to let him go.

18.

And so it was we found ourselves the following fall, addressing the new first-year class, scholarship students and rich kids and everyone in between, from the floor of the Rathskeller on Game Night. We replaced the awkward boy and girl who'd scared us with their intensity and their wide eyes and their teeth, though it was possible we were even scarier, given how many of us there were. We'd had the rest of the school year and the summer as well to think about our friendships and Eucalyptus and what forgiveness meant to us, whether love mattered more than survival or whether that was even the right question. We'd each come to our own conclusions, and here we were together, in front of the other students. All five of us.

After the games were over, after we'd watched the new students play Assassin and Truth or Dare, we turned the floor over to Wyatt. He'd spent a long time trying to come up with a new way to ask his question, a new way to identify kindred spirits for the reimagined version of Eucalyptus we planned to start, a group less concerned with what we put in our go-bags and more about how to use cooperation and empathy to prevent the things we were so scared of from happening. We'd be more about acting—protesting, canvassing, volunteering—and less about reacting, which meant we wanted to know different things about the students who might become our fellow club members and friends.

Wyatt had let his hair grow back, which made me happy, and he pulled at one of his curls as he stepped forward to speak. "If you thought it was possible the world could end in your lifetime," he began, "how far would you be willing to go to prevent it?"

He stepped back, and we waited to hear the answers.

ACKNOWLEDGMENTS

Thanks to everyone who helped this book come into the world. Particular thanks to everyone at HarperCollins, especially Elizabeth Lynch, who was very patient with what turned out to be a much more complicated drafting process than I'd anticipated. Thanks to Renée Cafiero, Christina MacDonald, and Tania Bissell for their copy editing and proofreading expertise and to Corina Lupp and Ben Fearnley for such a striking and appropriate cover. Both Jocelyn Davies and Christopher Hernandez were tremendously helpful in working through some of the ideas in this book with me while they were at HarperCollins as well. Thanks also to Richard Abate and Rachel Lee at 3Arts Entertainment and to Julia Borcherts and Dana Kaye at Kaye Publicity, who I didn't get a chance to thank last time around.

Thanks to everyone who helped with the writing process—I might put the words on the page by myself, but every other part of writing is a team effort for me. Thanks to Ragdale for providing a home away from home where I could be as productive as possible. Thanks once again to all the organizations that have provided community both online and off; I am writing these acknowledgments during the COVID-19 lockdown, and I value all of you more than you could possibly know. Thanks to everyone who read early drafts of this book, including Katherine Bell, Jessica Chiarella, Rachel DeWoskin, Marissa Falkoff, Sarah Lawsky, Elisa Lee, Brian Shelden, Judy Jane Smith, Brandon Trissler, Rebecca Johns Trissler, and Beth Wetmore. Thanks also to friends and family who continue to provide love and support: Nami Mun, the Dowagers, the Peabody High crew, my parents, my brother and sister, my future in-laws, and especially Brian. I didn't see you coming, but I'm so glad you're here.